Second

Story

seeing what's not being said

by

Anna Rapa

d[w]h

da[w]bar house
press

In memory of Pastor Tom, who died before his time in a tragic accident. His compassionate nature and unconditional love gave others the ability to overcome emotional barriers brought on by a world full of tragic losses, selfishness, misunderstanding, hatred, and shame. He openly admitted his faults and failures, exposing himself as a sinful man; one redeemed by God. His giftedness in telling stories allowed him to connect with all kinds of people who connected their stories to God's. Through his example, others could see true spirituality. Against all odds, he believed and hoped that lives could be transformed.

September 15, 1948-November 13, 2009

This book is dedicated to Tamara, Andrea, Travis, Molly, and Frank. Thank you for listening to my heart and for giving me the opportunity to learn to see all the things you weren't saying.

Table of Contents

Author's Note

I've been working in the secular world now for about nine years. Before that, I lived in a mostly Christianized world with friends who mostly believed what I did. When I made the switch to the big, wide world, it was hard to get my bearings. Where did faith fit into that secular existence? What was appropriate to talk about? How could I befriend people and not talk about faith? If they were my friends, and really wanted to know me, then why shouldn't I talk about my faith?

I struggled through these questions with a very good friend and then a community of people. As we talked about it, some patterns began to emerge. Being someone whose whole life and whose choices are all centered around faith in God, faith is a topic that I have to address at some point in any relationship. You can't know me without knowing what I'm doing and why I'm doing it, and the why is closely tied to what I believe about who God is and what my relationship with him is like.

But using the traditional methods of explaining faith, like the Romans road or the traditional tracts, wasn't really going to work for me. In addition, I learned that people's barriers to faith have moved from mostly rational barriers to mostly emotional barriers. With the help of my friend and my community, I wrestled through these ideas and have managed to find an authentic way to talk about faith and spirituality in my world.

I hope that the story both challenges and encourages you to think about these things in your own life and your own faith community. I know that there are some things that the characters encounter that are the focus of intense debate right now in the broader church culture—what truth is, how the church does and should treat homosexuals, and what the central message of the gospel is. This book is not meant to answer those questions. This book is meant to suggest some ideas for further discussion and exploration in our communities and in our context.

My greatest passion in life is to live as an ambassador of Christ in the world. My hope is that, through this book, you might be encouraged and challenged to figure out what that looks like in your own world.

2 Corinthians 5:17-21

A note about the genre

Although I grew up reading books like this and see a trend toward teaching through narrative, the publishing world hasn't come up with a separate genre for this type of writing. One author called a similar book wisdom literature, which he said is a delicate balance between narrative story and teaching. In other cultures, they call stories like these teaching stories.

Resources and information

For more information and links to resources, please visit www.annarapa.com. I would also love to communicate personally with you, so you can reach me at annarapa@gmail.com.

Second Story

Alex Cunningham flung open the door to the Second Story Bookshop, and the jingle bells announced his presence. He rushed up to the coffee counter, his leather jacket crinkling, and the scent of peppermint and a breeze of cold air followed along. He approached the counter, his reddish hair glinting under the Christmas lights.

"Sorry I'm late!" he said to no one in particular. Alex quickly shed his winter wear and went behind the counter, pulling on an apron. "What'll you have?" he asked the next person in line.

Alex was relieved to be at work. The smell of coffee and the sight of shelf after shelf lined with books seemed like a haven. He had just left his girlfriend Annie's place, where they had been in a desperate argument, the fifth that week. Things just hadn't been the same since his motorcycle accident last spring.

But it wasn't long before the bookstore worked its calming magic, and Alex turned his mind to the task at hand. Soon the lunch rush was over, and Alex was free to head upstairs to his office. It was Friday, and for Alex, that meant ordering and scheduling. Alex made his way between the tables and the stacks to the stairs. His office was upstairs, all the way in the back, and he shared it with Drew, the book purchasing manager.

Alex had worked at Second Story since July. Before

his motorcycle accident, he was a finance guy at a small local business. But after his month in the hospital, he was only able to work part-time. By the time he was ready to go back to full-time, the small business had folded. So here he was, the café manager. Certainly not ideal, but better than nothing.

As Alex entered the office, he noticed again the chaos that was his and Drew's office. Neither one was super detail-oriented, and they didn't have enough storage space. There were boxes along the wall, and piles of paperwork on every conceivable surface. They had a halfhearted filing system going in the big filing cabinet that stood on the wall between their desks. But it seemed like a lost cause.

Drew Reynolds was already in the office, hunched over his keyboard. "Hey Drew," said Alex.

"Uh, hello Alex." Drew didn't even look up. He was looking especially gaunt today, and there was a yellowish tint to his skin that made his dark hair look even darker. His Calvin Klein jeans and Abercrombie sweater hung loosely off his limbs. Drew was always well-dressed. But about a month ago, it had become obvious that he was a really sick guy. His clothes had begun to just hang off him, and his ordinarily lively face took on a more and more despondent look. Today Alex could see that Drew was failing fast.

"How are you feeling today, Drew?" Alex hesitated

to ask. Sometimes Drew would talk to him, sometimes he'd become angry, and sometimes he'd just speak in monosyllables for days at a time. Alex could never predict which it would be, so that made venturing to care a dangerous proposition. But Alex thought it was worth the risk. Drew didn't seem to have many friends, and with his recent break-up, he seemed to become more and more withdrawn from life with each passing day. Some days, Alex felt like he might possibly be the only person who cared a little bit about Drew.

"Well, Alex, I feel like shit, as a matter of fact. And my *!@& father picked last night to spring another lecture on me about the status of my mortal soul when I called to talk to my mom."

Drew paused, his face becoming redder by the second. "The jerk was supposed to be at a church meeting, but I guess it was cancelled, so he picked up the phone instead. I don't know why I even bother, anyway. Nothing good ever comes of those phone calls." Drew threw a challenging look over his shoulder at Alex and then turned back to his work.

"But your mom must have been glad to hear from you," Alex said.

"I didn't even get to talk with her. About five minutes through my father's diatribe, I couldn't take it anymore and hung up. No way was I gonna call back later to talk to her."

Alex raised an eyebrow. He ventured, "That's awful, Drew. But your dad must really love you, to talk with you about your spiritual life like that."

"Love me! If that's what you call love, I don't want any part of that." Drew swung his chair around to face Alex. "He doesn't love me. He can't accept me. He can't accept who I am. He can't accept that I don't fit that perfect image he laid out for me when I was two. All he was ever concerned about was whether all the people at church thought he was a good guy or not. And he's made it very clear that how I choose to live has ruined his picture-perfect family and life. According to him, it's amazing that the church even lets him collect offering now."

"Well, God l—"

"And don't even talk to me about God!" Drew's eyes flashed. "According to my father, God hates me as much as my father does. I don't want to hear about any of that B.S. today!" With that, Drew jumped up and stalked out of the office.

Alex's body sagged as his eyes followed Drew out the door. He sighed. He could not get this right. It had been quite a struggle for him to even get to this point. When he first started working with Drew, they'd hit it off. They had a lot of fun together because they shared the same sense of humor and love of mischief. They used to set up pranks for the other staff and watch as they usually went off without a hitch. But when Alex found out about

8

Drew's then-partner, Eric, well, he'd gotten really uncomfortable. It had never occurred to him that Drew could be gay. And what was he supposed to do about that?

Alex had grown up in a church where being gay was a "sin," and he was pretty sure that sin was supposed to be confronted head on. He knew that he was supposed to do something from Matthew 18–go to Drew alone first, or something like that. And then if Drew didn't repent, Alex could take someone else along.

Alex cringed when he remembered the time he'd tried to follow that plan shortly after he'd learned about Eric. It was a month before Drew had even talked to him again. But obviously this whole love-oriented message wasn't getting through either. Every time he so much as breathed a word about God, Drew blew up at him. And from the way Drew looked today, he might not make it much longer himself. He NEEDED to get right with God. And Alex was sure that he should be encouraging Drew to do that. Wasn't that what a serious follower of God would do?

Alex slammed his fist against his desk.

Agh! Why does everything have to be so hard?

Seriously, following God is supposed to lead to peace and love and happiness. But ever since I got out of the hospital, it's been one conflict after another. How am I ever going to keep going like this?

Alex turned back to his inventory sheets and tried

to focus. But he couldn't quite get rid of the nagging suspicion that he was missing something—some kind of skill or piece of information that could help him reach Drew. There must be some way, right?

God loved Drew, of that he was sure. God even wanted Drew to spend eternity with him. So how was God going to get through to him? And how was he, Alex, supposed to be a part of that?

Annie Russo had spent that day ferociously cleaning her apartment. She deep-cleaned the kitchen. She vacuumed the carpet. She did five loads of laundry. But no matter what she did, she hadn't been able to stop thinking about Alex and the fight they'd had that morning. It was stupid, really.

Now she and Alex were walking through a Christmas tree farm looking for the perfect tree for her apartment, and she was determined to make the best of the evening. She was tired of the tension and just wanted to have fun.

Alex and Annie held hands, walking through the trees, and Annie racked her brain for neutral topics of conversation. Alex had been unusually quiet on the way to the farm. Usually, he was quite a chatterbox.

"So," she said, "how was work today?"

But Alex didn't answer quickly enough for Annie, so she dropped his hand and started running through the trees. "Bet you can't catch me!" she yelled, darting here and there.

She looked over her shoulder, but Alex hadn't increased his speed. He didn't look like he'd even noticed she'd left. Looking down at the fresh snow on the ground, she grinned. She ducked behind a tree and waited until just the right moment.

Smack! Bulls-eye! It was a direct hit to the center of Alex's chest. But instead of making him lunge for the snow, as she'd expected, Alex just frowned and kept walking.

Annie frowned. How frustrating. What was going on with him?

When Alex caught up with Annie again, she asked, "Alex, what is going on? What's wrong?"

He kept walking.

Annie stopped abruptly.

Alex kept walking.

She shouted, "Alex! Stop. Would you look at me?"

Finally, he slowed to a stop and turned around and glanced at her. "Look, I had a really hard day. I don't want to talk about it. Let's just get your tree."

Annie shook her head, her brown curls bouncing around her face. "No, Alex. I'd rather not. Let's just go home."

Annie turned around and quickly started walking back the way they'd come. Her shoulders were tense and a frown played around her lips. After a minute, she heard his footsteps crunching through the snow. In another minute, he'd caught up with her. He gently grabbed her arm and pulled her to a stop. "Look," he said, "I'm sorry, Annie, I am. It's been a rough day. I really want to get your tree with you. Come on. It'll be fun."

Annie struggled to push down her feelings of frustration and regain her optimism. For a moment, the frustration was winning, and she longed to make a snarky comment about how he'd already ruined their fun. Instead, she said, "Fine, let's go. But if you're not going to talk about it, at least keep your bad mood to yourself. This is supposed to be fun."

They walked through the pines and headed toward the firs. Alex began to tell stories about the people he'd served in the café that day. Soon they were laughing and talking. Not about anything serious, of course, but at least they were talking. Annie felt the tension slowly leaving her body.

And then they came upon a slightly lopsided fir tree. Annie stopped in her tracks. "Ooh, Alex. This one's just right!" Alex seemed to be laughing at her choice, but he immediately bent down and began sawing at the trunk. It took just a couple of minutes, and the tree was theirs.

They slowly made their way back to the check out, Alex carrying the tree and Annie the saw. Annie asked quietly, "So, Alex, seriously, what's going on with you? Is everything okay?"

She looked over, and she noticed his jaw clench. Uh oh. But it was too late now.

"I had a rough conversation with Drew again. He had a bad conversation with his parents on the phone. I was just trying to explain to him how much God loves him. But he wouldn't hear it."

"Why do you even care about that guy, Alex? He's so mean to you."

Alex switched the tree from his right shoulder to his left. "It's really important, Annie. I feel sure that he doesn't really know God, and I think he's going to die soon. I just don't want to see him live his eternity in hell."

"But what's it to you? He's not even your friend." What was this obsession with God all of a sudden? After the accident, he'd been talking about spirituality all the time–and not just to her, but to people he knew didn't believe the way they did. She didn't know why. Church was fine for Sundays, and she was really happy that she'd found a moral guy. But to make it the topic of every conversation seemed a little much. And why couldn't he just leave Drew alone? It was obvious that he didn't really want to hear what Alex was selling.

Alex gripped the tree a little more tightly and started walking a little more quickly. If he hadn't been carrying the tree, Annie would have said that he was marching. Annie struggled to keep up with him. Finally,

13

he answered, "I wish I could explain this to you, but obviously I can't. It's important to talk about spiritual things with other people. God cares about Drew, and God wants him to know that. It's important that he make a decision to follow God before he dies."

"I get that it's important to you that people have their spiritual lives figured out. But it's not our job to figure it out for them. Drew obviously doesn't care about this stuff. So why even bother?"

Annie tried desperately to keep the cringe off her face as she approached the farm's hut to pay for the tree. When they got back into the car, their conversation moved on to other topics.

At work the next day, Alex could think of nothing but Annie. He was at a loss to explain to her why this was so important to him. He'd tried everything he knew. But things just hadn't been the same since his accident.

He stood at the café counter, waiting for customers. Alex remembered back to the days when their relationship had been all laughter and fun. Annie was that kind of girl. Her crazy, curly brown hair and her sparkling green eyes seemed to advertise her zany, bubbly personality. She was the life of the party, and together they were always cracking each other up. She was beautiful. She was fun. She was perfect for him, or had been. But his month in the hospital had sobered him a little, and Annie just didn't understand.

He loved that she wanted to start a snowball fight or play a game of chase through the snow. At least, he used to. But it seemed now like there were so many more important things to think about. Every day, people were dying without knowing Jesus. How could he just stand by and let that happen? It was just too important. It was time for them to take life a little more seriously.

He'd tried to explain to her that their old dreams of living for their own family and their own comfort was no longer enough for him. But she simply didn't seem to want to hear about the inward journey he'd been taking. She'd never seemed to want to hear about what he felt God was showing him. She'd always told him to "stop being so morbid" whenever he tried to bring things up in the hospital. And now, it seemed like all they ever did was fight. This was not good. Not good at all.

"Can I help you ma'am?" Alex asked without even looking up. But then he heard a familiar voice, "Alex. How are you?"

"Oh, hi Sara!" He gave a small smile. "It's been a while. How are you doing?"

"Fine, fine, Alex. But you look a little worried, honey. What's on your mind?"

"How long do you have?"

"Why, all the time in the world. I'll just get a cup of coffee and one of those whole wheat bagels, and I'll be

15

sitting right over there in the corner." Sara pointed to the table on the far side of the café area, right next to the stack of mystery books. "You just come on over whenever you have a minute, and I'd be happy to listen to anything you have to say."

Alex handed her the coffee and the bagel and caught her eye. Her warm brown eyes arrested his attention, and her angular face softened as she smiled. Her whole demeanor was open and welcoming as she gave him a knowing glance. Then she turned to take her food to her table. Alex stared after her, barely seeing her long jean skirt and wool sweater. As she made her way to her table, Alex shook his head to clear it and turned back to the next customer.

But his mind immediately turned to his youth group days. Sara Locke was one of his old youth leaders. She had always been the watchful, quiet kind of leader who saw so much more than what you said or did. How many times had she looked at Alex and asked him a question or challenged him to think about something that cut straight to the heart of his struggle? And she had been so kind to both him and Annie when he was in the hospital. Yes, she could be just the person to help them. Maybe she could help him explain things to Annie.

It was half an hour before Alex had a bit of a break. He looked over, and Sara was still there, sitting at the table in the corner. She sat properly, her back straight. Her long, thick brown hair hung just past her shoulders, lightly streaked with grey. She held a book in her left hand, and a journal lay on the table in front of her. Every once in a while, she'd stop her reading and write a few lines in the journal. As Alex approached, she paused and took another sip of her coffee.

"Sara?" Alex asked. "Is it still okay if I sit down?"

"Of course, honey. What's on your mind?" She smiled gently, put down her book, and gave Alex her attention.

Alex saw only warmth and understanding in her eyes and started sharing. He shared in fits and starts at first, struggling to find words. But as he warmed up, he was able to tell her everything.

"Sara, when I was laying there in that hospital bed, I just had so much time to think. And it seemed like I had this movie of my life playing over and over. The question that kept coming to my head is, was it worth it? Was what I had been doing and giving my life to worth it?"

"I felt like I'd been spared for a reason, you know? And I remembered that trip that we took to the Philippines, do you remember that?"

She nodded and smiled, so he continued, "Sara, I knew on that trip that God had a calling on my life. I knew that I was supposed to be a part of his plan to reach the world. And I don't know what happened. Somehow, during college I forgot about that. And it broke my heart to

17

realize that nothing I'd been doing was worth anything at all. I think I just got caught up in making myself a comfortable life. And Annie and I, we had these dreams of having a family and a life together. So I forgot about that calling for a while. But in the hospital, it all came rushing back. And I knew that something had to change."

"And what was that, Alex?"

"Well, I knew that I needed to give more thought to sharing about Christ with the people around me. And I wanted to make sure that Annie and I were living for something bigger."

Alex drummed his fingers on the table.

"But things got really hard when I left the hospital. I went back to my life–the life that didn't include much of God except for church on Sundays–and there's been a lot of tension since then. And Annie, well, I haven't been able to explain this to her. She doesn't understand why I'm so worried about all these people around me. And I don't really know what to do to help them, and I seem to be botching it all up anyway. Should I just give up on the idea, and go back to life how it was before the accident?" Alex paused.

Sara just took a sip of her coffee and kept silent.

"But I really don't think I can do that," Alex continued. "It's like all along, this is who I was supposed to be. I was supposed to care about the people around me. I was supposed to be living with purpose and mission. For a while, I forgot. But I remember now, and I can't go back. What do I do, Sara?"

Alex looked at Sara and then looked down again at his fingers.

Finally, she said, "Alex tell me this. Do you think that your new value system is incompatible with Annie's?"

"I think it might be. I don't want that to be true, but I think it's possible."

"Do you think that there's a chance to save the relationship?"

"I want there to be! But I've been trying to explain where I'm coming from, and I'm just not getting through."

"Do you think she shares your Christian faith?"

"Well, she definitely believes in God. She grew up Christian. I know that she thinks it's important to go to church because we do that together every week."

"Yes, that's right. I remember now. Hmm . . . . Well, do you think she'd be willing to think and pray about this and maybe learn with you for a little while–about this idea of mission and ministry and how that fits into her life, or how it fits into your lives together?"

After thinking for a minute, Alex replied, "Yeah, I think so. She's always wanted us to go to church and do stuff like that together."

"Well, what if we met together, maybe once a week, and talked about this? We can call it a Bible study or a discussion group. Or you guys can just come over to my house for coffee, and we can chat. But it sounds to me like there are some deep issues here and that it would be really good if you and Annie could work them out together. I'd be happy to help you if I can."

Alex leaned back into his seat, some of the tension leaving his frame. "Yeah, I think that sounds like a good idea. I really have no idea what to do. I don't want to break up with Annie. I love her. But this is not working, and we need help. I just don't know how to explain anything anymore."

"Okay, Alex. If Annie agrees to come, you guys just pick a night next week. You can come to my house. But before you come, I want you to read Luke 15 together, okay? And see if you can determine what the point of the three stories is."

"Thanks so much, Sara. I mean it. I'd better get back to work now, though. I'll call you."

"I'll talk with you soon."

As Alex got up to go back to the counter, Sara smiled to herself and then prayed quietly. "God, please be with Alex as he speaks to Annie. Help him to have clarity and sensitivity as he asks her to do this."

She picked up her coffee again. She was inwardly thrilled to have seen Alex here today, and she was excited to be a part of his journey. She'd always liked Alex. He had been the class clown of the youth group, always full of surprises and mischief. She'd always thought of him a little like a jester. He had that kind of goofy appearance that was made for laughter and fun. Everyone loved him, and he'd always had the ability to get other people to do crazy stuff right along with him. But there was more to him than that. His questions during Bible studies had always been deep and searching. It was clear that he had a deep desire to know and please God, and she'd always hoped that he would stay true to that.

And during the short time she'd sat with Annie during one of Alex's long surgeries, she'd sensed a very sincere person. She had no idea what Annie truly believed or what she cared about, beyond Alex, but she was hopeful. Yes, she would be praying for Alex and Annie.

Back at the counter, a new question was weighing on Alex's mind. How was he going to explain this to Annie?

New Hope

A few hours later found Annie finishing up her dinner at her dining room table. She had turned up the volume on the local soft rock channel, but no matter how loud she played it, she couldn't stop thinking about Alex. He could be so maddening! She didn't understand what more he wanted from her. She'd done everything she could for all these months to be supportive, to help him recover from his accident, and to get things back to what they'd been before. She just kept waiting for things to return to normal. But it seemed like after all that, after all the work she'd put in, Alex had changed the rules on her. Where before they seemed to be in sync in the way they wanted to live life and where they were going, now everything was a tug-of-war. If she wanted to go to the movies, he wanted to stay in. If she wanted to have a quiet dinner at home, he wanted to invite some of his work friends over for a party. It was like they were each speaking a different language. She just missed the times they had together–the peaceful, free, easy relationship they'd had before the accident. She missed her best friend. She didn't know where he'd gone.

She finally gave up trying not to think about it and went into her room. She opened the top drawer of her dresser and pulled out the note Alex had given her when he'd asked her to be his girlfriend. It was kind of goofy, actually. They'd been dating on and off for a while, and on this occasion, Alex had planned a scavenger hunt all over the college. He hid clues in classrooms, in dorm rooms, in the gym. He'd made her ask professors and friends for clue after clue. And during the whole hunt, he just followed her around, laughing at her attempts to guess and refusing to give out any hints.

When she finally found the last note, taped to the bottom of a bench overlooking the campus lake, she'd felt completely loved, treasured, and appreciated. She'd pulled out the note and read it, and when she'd turned to face Alex, he'd leaned over and given her a long, deep kiss. She'd kept the note in her top drawer for the last three years. Every time she looked at it, it made her feel special.

She brought it back to the table and looked at it again now. She ran her fingers over the creases, smoothing it out, trying to make herself feel what she always had before. It's not that she didn't love him anymore. She really did. And she knew that he still loved her. But those special, fun times had been replaced with tension and frustration. She believed in commitment, and she was totally committed to Alex. But her heart was breaking. It was just so hard right now. And she didn't know if it would get better.

She shook her head. She had to pull it together. Alex had called a few minutes before and asked to stop by on his way home from work. She'd said yes, of course. But she didn't really feel like seeing him tonight. Her emotions were too raw, and she was too worried about what the future held.

I just don't know how much longer I can do this. I don't know if I can keep fighting all the time.

Subdued, she placed the note in the pocket of her oversized sweater. She got up from the table and took her dishes to the sink. She slowly wrapped her leftover spaghetti and put it in the fridge. Then she heard the knock on the door that she'd been expecting. She sighed. There he was. She was just hoping that they could avoid another fight. She didn't have the energy tonight.

Annie took two steps from the kitchen to the apartment door, shook her head again to clear her mind, straightened her shoulders, and opened the door. But Alex wasn't there. In his place was a six-pack of Diet Coke, her favorite soda. She picked it up, noting that it was cold, and peeked out her apartment door. Alex was nowhere to be seen. Annie half-grinned and closed the door. She put all but one of the sodas in the fridge, grabbed a glass and some ice, and poured out a can. She probably wouldn't sleep well tonight now, but she couldn't resist. Annie was just sitting down in the living room with her soda when she heard another knock.

She put the soda on the coffee table, walked down the little hallway to the door, and gave another half-grin. She opened the door, a little more ready to face Alex. But instead of Alex, in his place she saw a giant glass vase she'd been admiring for weeks, filled to the brim with a cacophony of individually wrapped, snack-sized candy bars. This time she really smiled, picked up the vase, and brought it to her table. This was the Alex she knew and loved–full of fun and thoughtful surprises.

Annie was almost back to the couch when she heard a knock again. She tiptoed over to the door, yanked it open, and found herself face to face with a scarlet Gerbera daisy. Under the daisy was Alex's hand. But that and his arm were all Annie could see of Alex. He stood just to the side of her apartment door, flat against the wall. As she peeked around the doorway once again, she saw his impish grin and a sparkle in his eye. She grabbed the daisy and then grabbed his arm and pulled him into her apartment.

"Alex, what is all this?"

He, in turn, pulled her through the hallway to the couch, where they sat. He took a quick gulp of her soda, and proclaimed, "Annie, I love you. I don't want to fight. I know the past six months have been hard for you, and I know that I've changed. That can't be easy. But I want you to understand. I want us to change together. I want us to change for the better. I can never go back to the way things were before, but I can hope that when I get through this stuff, I'll be a better person and a better man."

"And, well, a better husband." He finished quietly. Annie looked at him, a question in her eyes. "Yeah, I know, we haven't really talked about marriage since the accident, but I still think about it, and I still want it. I still want you." Alex answered.

Annie was surprised by the tears that came to her eyes. Impulsively, she leaned over and gave him a hug. Pulling back, she said, "Alex, that's what I want too. But I don't know what else to do! What do we do?" She sank back into the sofa.

"I have an idea, actually," Alex said. "Sara Locke stopped by the bookstore today–you remember her from the hospital, right? Anyway, we ended up talking. She invited us to come to her house and meet with her to talk about stuff."

He jumped up and started pacing. "I can't explain it, Annie, it's like she's always known stuff about me without me saying anything. I think she might be able to help–maybe explain where I'm coming from. And maybe she can help us grow together." He stopped in front of her. "Will you give it a try?"

"Oh, I don't know, Alex. You know I don't really like to talk about that kind of stuff with other people, even someone as nice as Sara." Annie frowned.

Alex sat down beside her and grabbed her hand, tipped his head, and gave his most pleading look. "Please? Can we just give it a try? If we don't like it, we don't have to go back."

"I'll think about it, okay, Alex? I'll let you know

tomorrow?"

"Okay, Annie. Whatever you need. Just so you know, I think she was thinking it would be more like a Bible study. Not so much a counseling session."

Conversation moved on to other topics as they discussed their respective work days, their weekend plans, and updates on family and friends. They skirted the tension they'd been feeling for days by keeping things neutral. When Alex wanted to reserve some time to spend with his friend Kyle, he was careful to schedule around the plans that Annie'd wanted to make for them. In this way, they passed an hour or two, and then Alex got up to leave for the evening.

Annie walked him to the door. On the way out, he caught her in his arms, brushed her lips with his, and said quietly, "I love you, Annie girl. Have a good night."

"Good night," she whispered as the door closed behind him. She turned and leaned with her back against the door as she was suddenly caught up again with sadness and uncertainty. He couldn't go back, he'd said. He could only go forward. But forward to where? And could she really go with him? He said he wanted her to come along.

But how could she go forward when she didn't know the destination? And did she even want to go there? She'd loved her life. She'd loved her Alex. But this was a different Alex–different, yet the same. Still standing with her back to the door, she glanced to her right through the galley kitchen to the dining area, and saw the vase of candy sitting there. She wondered if she could ever find someone as great as Alex again.

She flipped the lights out and moved slowly through her apartment in the dark. She got ready for bed, praying all the while that God would somehow make it clear to her what she was supposed to do.

Alex arrived at work the next day a little more hopeful about his future with Annie. He knew there was a chance she might decide to say no to the time with Sara, but he thought she'd be willing to give it a shot. They were both still fighting for this relationship, and he was pretty sure that she still saw it as worth fighting for. If they could just get through this tension and uncertainty, he was sure that it would be okay. At least that's what he was telling himself. Alex was nothing if not optimistic.

Annie had slept peacefully the night before, and she had a renewed sense of hope about her relationship with Alex. He still loved her, he still wanted to marry her, and in the bright light of day, it seemed like anything was possible.

Annie's shift at the hospital started at noon, so she'd had an easy morning. As soon as she got up, she went for a jog. She came back, showered, had a leisurely breakfast, and skimmed the paper. Dressed in her baby blue scrubs, she grabbed her gigantic, black leather purse and rummaged around for about 30 seconds to find her keys. Once they were secured, she blew a kiss to her goldfish Herman, who sat on the bar between the kitchen and living room, and made her way out the door.

Still smiling, she walked through the hall. When she got to the steps, she saw her neighbor, Patti Conrads, on the way up. She gave a bright smile, "Hi Patti." Patti glanced up quickly, said a quiet "Hello" in return, and just as quickly looked back down at her feet. Patti's long stringy brown hair hung limply to her waist, and every move that Patti made was aimed at making herself less noticeable. She kept her arms close to her side and took very small steps, as if to take up less space. She seemed to hate the very thought of human interaction. And her clothes! All drab browns and grays and never any color at all. Annie shook her head. The woman was a mystery to her. And she always had this slightly haunted look about the eyes. She'd barely said ten words to Annie in the two years they'd lived next door to one another, and all ten of them had been a "hi" or "hello" in response to one of Annie's greetings.

Patti's daughter Josie was just a little bit better. She was almost as quiet as her mom, but she held herself aloof. Rather than being haunted, Josie always looked angry. At the same time, there seemed to be a hunger in her eyes that longed for someone to notice her. And her dad, boy, her dad was something else. A cop, or something, Annie thought. He was a big, burly guy who never smiled. Maybe that's why Patti was such a mouse.

Ah, well. You can't make anyone love life. They've got to choose it themselves.

And she walked out and got in the car to head to work. It was unseasonably warm for November, and that lightened Annie's mood even more. Yes, today would be a good day.

Annie's car was a brand new, yellow Volkswagen Beetle. As she slid behind the wheel, her eye caught the little photo-booth picture of her and Alex that they'd had made during a trip to Cedar Point before Alex's accident. It was the one where they were sticking out their tongues and looking at the camera cross-eyed. It never failed to make her smile and to bring up happy memories. She smiled again, and then said aloud, "Yes, what I am I going to do about Alex?"

She started her car and pulled out of the parking space, and then onto the road, heading to work. It was just a short ten-minute drive to the hospital, and at this time of day there shouldn't be too much traffic. She was soon mulling over what to do about Alex's invitation to meet with Sara.

Alex was in earnest about wanting to involve her in his life and in the changes he'd experienced, of that she was sure. And it was definitely true that they'd been having trouble communicating through all that. But really, let someone else into the conflict? Asking questions, butting into their business?

But Sara really was nice. No, she was kind. Annie remembered those long hours in the hospital and how Sara simply sat beside her. She'd actually already seen Annie at her absolute worst. And Sara hadn't seemed judgmental. She certainly hadn't lectured anyone. So what was the worst that could happen?

She sighed again.

She really was going to have to give it a try. There was no harm in that. And if it didn't work–but no, she wasn't going to think about that just now. She would cross that bridge when it came. Today she was going to be hopeful.

With that, she nodded her head and turned up the music. She'd call Alex a little later to let him know.

After work, Alex and Annie had a late dinner together at Annie's place, and then they sat down on the couch to read Luke 15 together. Sara had asked them to read it before they came to her house, and tonight seemed as good a night as any to get started. Both were feeling a bit nervous about the potential for conflict, though. Any time either had brought up spiritual things the last couple of months, it seemed like they could never quite see eye-to-

32

eye.

"So what are we supposed to do, Alex?" Annie asked.

"Well, Sara asked us to read this chapter and see if we can figure out what it's about. So we can read it silently, and then I think we should talk about what we notice or what we think it's saying."

So they each got out their Bibles and sat for a little while reading. All that could be heard was the tick of the living room clock, the hum of the refrigerator, and an occasional bark from the dog that lived across the street.

Finally, they both looked up. "Well," Alex said, "I thought that was interesting. I remember the story of the prodigal son, but I'd forgotten about the lost coin and the lost sheep. I thought they were really interesting because they seem to be talking about how much God loves people and wants them to know him."

Annie furrowed her brow, "Where do you see that, Alex? Those stories don't say anything about God or love or anything."

"It's a parable. So it has a deeper meaning."

"Don't you think we should start at the top? I mean, shouldn't we look at the surface meaning before trying to delve deep?"

"Well, we can. But don't you think that, along with the prodigal son, it's all about how much God loves people?"

33

"Maybe. But I'm not sure, Alex. I'm not sure."

"Okay, so what did you notice about the passage?"

"Well, one thing I noticed was that, for the sheep and the coin, the person who lost it worked really hard to find it again, and then with the lost son, the dad waited for the son to come back by himself. I'm not sure that running out to meet the son is exactly the same thing as searching high and low for the sheep and the coin."

"I didn't see that, Annie, that's good."

Annie continued, "Well, if that's true, what's the point, do you think? Do you think they're all trying to say the same thing about God or that they're saying different things?"

"Well, my Bible has them titled as the lost coin, the lost sheep, and the lost son. So I think we can probably infer that they are about the same topic. But I never actually read all those stories together. When I read that story about the prodigal son before, I always identified with the son, and it always seemed like maybe I was trying to run away from God. But that certainly doesn't fit with the coin situation—coins can't run anywhere."

"So what's the point?"

"Well, it can't be the seeking, because the dad doesn't seek in the last story. Maybe it has more to do with the emotion—like the pain of loss and then the joy of finding again. Even in the super-short story, there's time enough for the woman to tell her neighbors how happy she was

34

that she found the coin."

"That could be. But how upset could you be about losing one sheep if you have 99 more? And one coin? A lost son, I could understand–but then if he cared so much, why didn't the dad go and find the son? I don't know, Alex. It doesn't really make sense to me."

"I think the point is that God cares about sinners and is happy when one comes back to the family. That's why it's so important that we care about that too."

"Sure, I guess." Annie shrugged. "What do you think Sara's going to want to talk with us about? Do you think she'll be able to shed any light on it?"

"Definitely. She was always pretty good about explaining things well, and she has a lot of experience teaching this type of thing. So I think it'll be good."

"Alex, what exactly do you think she'll be able to help us with?"

"Well, I'm hoping that she'll help me to explain where my heart is a little better. Like I told you before, she always was able to kind of see through me–to see right to the heart of what I was thinking and feeling. And because so much of what has changed in me really goes back to who I was and what God did in my life in high school, I was hoping she might be able to help me explain. I want to be able to share where I feel like I'm headed and see if it's possible we could go there together, you know?"

Annie nodded. "All right. And I guess it doesn't

ever hurt to spend time praying and talking about spiritual things, right? Maybe there's something that she can teach us too. That could be good."

"So, all right." Alex said. "I guess that's it for now. We'll have to see what she says on Wednesday when we go over there." With that, the conversation turned to other matters, like another disturbing conversation with Drew that morning and their plans to hang out with Annie's family on Sunday. There seemed to be a cautious optimism on both of their parts and maybe a renewed security in the fact that they were both still in this relationship for the long haul. A little of the tension had dissipated.

Lost and Found

The following Wednesday, Annie and Alex pulled up to Sara's house in Annie's little yellow bug. Annie shifted into park, turned off the ignition, and looked over at Alex.

"You ready?" Alex asked.

"Sure. Ready as I'll ever be," she replied. "Let's do it."

They got out of the car, and Alex led Annie by the hand up the snow-dusted path. Here and there a piece of salt was sprinkled, and everywhere the salt was, the snow wasn't. The path to Sara's door was framed by fat green bushes, their little red berries presenting a splash of color against the white snow. The house was a cape cod. Each window was framed with shutters, and a single candle glowed on each windowsill.

Alex and Annie stepped up the single step to the porch, and Alex just raised his finger to push the doorbell when the door opened. "Hello Alex. And Annie–so good to see you again! Come on in," Sara said with a big smile. She swung open the outer door and let them in. As Annie stepped through the threshold, she at once smelled the rich, spicy scent of mulled cider and felt welcomed by the warm colors. She glanced at Sara, noting her warm smile and the sparkle in her brown eyes.

Then she noticed the steps heading upstairs just to

her right, with a closet to her right closer to the door. Looking straight ahead, she could see into the kitchen, and beyond that, into a formal dining room. Off to her left was a big living room with oversized chairs and a couch and love seat all arranged to frame a gigantic fireplace. All the furniture was in browns and tans, with splashes of color in the throw pillows and the wall decorations. The carpet was a plush tan.

"Here, let me take your coats," Sara said. She swung them over the banister. "Do you want any tea, coffee, or hot cocoa?"

Annie asked for some fruity tea, Alex asked for coffee, and Sara directed them to have a seat in the living room. Annie at once made for the oversized love seat, and Alex was right behind her. They settled in, and Annie pulled a throw off the back of the couch. She wasn't so much cold as comforted by the weight of the blanket.

"Here you go," Sara said, as she handed them each a mug. She placed coasters down on the coffee table and took a seat opposite the love seat in an oversized recliner. They exchanged pleasantries for a couple of minutes as they all adjusted to the environment. Finally, Sara said, "Well, Annie, we don't really know one another very well. And Alex, it's been a while since we've had much time to talk. Why don't we start with some life history—a little background, if you will. I can start, and then Annie maybe you can tell me a little bit about yourself. I didn't really get to hear much about you when we were at the hospital. And Alex, you can fill me in on what's been going on with you lately."

Alex nodded and Annie gave a bit of a shrug and so Sara went ahead. "Well, I guess I'll start kind of at the beginning. When I was young, my dad wasn't a Christian, but I usually went to church every Sunday with my mother. It was a small, country church, and I was a country girl. Church was where I learned all these stories about the God in the Bible, but it wasn't until I saw my dad's life radically changed that those stories became real to me. My dad was an alcoholic, and he was often abusive to both me and my mother."

Annie's heart skipped a beat. Oh no. This is exactly what she was afraid of! Sara was already giving her whole life's story about abuse and heartache. Bonding through hospital trauma was one thing, but this was a lot of personal information. How was she going to survive the whole night?

Annie started swinging her leg quickly, keeping time with the tick of the clock on the mantle.

Sara continued, "When I was about eight or nine, my mom must have had it, and she kicked my dad out of the house. I don't really know where he went or what he did, but when he came back a couple of weeks later, he was a totally different person. He was sober for the first time in years, and there was a gentleness and humility where his anger had been before. All he would say is that he went away and met Jesus. My mom let him come back, of course, and that was the beginning of our family's faith journey. It wasn't long after that that I decided that any God who could change my dad was the kind of God that I wanted to give my life to."

"We kept going to church, and every so often we'd have missionaries come and speak about their trips overseas. I was at once captivated by the idea of traveling to tell people about Jesus, and I told God that I would go, if he would send me. I ended up at a Christian college, studied English and missions, and met my husband, Barry, there. We served about two years in China, and then my health gave out and we had to come back."

"I went back to school and eventually ended up teaching English at a local community college, and Barry did nonprofit work. I'm still working at the college part time, but my husband passed away from cancer about two years ago. I now go to a small house church." Sara grinned. "I guess that's enough for now. How about you, Annie? What can you tell me about yourself?"

Annie hesitated. Usually she loved to be the center of attention, but that was when she was telling stories or jokes. This kind of sharing made her uncomfortable, and she wasn't sure how deep to go.

"Well, I'm the youngest of six kids. My mom was raised on a farm, and I guess she wanted to have as many kids as she'd had brothers and sisters. My dad is a dentist, and we lived in a pretty nice neighborhood. There are ten years between me and my oldest brother, so by the time I was starting school, he was just about driving. The sibling just above me is two years older–Jason–he's the one who named me, actually. My real name is Anne Marie, but he was too little to say the whole thing, so he called me Annie, and it stuck." Now why had she said that? She reigned herself in.

"So anyway, we had kind of a busy, crazy household, with all my brothers and all their friends. I played soccer and starred in school plays in high school, and then went on to college, where I met Alex. I studied nursing, and I work at the hospital on the pediatric ward. I went to church with my family all my life–it was a pretty big church. They had great youth programs, and some of my best friends were there. I showed up pretty much every week, and now I still go to church and go with Alex to a small group every other week. That's about it for me."

Sara smiled. "Thanks so much, Annie." She turned to Alex.

"Well, you both know where I grew up," Alex said with a grin and looked at Sara. "But I don't know if you know how we met." When Sara shook her head, he went on, "So, after high school, I went to the same college as Annie. We met our freshman year in biology class. Annie was pretty darn good at biology, and I was pretty darn bad.

But we really hit it off when it was time to dissect the frogs and Annie hid one of her frog's legs in another girl's backpack. You know me, Sara, I was in love! Everything was going great until the accident, and then I lost my job. So that's how I ended up at Second Story. And that's how we got here."

Alex glanced at Annie and said, "After my accident, I had tons of time to think, and I had nothing to do, so I guess God finally had time to get through to me. I realized that I really wasn't living much with him in mind. I mean, how can I say this? I thought about God." He turned to Annie, "We were going to church; we were doing all the right things. But the kind of time I had with God in high school, being able to hear his voice in my life, I guess I just got too busy for that. So the accident gave me nothing but time, and God finally got through. I started thinking about my life–about our life–and about what it's worth. I want it to count for something, Annie. I saw God change lives, and I want to see him change lives still–through us."

He turned back to Sara. "But I'm botching it all up all the time, Sara. People aren't responding the way that I hoped they would. So I really want to talk about this here. And I want to be able to explain to Annie where I'm coming from." He grabbed Annie's hand. "And really, I want to have a chance for Annie and me to be walking on the same path together, toward something. But I'm doing such a terrible job explaining where I want to go that there's no way that Annie can decide if she wants to go there too." Alex shrugged. "That's the best I can do right now, Sara. I'm not sure what else to say."

"Thanks, you guys. That helps." Sara paused, tapping her lips with an index finger. She seemed to be considering something.

"All right," she said. "I think what I'd propose is this: let's get together for the next couple of months, maybe once a week. During that time, I'd encourage you both to pray that God will speak to you both about your future together and about what he wants you to do, given what Alex is learning and feeling. Is this something that God wants to do in both of your hearts, to give you a common vision for the future? I think we can talk about God's heart for people, about sharing the gospel with others, and I think we can do it in a way that will give you opportunities, Alex, to share your heart with Annie. And Annie, it should give you opportunities to hear from God and to discern whether Alex's direction is a direction that you also want to go. How does that sound?"

Annie hesitated to commit herself, so Sara quickly continued, "You don't have to decide right now. Let's go ahead and talk about the passage I asked you to read for this time, and you guys can get back to me on whether you want to continue."

Annie gave a sigh of relief. She still wasn't sure she wanted to commit. This would give her a little more time to decide outside of a pressure-filled environment, and if she said no, she wouldn't have to hurt Sara's feelings.

Sara continued, "For today, though, I'd like to walk through those stories from Luke 15 that I asked you to read. But I want to do it in a special way. I want us to read the story and then retell it to each other. And I want us to focus on really putting ourselves inside of it to experience it along with the people in it. So I'm going to read it, and I'd like for you to imagine yourself in it."

She began, "Now the tax collectors and sinners were all gathering around to hear Jesus. But the Pharisees and the teachers of the law muttered, 'This man welcomes sinners and eats with them.' So Jesus went on to tell three parables." And Sara told the parables.

After she'd finished, she waited just a moment. And then she asked, "Okay, so what happened in the story?"

Annie answered, "Well, it was three stories within a bigger story, right? Jesus was hanging out with some people and went ahead and told them some stories."

"Okay. So what was going on with Jesus?"

Alex said, "He was hanging out with tax collectors and sinners, and the religious people were getting upset."

"What happened next?" Sara asked.

"He told the story about the lost sheep."

"And what happened there?"

"Jesus was pretty up front about things. He said

44

that just like they would go search high and low for a lost sheep, and when it was found, be so happy they would have a party, there's more joy in heaven when a lost person repents."

"Annie, what happened in the next story?"

"Sort of the same thing. Except there was a lost coin instead. And a woman, who had just ten coins to start, lost one of them. She cleaned the whole house and finally found the coin. When she did, she got all the neighbors together to have a party. And then Jesus told the religious people that, in the same way, there would be joy in heaven over one sinner who repents."

"All right. Last one. What happened in the parable of the lost son?"

Alex said, "So this young guy decided that he wanted his inheritance before his dad died. So he asked for it, and the dad gave it. Soon, he left on a trip and went out of town. He spent all his money, and then there was a famine. So he started working slopping pigs. But he couldn't eat their food, and no one would feed him. So he remembered his dad and how his dad's servants lived way better than him. So he decided to go back and ask his dad if he could be a worker in his dad's fields."

"So then, while he was still walking up the driveway, the dad saw him and came running to meet him. The dad was so happy, he handed over his jacket and his ring, and then threw this huge welcome-home party." Alex

45

fell quiet.

Annie said, "You forgot the part about the brother." She continued the story. "So when his dad threw the big party, the guy's older brother was really upset. He wouldn't even come to the party. So the dad went outside and tried to get him to come in. So the brother asked why the dad never threw him a party. And the dad basically said, 'Grow up, dude. Everything I have is yours.'"

"Great job, guys. It's not always easy to remember all those details. But you did a great job. So now I want to ask some questions about this. Tell me. What did you really notice about the story?"

Alex said, "I thought it was interesting that Jesus was telling these stories in response to the Pharisees' question. I'd never really noticed that before."

"And what was that question? They didn't actually ask a question, did they?"

"Well, now that you mention it, no. But they seemed to be wondering why Jesus was wasting his time with these 'sinners.'"

"What else did you notice?"

Annie said, "I thought they sort of told the same story. Well, the first two were almost exactly alike. But the third was different."

"What was different about the third one?"

"Well, in the first two, the owner of the object looked really hard for the item. In the third, the son came home. Even though the dad ran down the road to meet him, he didn't go searching. But he seemed to have the same kind of joy about finding the son as the other people had–the ones who actually looked for the sheep and the coin."

"Interesting. Was there anything you wondered about?"

Annie said, "I wondered why the first two were so happy about finding the lost stuff. What's the big deal about finding a lost sheep if you have 99 other ones."

"Great question, Annie. Did you think of any possible explanations?"

"The only thing I could think was that maybe they didn't have much else. The woman with the coin only had ten coins. So losing one of them would be one tenth of her wealth. I guess I'd be pretty upset if I lost that much too."

"Did you put yourself in the story? Did you imagine how it might have felt to lose something that valuable?"

Annie nodded, but said nothing.

Sara turned to Alex and asked, "How about you? Did you wonder about anything?"

"I wondered how mad the Pharisees were when Jesus finished with the stories. That last one seemed to be a pretty harsh criticism of their values."

"I wondered that too, Alex," Sara said.

"I had another thing," Annie said. "I wondered

47

about how I've actually heard people use these stories before. I mean, a lot of time people focus on the lostness of the coin and the sheep and the son. They try to say that without the finder, those things would be lost forever and worthless. I kind of feel like that leads to making people objects, you know? Like if we take that and apply it to our lives, then that would mean that we're the heroes of the story—rushing off on a white horse to find something. And the lost things, in this case, the people that we're reaching, they're helpless and hopeless until we come." Annie wrinkled her nose. "I don't think that's right."

"But Annie," Alex said, "people are lost, and they do need to be found. If there's no one to find them, how will they ever get found?"

Annie said, "But what about the son? He came back." Annie felt the familiar tension rising again, but had to continue, "Alex, I just don't think that we can walk around like the saviors of the world. I think it makes people feel used and objectified. I think it's horrible."

Sara broke in. "Let's go back to the context of the story. That's pretty important for properly interpreting it. Why was Jesus telling these stories?"

Alex and Annie looked again at their Bibles. Then Alex answered, "The story was for the Pharisees."

"And who were the Pharisees?"

"They were religious leaders who were pretty mad that Jesus was spending time with people they thought

48

weren't religious enough."

"So what is the heart of the message of this story?"

"I know," Annie said. "I think it was to give the Pharisees the reason for Jesus's actions. They wanted to know why he was doing what he was doing. He was explaining that God really cares about the people who are lost. He cares so much that he wants to throw a party when someone is found or comes back."

"Given the context, I think that you're right, Annie. If there's any truth to what you're saying, Alex, it's not found in this story." Annie looked over and saw that Alex was focused intensely down at his Bible, but his eyes weren't moving. She didn't think he liked Sara's answer very well. But she was interested now.

Sara continued, "So what can we take from this passage? How can we respond to the story?"

Alex stared, and Annie thought. She said, "I wonder if there's any way that we can have the same emotion or response as God does about lost people being found. We certainly don't want to be the Pharisees. But how do we do that?"

"Good question, Annie. Do you have any ideas?"

She shook her head. "Not really. I don't know if it's possible to create an emotional response out of thin air. So I'm not sure where it comes from."

Sara said, "We could start by praying. We could ask God to give us the same heart for lost people that he has."

Annie asked, "Do we have to label them lost, though? Doesn't that lead to the same kind of feeling of superiority that the Pharisees had?" Annie looked over at Alex again. Now he was quietly tapping his foot. Then his foot stopped and he shook his shoulders and he seemed to reenter the conversation.

Sara said. "One of the toughest things to do is to navigate these ideas without making ourselves superior. But if your spirituality and your relationship with God is important to you, then I think it's natural to wonder about and be concerned about how that plays out in the lives of those around us. If spirituality leads to peace and joy and other good things in our own lives, it's natural to want to see those same good things in other people."

Alex said, "That's exactly it, Sara. That's totally why I'm so passionate about this issue. God has done so much in my own life. And he's given me such peace and purpose in life that I just want to share that with other people. I want others to see and experience the same things I do." He gave a nod and then fell still.

"Okay, then, do you think it is appropriate to ask God to give us the same heart for other people as he has?" Sara asked.

"I think so," said Annie. Alex nodded.

"One thing that might be helpful is to think of some specific friends to pray for. As we're learning and growing and being challenged in our own spiritual lives, it is good to be thinking about who we can share those things with. Part of the process of growth is being able to articulate what we're learning and thinking about."

Annie raised her eyebrows. "Why do I get the impression that you mean people who don't consider themselves Christians?"

Sara smiled, the corners of her eyes crinkling. "You're right, Annie. I was thinking about people who don't know about or care about Jesus."

"But why would I want to share my spiritual journey with people who don't believe the same thing?" Annie shuddered as she thought about the possibility. She was afraid, really. She didn't want to be judged by the people around her. And she really didn't want to make anyone feel uncomfortable. "I guess I just don't want to rock the boat. It seems really offensive to just start spouting off what I believe all the time."

"That's not quite what I'm suggesting. But I do think it's possible to share our own stories as we walk through life with people. And there's a lot of power in that. Who knows what God will do in the hearts of other people as we open up and share what he's doing in ours. I just think it's good to be thinking about the people around us and how our stories could intersect with theirs. And one way to increase our sensitivity to them is to pray for them."

Annie tipped her head to the side. She still wasn't sure she understood. "So you're not saying that the goal is

51

to make these people believe the same things as us?"

"No, Annie. I don't think anyone can make anyone else believe anything. But I do believe that we're meant to walk in community with other people. We're meant to share our stories with those around us. And that means with people who believe in Jesus as well as those who don't."

Annie nodded. "I think I can see that." She looked over at Alex, and he was nodding too.

Sara said, "So lets spend some time this next week thinking about who is around us that we might be called to walk alongside. And if you think of someone, start praying for him or her. Let's pray that God will bless them. I'll do the same thing. And we can talk some more about this when we get together again. If we get together again." She gave another warm smile.

They chatted for a few more minutes, and then Alex and Annie said their goodbyes.

As Alex and Annie settled into the car to head home, Alex looked over and grinned at Annie. "Thanks for coming with me, Annie girl. Was it as bad as you expected?"

Annie returned his smile and said, "No, not really. Sara's a really nice woman, Alex. She seems genuine. I think I'd like to come again. If this is really important to you, then I'm willing to give it a try. One can survive just about anything for a couple of months, after all."

Alex settled back into his seat, satisfied. Although there were some things he wasn't sure he agreed with tonight, it was really good that he and Annie were talking about spiritual things. There hadn't even been one vocal disagreement. There had been a little tension, but it wasn't too much to wade through. This had been a great idea.

One Prayer at a Time

That night, another couple of inches of snow fell, blanketing the world in white. As morning broke, the snow clouds moved out, uncovering the sun, so Annie woke up to a bright, cheerful winter wonderland. When her alarm clock rang, she peeked out the window next to her bed to determine how early she'd have to leave for work. Seeing the blanket of new snow, she leaned back against her pillows and sighed contentedly. She loved waking up to a whole new world.

As she got out of bed and prepared for her day, she considered the conversation they'd had with Sara the night before. When Sara had asked if she'd pictured anything she loved and lost during the story, she'd thought immediately of Alex, of course, and his motorcycle accident. She'd thought back to that first phone call–Alex's mother calling to tell her that he'd been in an accident and he was in the hospital in critical condition. All the way there, her heart had beat quickly, her mind had raced over the three years they'd shared together, and she had been devastated by the possibility of losing him.

She wondered, now, at the possibility that God felt that way about all people who don't have relationships with him. Could it really be that he is so involved in life and the world that he would care that much about the fact that the relationship between himself and most of mankind was broken?

If so, then God's willingness to sacrifice Jesus made a little bit more sense to Annie. It was true, when Alex was hurt, she'd been willing to trade just about anything to see him get better so that she wouldn't lose him. She could well remember the kind of relief she felt when Alex got better. She'd definitely felt like having a party!

She thought too about Sara's challenge about how this was supposed to impact her life. Even if she accepted the fact that God feels this immense connection to humanity, and deeply longs for relationship between himself and all people, Annie knew that alone wouldn't make her want to share her spiritual journey with everyone around her. It wasn't really enough for her to know how God felt about people. Maybe she'd gotten a glimpse of that feeling as she'd imagined herself in the story of the lost coin and the lost son. But already this morning, in the clear light of day, the bare facts didn't give her any motivation to go out and talk to the first person she met, particularly because of how uncomfortable that kind of conversation would be. Annie had no desire to have deep personal conversations about spirituality with strangers, and she struggled to have those conversations with her closest friends.

No, she'd need something more than just knowing God's heart for people. But what? Didn't Sara say something about praying that God would give them the same heart for people? That made sense. Maybe if she actually felt the same way about people, she'd be willing to take a risk to say something to somebody.

But the next problem was who to even share with. Annie had gone to a private Christian college, and she and Alex spent a lot of time with church friends. Who did she even know who wasn't a Christian? Maybe she should pray about this too.

So as she leaned over the sink to put on her make-up, Annie prayed simply, "God, if Sara's really right about this stuff, and you really want me to be passionate about sharing your message with other people, then I'm going to need a little help here. I don't think it's enough for me to know how you feel. I think I've got to start to feel the same way. But I don't know how to make that happen. So you're going to have to give me the same heart for people that you have. I'm not exactly sure how this works, God, but whatever you need to do, just go ahead. And I don't really know who I know who even needs to hear about you. Most of the people I know are Christians. So help me to see the people that you already have in my life, or bring other people into my life. I guess that's it, God. I'm not really sure what else to say."

As she made her way out to the car a few minutes later, she passed her neighbor in the hallway again. Annie said a bright "Hi," as always, and, as always, Patti said a very quiet "Hello" to her own feet as she passed. For just a moment, Annie wondered whether Patti knew God. Then Annie swung the apartment building door open and headed out to her car to go to work. She was quickly lost in thoughts about Alex, work, and all the things she had to do that day.

Annie worked as a nurse in the pediatrics ward of a local hospital. It was kind of an upscale place near a very nice suburb and about 15 minutes away from the city proper. There were several doctors with privileges there. Annie worked mostly with one doctor, Dr. Franklin.

That morning at the hospital just flew by. As it was late November and cold, kids and their families kept showing up with terrible flus, high fevers, and bad ear infections. Annie was busy giving shots, taking notes, and doing rounds with patients until half an hour past her scheduled lunch break. Finally, she got through the last patient she had to check up on and arrived at the break room energized from all that social interaction. As she walked through the door, she glanced around and saw her friend Oliver Lee seated at the table with his brown bag lunch. His dark hair was recently cut and emphasized his Korean features. He hunched his compact body over the table as he filled out the community crossword puzzle. As Annie walked toward him, he asked, "What's a three-letter word starting with 'Y' that fits the clue 'coniferous hedge'?"

Sitting down across from him, Annie said, "You

know I don't do crossword puzzles, Oliver. Boring! How's your day been so far today? I had like 52 kids with infections and another 30 with fevers. And that was only after Mrs. Robinson brought in little Tommy for chemo, again, and he threw a tantrum up and down the hallway, again. It took like 25 of us to calm him down and get him back in his room. Well, that might be a slight exaggeration; but still, it's been crazy." Annie finally took a breath.

His glance having never left the paper, Oliver muttered, "Hmm, a vowel must come after the 'Y.' Yet, yam, yip, you . . . ."

"Oliver, are you listening?" Annie knocked on the table, "Hello, are you there?"

Oliver finally looked up from the puzzle, a puzzled look on his face, and said, "Oh, hi Annie. I've been trying to figure this thing out for the last 20 minutes. Sorry." He put down the paper. "What were you saying?"

"Well, I was just telling you about my fabulously crazy day and our continuing adventures with Tommy Robinson, but I see that you're far too busy to care about that." Annie rolled her eyes and grinned and said, "Besides the crossword puzzle, what have you been up to lately? Anything interesting? Any new girls on the horizon?"

Oliver's face fell. "Come on, Annie, let it go. You know that I'm not ready for that yet. Heather and I just broke up a month ago. I don't even want to think about anyone else. I'm still trying to figure out what went wrong.

In fact, work is just about the only place I don't think about her every moment, so thanks for ruining that for the day."

"Sorry, Oliver. I was just kidding, really. And you know I just want you to be happy, right?"

"Besides," Oliver continued, decidedly not answering Annie's question, "aren't you and Alex having a little trouble of your own? I don't know how you can be pushing something on me that's not working out so well for you."

Annie paused before answering. She'd met Oliver about a year ago, when she first started at the hospital. He was a smart guy, and funny, and they'd immediately had a million things to talk about. For one thing, they were the only young people in the pediatrics ward; everyone else was at least 40. So while everyone else wanted to talk about their kids or their spouses, Oliver and Annie were still talking about dating, their college days, and how to get ahead. At the same time, though, she and Oliver didn't talk all that deeply. She wasn't really comfortable with the thought of delving into her personal life. The only reason Oliver knew that she and Alex were having problems is because after one particularly bad fight they'd had, she was in a foul mood at work and had exploded to Oliver about it. She wasn't sure she wanted to discuss what she and Alex had been fighting about, and she certainly didn't want to try to explain how they were trying to fix it. She didn't know much about Oliver's spiritual life, but she knew enough that he wasn't religious and that he generally didn't like religious people. He would definitely not understand.

She finally answered, "We're working on it, Oliver; we're working on it. He's a really sweet guy though, and I think we're really good together. We're just not seeing eye to eye on everything right now. But I think it'll get better. And anyway, even if this doesn't work out, I think life is always better shared with someone else. Like I said, I just want to see you happy."

"Yew!" Oliver exclaimed, slapping his thigh. "That's what it is."

"Me?" Annie asked. "What about me?"

"No—Y-E-W, that's the answer to the crossword puzzle. Now maybe I can figure out 14 down. You don't mind, do you Annie?"

"Nah, that's okay. I've got to get back to work anyway." Looking at her watch, Annie said, "It looks like I'm late getting back as it is. Have a great one, Oliver. Maybe I'll see you tomorrow."

"All right," Oliver muttered, already enthralled in the crossword puzzle again.

Annie went back to work, and the second half of the day flew by just as quickly as the first, though without all the excitement that Tommy Robinson brought. She finished the day worn out, but happy. For Annie, a day with people, even sick and whiny kids, was a good day, and she was actually looking forward to hanging out with Alex that night over dinner at her place. She was supposed to be cooking dinner for him, so she stopped for groceries on the way home.

Alex arrived at Annie's apartment that night about 15 minutes late, as usual. For some reason, he could never be on time. As he approached Annie's door through the beige apartment hallway, he thought he smelled bacon, or was it sausage? Ah well, he would know soon enough. Annie answered his knock with only about a second's delay, and he walked in her apartment to see her leaning over the refrigerator door to unlock the front door. She leaned back, picked up the eggs she'd been reaching for, and greeted Alex, "Hey Alex. How are ya?"

The front door slammed itself closed, and Alex came around to the bar in the living room that faced the kitchen sink. "I'm doing great. How're you, Annie girl? Did you have a good day?"

"Sure I did, although it was absolutely crazy. You remember little Tommy R., right? The one I always tell you about? He came in and threw a tantrum the size of Texas, and poor Dr. Franklin looked like he was about to croak because of all the screaming. I know that he likes kids, but, for a pediatrician, he seems to have an unnatural aversion to the screamers. Anyway, it was otherwise uneventful. How about you?"

Alex watched Annie beat four eggs and then turn to the stove to pour them into her omelet pan. "Nothing much to report, actually. Everything went pretty smoothly at the store, and Drew was even in a pretty friendly mood, so the day went pretty quickly. Hey–can I help you set the table or something?"

Annie welcomed the help, and in no time they were eating bacon and mushroom omelets. After taking a bite, Annie said, "So, Alex, I've been thinking about last night. And I just don't know what to think about those stories. I mean, I think it's really great if it's really true, that God is really passionate about lost people being found, or finding him, or whatever. But I'm not sure what it means to my life, you know? Like, just knowing that about God doesn't really change me in any way. But didn't it seem like Sara thought it should–change us, I mean? I don't really get that."

Alex said, "I think knowing things about God's character should change us. We should be always growing to look and act more like him. As for how that happens, we certainly have to pray and ask God to change our hearts."

"Well," Annie said doubtfully, "I did pray about it this morning. But I wasn't sure if that was enough. It seemed like maybe I should have done something more."

"Well, God can use experiences to change our hearts too. That's what happened to me on that trip to the Philippines. What made it so powerful was that I was

63

confronted over and over again with how many people don't know Jesus and how deeply they need things. Not just spiritual things, but things like water, and food, and clothes. Everything. And my heart broke for them. But even then, God was the one who was changing my heart."

"Well, maybe he'll change mine too. I don't know." Annie paused, "Actually, practically the next minute after I prayed, I walked out the door and saw my neighbor, Patti, you know, the really weird, quiet one? Anyway, I had the thought for a second that I wondered if she was a Christian. Maybe that was God."

"Of course it was, Annie. But we can keep praying. Did you start thinking about other people to be praying for?"

"Well, I thought I might be able to share some things with Patti, if she'll ever say something more than hello. But I'm not really sure who else. Most everyone I know is from church or school. You know we don't really hang out much with other people."

"How about at work, Annie? Because I was thinking about that too–about how we don't really have many non-Christian friends. But I do know Drew from work. And then there's a new guy working there, Omar, and he's definitely a Muslim, or a Hindu, or something. He's from some Middle Eastern country, and it's pretty clear that he's practicing another religion."

"There's always Dr. Franklin, I guess. But that

might be kind of weird, because he's my boss. Maybe Oliver. You know Oliver, right? The other young nurse at work? He came to my birthday party last year. We talk a little bit when we happen to have lunch at the same time, so there's some potential there."

Alex said, "Sure, yeah, I remember him. Hey Annie, do you want to pray after dinner for these people, together?"

"I guess so."

So after dinner, Alex and Annie sat together on the couch, holding hands, and they prayed that God would be with these four people. They prayed that God would bless them and that God would give themselves eyes to see their friends the way that God sees them.

Alex left a few hours later, totally encouraged by their conversation and interaction that evening. It was almost like they were beginning to speak the same language again. It was so exciting to think that they might actually get on the same page and that all the fighting and disagreement could be over. Well, maybe not over, but at least over things that were less important than those things he thought were becoming dear to his heart.

An All-Consuming Calling

The following Wednesday, Annie and Alex pulled up to Sara's house in Alex's truck. Alex was excited to see if this week would lead to the same kind of positive discussions that they'd had last week. Hand-in-hand, they approached the front door. This time, Annie rang the doorbell. In the hand not occupied by Annie's, Alex held a loaf of his mom's banana bread.

Sara opened the door and welcomed them. Alex presented the bread: "From my mom, Sara. She said to say hi."

"Thanks, honey. That was really sweet. We'll just cut this up to eat while we talk. What can I get you guys to drink?"

Alex glanced at Annie. "A couple of hot cocoas?" Annie nodded.

"Make yourselves at home," Sara said, motioning to the living room. She went to the kitchen while Annie and Alex got comfortable on the love seat.

Sara soon brought in a tray with a couple of mugs of hot cocoa and a plate of Alex's mom's banana bread. They chit-chatted for a couple of minutes and caught up on Alex's family news. Finally, there was a lull in the conversation, and Sara started them off with prayer. Her words were quiet and confident, inviting God to be a part of their conversation and to lead their thoughts and discussion that night.

After praying, Sara said, "I've been thinking a lot about what we talked about last week. Actually, I've been thinking about something you said, Annie. You talked about how we don't want to be like the Pharisees, having an attitude of superiority about other people or objectifying them because we think they are 'lost' or don't believe the right way. That showed a lot of insight."

Sara took a sip of tea and then continued. "I've been trying to think of a way to reframe the idea of sharing Christ with those around us. I grew up with that paradigm we talked about last week: people are lost and need to be saved, and I have the message that will save them."

"But I think you're right, Annie. I think that thought pattern really does lead to an attitude of superiority and objectification–the last thing that God would want from me. I thought then about those stories we read, about how much God loves people and wants to have a relationship with all of us. And I prayed, a lot, that God would give me his eyes to see the people around me."

"And I really had this sense that my life is a story that I've been entrusted with. As I walk through life and get to know more about the God in the Bible, I see myself more and more a part of his greater story. And stories are meant to be shared. So instead of being a savior come to give someone information that will save and transform them, I'm wondering now if I shouldn't see myself as a storyteller entrusted with the story of my life and God's activity in it. In that framework, sharing what he's been doing in me seems to be much more about relationship-building than information-giving."

Sara smiled and shrugged. "You really challenged me, Annie. So thank you for that."

Annie smiled and said, "You're welcome."

Alex wondered about Sara's comments. He didn't really see much of a difference between the lost/found mentality and the storyteller mentality, but he didn't say anything. He didn't want to interrupt because Annie seemed to be responding so well. There was an interested light in her beautiful green eyes that he hadn't seen for a while. He didn't want to put it out, so he held his peace.

Sara brought her hands together in a single, soft clap. "So anyway, what I wanted to talk about tonight was a little bit more about God's story. What have we been called to? How do we communicate what God has called us to? Alex, can you read Mark 12:28-34 to us?"

Annie handed Alex his Bible, and Alex flipped to the right page. Then he read:

> One of the teachers of the law came and heard them debating. Noticing that Jesus had given them a good answer, he asked him, "of all the commandments, which is the most important?"
>
> "The most important one," answered

Jesus, "is this: 'Hear, O Israel, the Lord our God, the Lord is one. Love the Lord your God with all your heart and with all your soul and with all your mind and with all your strength.' The second is this: 'Love your neighbor as yourself.' There is no commandment greater than these."

"Well said, teacher," the man replied. "You are right in saying that God is one and there is no other but him. To love him with all your heart, with all your understanding and with all your strength and to love your neighbor as yourself is more important than all burnt offerings and sacrifices."

When Jesus saw that he had answered wisely, he said to him, "You are not far from the kingdom of God." And from then on, no one dared ask him any more questions.

Sara asked, "Does anything strike you about this passage?"

Annie said, "Well, it seems pretty all-encompassing. All your heart, soul, mind, and strength. It doesn't sound like there's anything left. It seems like everything. And that seems like a pretty huge burden."

"Interesting that you would use the word 'burden,'

Annie," said Sara. "Some of Jesus's parables might speak to that. Shall we look at some?"

Annie and Alex nodded, so Sara directed them to Matthew 13:44-46. There they read about the parable of the hidden treasure and the pearl of great price. Then she asked, "What did you notice about these stories?"

Alex answered, "The two people found something that seemed valuable enough for them to give up everything else for."

"Did it seem like they minded the sacrifice?" Sara asked.

Annie shook her head, "No, there was no hesitation."

"Why do you think that was?"

Alex answered, "Well, maybe because they realized that they were getting something more valuable. It was like a value-for-value transfer. The treasure was buried, so no one else knew about it. The guy got a great deal. And money for a pearl, well, at least the person still had something to sell, if he needed to."

Annie interrupted, "But how does this relate to loving God with everything? It's not like I can trade that in for a hundred dollar bill."

Sara said, "Okay. I'll try to put the same idea into more intangible terms. When Alex was in the hospital, what do you think it was worth to his family to have him back?"

Alex saw Annie smile, "Ah, I see. Everything. They would have mortgaged their house; they would have worked 24 hours a day; they would have done anything."

Sara asked, "Even though he was injured and couldn't pay them back?"

"Of course. They just wanted him. Interesting."

Sara let that sit for a minute. "So we've seen that we are called to love God with all that we are. But that's not everything. What else did the guy say when Jesus asked him that question?"

"We're to love our neighbor as ourselves," Alex answered.

"And what does that mean?"

Alex looked at Annie, but her face was blank. He shrugged.

"Do you remember the story of the good Samaritan?" Sara asked.

"Oh, yeah," Alex said. "Of course. A Jewish guy got beat up and robbed and was laying on the side of the road. A religious teacher walked by, saw him, but didn't help; another Jewish guy did too; and then a Samaritan came by. He picked up the Jewish guy, carried him to an inn, and paid for them to take care of him."

"And what was the big deal about that?"

"Well, the Jews and the Samaritans hated each other fiercely. It would be like how Americans feel about radical Muslims. Maybe it would be like, the day after September

11 if someone from New York came across a suicide bomber that was injured but not killed. If he took that guy to a hospital and said he'd pay for all the procedures, that would be like what the Samaritan did."

"Wow, Alex," Sara said, "that's a great picture of what Jesus was trying to say. So what do you think his point was?"

"To love your enemies?" Annie answered.

Sara asked, "Do you remember how the story came about? Who was Jesus talking to and what did they want to know?"

Alex said, "It was after they talked about loving your neighbor as yourself. Someone asked Jesus who his neighbor was."

"Yes, that's right."

"Hmm, that's interesting," said Annie. "So Jesus didn't really answer the question. He just told them this story."

"Exactly. And when he was finished, he didn't say, 'so love your enemies.' He said, 'who do you think the neighbor was in this story?'"

They all sat for a moment, and Alex pondered this. It seemed strange to him that Jesus didn't answer the question. Why wouldn't he just tell them who their neighbor was? He supposed that it was an important point that they should love anyone and that maybe it was more important how they loved than who they loved. But that guy had a real question, and Jesus didn't answer. You should always answer a person's questions, right? Alex shook his head and heard Sara continuing:

"There's one more aspect of this calling that I want to discuss. I actually want to read to you a paraphrase of part of 2 Corinthians 5. It's a mix of my own paraphrase and the Message translation,[1] but it captures what Paul calls the 'ministry of reconciliation' very well. Here it is:

> Therefore, if anyone is in Christ, he is a new creation; the old has gone, the new has come! All this is from God, who reconciled us to himself through Christ and gave us the ministry of reconciliation: that God was reconciling the world to himself in Christ, not counting men's sins against them. And he has committed to us the message of reconciliation. We are therefore Christ's ambassadors, as though God were making his appeal through us. We implore you on Christ's behalf: Be reconciled to God. God made him who had no sin to be sin for us, so that in him we might become the righteousness of God.

---

[1] This passage is a mixture of the author's paraphrase, the NIV, and The Message, which is copyright 1993, 1994, 1995, 1996, 2000, 2001, 2002 and used by permission of NavPress Publishing Group.

Our firm decision is to work from this focused center: Jesus died for everyone. That puts everyone in the same boat. He included everyone in his death so that everyone could also be included in his life, a resurrection life, a far better life than people ever lived on their own.

Because of this decision we don't evaluate people by what they have or how they look. We looked at the Messiah that way once and got it all wrong, as you know. We certainly don't look at him that way anymore. Now we look inside, and what we see is that anyone united with the Messiah gets a fresh start, is created new. The old life is gone; a new life begins! Look at it!

Instead of selfishness, we now can be selfless. Instead of greed, we now can give generously what we have. Instead of being filled with lust, we now can love people who are ugly. Instead of being prideful, we know that everything that we have and are comes from God. Instead of seeking the approval of others, we now know that we have God's approval.

All this comes from the God who healed our broken relationship with him, with ourselves, and with each other. He now asks us to spend our lives working to help other people heal their broken relationships. If we choose to walk with God, then our job is to also walk with others and bear their burdens and help men and women drop their differences and enter into God's work of making things right.

But how is this possible? It's possible because God made Jesus, who had no brokenness, to be broken for our sakes, so that through his body and blood, we could become the children of God.

Annie and Alex were silent. Sara said quietly, "This is the mission that we have been given. To love God, to love other people, and to be about the business of reconciling others and the world to God. There's a whole broken world out there. There is evil; there is brokenness; there are people who are unloved and people who are hurting. God longs to have a relationship with all people. He longs to see all people come to know him as Father and as God. We get to be a part of that! We get to be a part of that by sharing the story of the reconciliation offered by Jesus through the cross and by doing the ministry of reconciliation. That ministry is made up of loving other people and helping to heal the brokenness of our world.

What a calling!"

Alex jumped up and started pacing. "Annie, that's exactly what I've been talking about! This is exactly what I feel like God has called me to. When I was laying there in the hospital, I just kept seeing the broken and hurting people in my world flashing through my memory. I kept thinking about those Filipino children I met in high school and about how they had nothing. This is what I want to give my life to. Do you understand? The world is lost and dying and broken, and it needs to be fixed! And I just know I'm supposed to be a part of it. There's so much to do!"

Annie was fidgeting, and she didn't immediately answer. Sara gave her a minute to respond, and when she didn't, said, "You know Alex and Annie, this is a huge calling. It's enormous. It is a whole life's worth of surrender and commitment. While this is clearly the calling that Jesus gave in Scripture, people don't get there overnight. It takes time, sometimes many years. As we continue to talk about this, I'm going to challenge you and myself to continue to take steps toward living out this mission, one step at a time. And I also want to remind you that this is a calling to sacrifice. It's not to run around trying to fix things, but to love and sacrifice for those around us. Jesus spoke of picking up our cross and losing our life to find it. It is not an easy road."

"So for the next week, I would really like for us to

think about what might be holding us back from loving God with everything that we are. We can also think about practical ways to love those around us, whether Christians or not. When we come back next time, let's talk some more about loving God this way and walking in this mission. Alex, can you pray for us?"

So Alex prayed aloud while Annie fidgeted. No one said much of anything after the prayer, and Annie and Alex soon left. Alex made a couple of attempts at conversation in the car, but Annie's responses were monosyllabic. Soon they arrived at Annie's and parted with a hasty kiss. As Alex left, he worried about Annie because she was usually such a verbal processor. It wasn't normal that she didn't want to talk. He also felt vindicated. What he'd been trying to express for several months now to Annie was right there in the Bible. He was right about the place this was supposed to have in their lives. He was right where he was supposed to be. So at least he had that. He just hoped now that Annie would get on the right track too.

Meanwhile, Sara was still in her living room at home. She hadn't moved from the living room since Annie and Alex left. She sat, quietly praying. She had sensed a great spiritual battle was upon them that evening. She was concerned with Annie's silence and with Alex's exuberance. Each seemed problematic in its own way. As little as she knew Annie, she did know that Annie was usually talkative. Alex, though passionate, could be very overbearing in his own opinions. She thought that perhaps this was where some of the tension in the relationship was coming from. Although Alex seemed sincere in his transformation, Sara knew that he had a tendency to be extreme. The extremeness of his opinions made everything seem totally defined, totally black and white. Annie did not seem to be that type of person. She was praying that Alex's certainty would not be a hindrance to the work of the Spirit in Annie's life.

Heart, Soul, Mind, and Strength

Although not usually prone to introspection, Annie lay down to sleep that night with "all your heart, soul, mind, and strength" running over and over through her brain. She couldn't stop thinking about those words and what they meant. She wondered whether she had ever been consumed with anything to that level in her life. She wondered if that kind of all-consuming commitment was even possible for her. Admittedly, she liked to flit from one thing to the next. A social butterfly, she rarely got close to anyone, but she knew everyone. She had a million hobbies, but wasn't an expert at anything.

Annie tossed and turned and wondered. She really wanted to do the right things. She grew up going to church, and she'd taken on those moral values that the church taught. She was concerned about her spiritual life, and she had inconsistently read the Bible and gone to church as an adult. She always meant to do those things, and she was pretty committed to the small group she and Alex went to. But in her spirit, she knew that was because of the people and the social aspects and not because she actually cared about the Bible studies. She couldn't actually remember another time in her life when she had been so impacted by any words from the Bible.

Heart, soul, mind, strength.

Her family was religious. Her parents made her go to church. Her mom was even involved in the nursery, and her dad did the offering thing most weeks. But they weren't that committed to Jesus. At home, they fought a lot. They didn't talk about God, and some of the things she knew were in the Bible, well, those things didn't always happen at home. In fact, she had known from a young age that her parents' first priority was money. She wasn't sure where that came from. They talked a lot about retirement and how to have nice things, and they redecorated the house about once every three years. No, God was not first in their lives, and he certainly wasn't all-consuming.

And Annie herself. She was a good person. She didn't have stuff like her parents did. She was generally nice to other people and even gave some of her money to support a kid in South America. His picture was hanging on her fridge. Her parents had never done that.

But was that enough?

She was sure that God did not have first place in her life. And she wasn't sure that she wanted him there. Look what it had done to Alex. He went from being a perfectly normal, reasonable guy to someone who only ever talked about God and his own mission in life. And in fact, he'd begun to sound a little self-righteous. If that's what it meant to love God with all your heart, soul, mind, and strength, she wasn't sure she wanted it.

But there was Sara. She seemed reasonable. There

was no denying she was kind and thoughtful. She talked passionately about God, but she hadn't lost her ability to talk about other things. She was actually very sweet, and she had such a peace, even about her husband dying. She seemed like she really loved life and was genuinely happy with things.

Annie eventually drifted off into a fitful sleep. She dreamed that she was at church the next Sunday, and God called her out of her chair to come to the front and commit to going to Africa to tell other people about Jesus. She spent the rest of the dream running away from something she couldn't see.

The next morning, Annie awoke in a terrible mood. She hadn't slept well, and she was annoyed. The first thing she'd thought of when she woke up was those same four words. *Heart, soul, mind, and strength.* She hoped that her whole day wouldn't be like this.

Annie went for an early morning jog before getting ready for her shift at the hospital. Unfortunately, the run didn't do a thing to clear her mind. She returned to her apartment building, exasperated. She approached her front door, and the neighbor's daughter, Josie, was sitting on the steps. She wore torn, black jeans and a puffy, black coat. She had ear buds in her ears, and she was scowling at her phone while she messaged someone. The early morning sun gently highlighted the purple streaks in her hair.

Annie asked, "Hey, Josie, what are you doing outside in this cold?" Josie raised her head and one eyebrow, giving Annie an icy stare. Finally, she answered, "It's Jo, actually. And I'm waiting for my ride to school, if it's any of your business." She went back to messaging. Annie took the hint and just went inside rather than trying to carry on the conversation. She was exasperated enough already. She wondered for a moment if God actually loved Josie and wanted her to know him too. She was certainly less than pleasant to be around.

As Annie's day progressed, one wrong thing happened after another. She burned her breakfast and didn't have time to throw it away and start over. She had a horrible time finding veins to start IVs or take blood. Only the grumpy warden-like nurse was working on the floor that day–none of her friends were there. Her least favorite chronically ill kid was admitted and assigned to her section. And through it all, she kept thinking about how God wanted to be the biggest priority in her life. She kept thinking about being called to the ministry of reconciliation. What would it look like if she was committed to helping people like Josie or the warden-nurse to know God better? How could that even work? The very thought made her uncomfortable.

Annie arrived home around 8 p.m., still miserable, and still introspective. There was a message from Alex on the phone, but she didn't feel like talking to him. As she couldn't get it out of her head anyway, after changing clothes and heating up leftovers, she sat down and read the passages that they'd looked at the night before.

She was struck this time with the passage from 2 Corinthians. She was struck by that picture of a new life with hope and purpose. It sounded good. It sounded like something worthwhile, something worth seeking. But at what cost? And then she was back to the heart, soul, mind, and strength. What did that even mean?

Drumming her fingers on the table, she picked up the phone. She put it down again. A few seconds later she picked it up again, looked at it, and put it down. Finally, she actually dialed Sara's number. She hoped it wasn't too late. But Sara picked up on the first ring. When she realized how distraught Annie was, she offered to come over. Annie agreed, and then sat waiting for Sara to come.

When Sara arrived, she set about making tea while Annie paced and began her story. Annie explained her frustration and her doubts, and finally asked, "Sara, how is it even possible? I mean, I know my life hasn't been perfect, but I've been doing what I can. And I'm better than a lot of people. But somehow I get the idea that it's not enough. I am seeing for the first time that maybe my priorities are wrong. But I don't know what to do about it. I mean, how do you love God with your whole heart, mind, soul, and strength? It seems enormous. And what is it supposed to look like, anyway?"

As soon as Sara finished making the tea, she set two cups down on the coffee table in the living room and said, "Why don't you have a seat." Annie sat.

"Annie, look," she continued. "You're right that being called as a child of God is an enormous, all-consuming thing. To love God with your whole heart, soul, mind, and strength is like saying that you're to love God with all of who you are. But it's not something that you can make yourself do. And it's not something you do all at once. Your love for God is something that grows and develops one day at a time. It grows as you spend time with God, getting to know who he is. It grows as you understand the whole story of God and how all the little stories fit together. It grows as you spend time praying and sharing your heart with God and trying to listen to what he has to say to you. It grows as you try to listen."

"But the first step is to be open to God. The first step is to lay your heart out there, telling God what you're thinking and feeling. You can ask him to help you to learn to love him like that. And then, Annie, you have to get to know him and his ways. You have to pray that he will give you his heart for the people around you, and you have to be willing to let him do that work in your life."

"It's a lifelong process. But it's one you can take one day at a time. Today, you can say to God, 'God, I want to love you with all my heart, mind, soul, and strength. But I don't know how. Please help me.' And then tomorrow you can pray the same thing. You just take one day at a time."

"But Sara, what does it look like? I mean, I think you're a great person and all, and it seems like this is what you are trying to do with your life. But so is Alex. And he's changed, Sara. He used to be so fun-loving. He used to be fun to be around, and everyone liked him. But he's so strongly opinionated now about right and wrong that I see him alienating the people around him. And he often alienates me. I don't want to be that kind of person."

"Annie, I don't pretend to know what's going on in Alex's heart. But I do know that God wants you to be the you he created you to be. Allowing him to have first place in your life should allow you to live more freely out of who he created you to be. But sometimes people who are touched by God attach themselves to the wrong things. Sometimes they get caught up in the external things that the Church or even the Bible tells them are good. I fear that Alex may have gone that direction and may be focused more on his mission than on knowing and loving God. Only time will tell." She reached over and squeezed Annie's hand.

"But you don't have to become like that. If you continue to seek God, to surrender yourself to him one day at a time, he'll lead and guide and grow both you and your love for him."

87

"You make it sound easy. How do I know I can really trust God, though? How do I know what he'll ask me to do? I had this dream last night that he called me to go to Africa. I don't want to go to Africa, Sara. I know I should be willing, but I'm really not right now."

"Today Annie, maybe that's all you need to surrender. You can offer your fear to God, and say, 'God, I want to trust you. But I'm afraid. I want to love you, but I'm afraid of what that means.' He'll meet you right where you are, Annie. He wants to do that. He wants you to bring those things to him too."

"I guess I can try that." She gave a watery smile. "You can go home now, if you want to. I know it's late."

"Okay, Annie. But you call me any time, honey. I'm happy to come over and talk with you. I'll be praying for you tonight."

So Sara left, and Annie got ready for bed. Tonight, as she lay down to sleep, she simply prayed that God would meet her in her fear. She told God that she wanted to love him and she wanted to trust him, but she wasn't sure if she could. She asked God to help her. And then she went to sleep.

The next morning, Alex made his way to Second Story for his ordering and scheduling shift. This was actually his least favorite part of managing the café. He loved managing people, and he thought he was pretty good at it. But today's work would be poring over inventory sheets and schedules with little to distract him. He could only hope that Drew would be in a good mood. And then he remembered–he was supposed to be praying for Drew. Drew was part of his mission of reconciliation. So he spent his commute to the bookstore praying for Drew and praying that God would give him an opportunity to talk with Drew.

He made it into their shared office first, so he got out his inventory sheets and started going through them. He was marking up his paperwork and humming a little tune when Drew walked in. Drew looked ghostly pale. His shoulders were slumped, and his limbs moved without energy. He made his way through the clutter to his desk.

"Hey Drew!" Alex said. Drew nodded, but didn't reply.

"Is something the matter?" Alex asked.

"Not really. I feel awful is all. The doctors have me on this new medicine, and it makes me feel really nauseated."

Alex said, "Drew, you've been looking really sick. What's going on?" Alex wasn't sure if it was appropriate to ask, but he thought he'd take the plunge.

Drew sighed. "I have cancer, Alex, okay?"

"Oh." He paused. "Wow, Drew. I'm so sorry to hear that." Is that what he was supposed to say? Now what should he do?

"I really don't want your pity. Can we just get to work?" Drew pulled his chair up to the desk and turned his back toward Alex.

Alex went back to his inventory sheets, but he couldn't concentrate. He'd been right. Drew was basically on his deathbed. He clearly didn't want to talk about it or to talk about anything, really. But his time was short. Alex had been placed here for just such a time as this, he knew it. So now what should he say? How should he approach it? Drew clearly was not reconciled with God.

"Drew, I understand that this must be a really hard time for you. But have you thought about where you are spiritually? I mean, if you die from this disease, are you going to show up in heaven or hell?" There. At least he had gotten something out. Maybe it wasn't perfect, but it should open up the conversation.

Drew slowly turned around in his chair. He took a long, sweeping look at Alex and said, "According to my dad, I'm on my way to hell." Drew kept eye contact with Alex for a minute, almost daring him to speak, and then turned back around to his work. He said over his shoulder, "Enough of this bullshit, Alex. You know and I know that God doesn't give a damn about a gay man."

To Drew's back, Alex bravely went on, "But that's where you're wrong, Drew. God does care about you. He spent all of his time on earth with sinners–the lowest of the low–the prostitutes, the tax collectors. Sure he loves you."

Drew remained tense, but he didn't say a thing. He just flipped on his radio and kept working. Alex was crushed. Where was all this hostility coming from? He was talking about God's love–not even about God's judgment of sin. Why didn't that make a dent in Drew's attitude? And why was he holding Alex responsible for what his dad had said and done. His dad was clearly a jerk. But that had nothing to do with God.

The morning wore on, and Alex mulled it over in his mind. What a train wreck. He had to figure out a way to reach Drew before it was too late. But obviously what he'd been saying wasn't working. Maybe he would ask Sara about it the next time they got together.

His thoughts moved on to Annie. She'd been acting strangely since their last meeting with Sara. They'd talked briefly this morning before work, but Annie was a little distant. He hoped that dinner at his place that night wouldn't be too awkward.

Annie's day was going much better than yesterday. She was almost back to her old cheerful self. She woke up that morning still wondering about things, but she just prayed again that God would meet her in her fear.

I really do want to love you most of all, God, and to put you first in my life. I just don't know how.

At work, her least favorite patient was still there. Jenny was a little girl who had a horrible blood disorder.

She had to come in regularly for transfusions, and sometimes she had bad infections that brought her very near death. Jenny was okay when she was too sick to talk, but the minute she started feeling better, she started whining and complaining and generally trying to manipulate all those around her. Annie knew she was a sick little girl, but she couldn't stand the way Jenny's parents catered to her and let her get away with murder. She would push the nurse's call button every five seconds, and she always had Annie running the whole shift.

About an hour into her shift, Annie was already annoyed with Jenny and fighting to keep a professional demeanor as she, too, had to cater to Jenny's every whim. She was giving herself a little pep talk on the way to the ice cream machine they kept around for the kids, when she thought that Jenny was sort of like her enemy right now. Sure, Jenny wasn't really hurting Annie, just annoying her. But Jenny made Annie want to scream.

So what did it mean in this situation to love Jenny? She certainly couldn't do it on her own. So she stopped for a second and prayed, "God, this little girl is driving me nuts right now. But I know that you created her and you love her. Help me to see her the way that you do today." She continued to the ice cream machine and got a little cup of twist ice cream for Jenny, and she returned to Jenny with a slightly lighter step.

Jenny, of course, met her with complaints about

how she wanted chocolate instead of twist. Instead of being short with Jenny (or throwing the ice cream at the wall, as she was tempted to do), she just smiled warmly and went back for a chocolate. She cheerfully returned with Jenny's ice cream and told her to ring if she had any other problems.

Annie left surprisingly pleased with herself. Jenny was still a little punk, but it wasn't her job to fix that. Her job was to make a really difficult situation a little bit better for this little girl and her family. She could do that.

As the weekend progressed, Annie and Alex shared a few meals and attended church together. They didn't talk much about what was going on, though. Annie was still trying to make her way through this question of how to love God with everything that she was, and it seemed a little too raw or too fresh to expose to another person, even Alex. Alex was trying to puzzle out how to reach Drew, and he just wasn't sure Annie would understand. They'd fought so much about stuff like this. He thought that Sara might be getting through to Annie, but he wasn't sure and he didn't want to cause any tension. So he didn't mention it, and they had a relatively peaceful weekend.

Monday dawned bright and clear, though cold. Annie bundled up and then went for an early morning run and passed by Josie on the way out this time. As she was running, she thought about Josie and Patti. They were such an interesting family. The dad was really intimidating. She heard him shouting sometimes and basically tried to stay out of his way when he was around. But he didn't seem to be around much. And Patti was so quiet, she barely said two words. Annie wondered what was going on there. And Josie. Josie was always alone. She'd never seen any teenager friends hanging around. There were no parties, nothing. And she wasn't very friendly at all. Annie wondered how they all got along in such a small space and why they were in an apartment anyway. Couldn't they afford a house? She prayed for them as she jogged home, asking God to help her to see them the way he did and to give her opportunities to be a friend to them.

She arrived back at her apartment to find Josie still sitting on the stoop. "Hey Jos—I mean Jo," she said. "How's it going?" Josie just looked at her and then said, "Fine."

"Well," said Annie, "if you ever want to drop by my place for a cup of hot cocoa or something, feel free. I love to have visitors!" She smiled warmly and then headed in. She wasn't surprised at the lack of response from Josie.

She was surprised that evening when, about ten minutes after she arrived home from work, Josie knocked on her door. "Come in!" Annie said.

So Josie came in and made her way to the living room. She glanced around at the modest furnishings and

94

plopped on the couch.   Annie asked, "Do you want anything to drink?"

"Do you have any beer?" Josie asked.

"Ah, no." Annie replied. "How about some soda? Or some coffee?"

Josie shrugged, "Soda's fine." As Annie retrieved the soda from the kitchen, Josie made a closer inspection of the contents of the room. Annie wondered if she was casing the joint but brushed that thought aside.

"I'm glad you stopped by." Annie handed over the soda and then sat down, crossed her legs, and started swinging the top one. She looked at Josie. Josie glanced at her, glanced away, and glanced back.

"So, what brings you by?" Annie asked.

Josie wrinkled her brow. "You invited me over." She looked at Annie.

"Of course I did. Of course. How was school today?"

"Boring. It's always boring. What do you have to do around here? Movies? Cable? Music? You must have the internet."

"Sure I do. My iPod is right over there by Herman." Annie pointed at the goldfish. "You can hook it up to the speakers if you want." So Josie went over to the bar and got the iPod all plugged in. She flipped through the files, looking for something she recognized.

"What is all this crap? The Passion Worship Band?"

She whipped her head around to look at Annie. "You're not a Christian, are you?"

"Well, yeah. Aren't you? Don't I see you guys getting back from church sometimes, on Sundays?"

Josie rolled her eyes. "My parents make me go. What a load of crap. The pastor just stands up there every week, whining for money because if we don't increase the budget, the roof will cave in and he'll have to get a real job. If people need a crutch to get by in life, that's fine for them. But I don't need that. I don't need anyone." Josie sat down again, arms crossed.

Annie wasn't sure what to say. Josie seemed to despise the idea of church and of God. So she just said, "Okay. Would you rather watch a movie? I think there's a couple coming on in a second."

Josie loosened up a little bit. "Well, if you have cable, there's a new Dr. Who on the SciFi channel. My dad is always hogging the TV at night, so I never get to see it. Do you mind?"

Annie shook her head and handed Josie the remote. After the show, she headed back home. As she closed the door behind Josie, Annie shook her head. What was that all about? The kid barely says a single word to her for a year, and then she comes over? Weird.

Annie shrugged, and then made a quick call to Alex. She told him about Josie and about how hardened she'd been to talking about God.

Alex asked, "What did you say?"

"Nothing, really. We just watched some TV together and then she went home."

"Annie, why didn't you say anything? That was your chance to tell her about God–to be part of the 'ministry of reconciliation' that Sara was talking about. How could you let the chance slip away?"

"It didn't seem appropriate, Alex. She as much as told me she didn't want anything to do with it. I didn't think saying anything right then would do any good. But she clearly wanted to stick around, so I let her."

"But what if she dies in her sleep tonight? Won't you feel bad that you didn't say anything?"

"Alex, don't be ridiculous. She's not going to die in her sleep. I just don't think that she was ready. I know I wasn't ready. What's wrong with just being nice to her and letting her come over? She's just a kid."

"What's wrong is that in order to become a Christian she has to know the message of God. And someone has to tell her the gospel."

"Alex, she's been going to church for years. Don't you think she's heard it all before?"

"Well, maybe. But still. It was a lost opportunity."

"Maybe it was. But I didn't feel like it was good timing. And I didn't want to make her hate me more than she already did when she found those songs on my iPod. So I just wanted to give her some space. I don't think that was the wrong decision."

Before Alex could disagree with her again, Annie told him she loved him and got off the phone.

Alex was disappointed. Annie was still not seeing things from his perspective. He'd been so hopeful that they were going to start seeing eye to eye after starting this study with Sara, but it didn't really seem to be helping. It was great that Annie'd had that kid over. But how could she just let a chance like that slip away?

The Barrones vs. The McDougals

Annie arrived at Sara's first that Wednesday. She and Alex had to drive separately because Alex was working a late shift at the café. He was going to be a couple of minutes late, and Annie wanted to see Sara for a few minutes anyway.

When Sara answered the doorbell, she gave Annie a quick hug and invited her inside.

"How are you doing tonight, Annie? Are you feeling any better about life than last week?"

"I think so, Sara. It's been a weird week. I did what you said and just started praying about where I was at. I was able to be honest with God about what I was feeling, and I guess it helped. I mean, I don't feel like things are all that much different. I can't honestly say that I do love God with all my heart, soul, mind, and strength. But I do ask God to help me with that every day. And I've been praying for opportunities to talk to the people I know."

"Have you had any?"

"Yeah, actually, I did. I had this really weird interaction with my neighbor's daughter. She came over for like an hour this week. She's barely said a word to me before, but I ran into her on the way into the building one day and invited her over. She actually came later that day."

"That's really great, Annie. I'm so glad to hear that. And it looks like you're more at peace than you were when

I saw you last."

"Yeah, I really am. Like I said, I don't actually have all the answers, but I feel like maybe I'm headed in the right direction."

They continued talking, and Sara put some water on for tea. After about 20 minutes, Sara answered the door to a loud, persistent knock. "Oh hi, Alex. Come on in."

Alex rushed in, threw his coat over the banister and said, "Sorry I'm late! It was a zoo over at the café. The mall is really busy right now because of Christmas shopping, and we're getting a ton of overflow traffic. Good for business, but tough on me."

Alex sank into the love seat and threw his arm over his brow, sighing. Annie smiled and patted his knee, and Sara handed him some tea.

A few minutes later they were all settled again. Annie was wrapped up in the throw from the back of the couch and Alex was lustily gulping his tea. He had already downed two of Sara's chocolate chunk brownies.

Sara asked about how things had been going with them and whether they had thought of anything that caused each of them to have a hard time surrendering to God.

Annie spoke first. "Well, I think I figured out that I was afraid. I'm afraid of what God will ask me to do, and I'm afraid because I don't know that I've ever loved anything with all my heart, soul, mind, and strength. So

100

that's what's standing in my way."

Sara said, "I took some time to really think and pray about that this week. I sensed that I am having some trust issues with God. After my husband died, I basically didn't want to get close to anyone again. The pain of the loss is just too hard. So I withdrew from my relationships, including my relationship with God. The Spirit really spoke to my heart about that this week, and so I prayed that God would help me to let go of that fear and that pain and trust him again. It's really not easy."

Alex thought for a minute and said, "You know, I don't think there really is anything standing in my way. I think that there used to be–mostly because I just didn't care that much. I didn't remember what's important, so I just didn't pay attention. But after the accident, well, I'm reading the Bible every day, and I'm really looking at every day as a mission and every person as a mission field. So I don't think there's really anything holding me back."

Annie rolled her eyes. Alex sounded so conceited when he talked like this. It was like he didn't think he had anything to learn from God or the people around him.

Sara just moved them on. "So, was there any time that you had this week that you were able to love an enemy?" Annie filled them in on Jenny, and Alex mentioned how he'd tried to reach out to Drew. Sara shared how there was one really difficult neighbor named Clyde who was constantly phoning in complaints about her lawn to the city. She'd had a hard time keeping up on yard work since Barry died. So this week she'd baked a loaf of pumpkin bread and brought some around to her neighbors, including Clyde.

"Good," Sara said. "I'm glad that we're trying to put into practice the things we've been talking about. I don't think we ever want to gain more knowledge than what we're actually applying in our own lives." She smiled.

"So this week, I'd really like to speak with you about culture. First, I want to talk about how our broader culture views us as Christians. Then I want to talk a little bit about how we can deal with this hostility and how we can open up our lives to include more people who might not believe exactly like we do."

"So first, I'm going to show you a couple of clips from the internet. I want you to watch them and especially pay attention to how they portray Christians. The first clip is from *Everybody Loves Raymond*."[2]

Sara set her laptop on the coffee table between the mugs of tea. She flipped open the top, and typed in an address. "Here you go." Alex and Annie had to sit forward a little to see the screen. They watched intently as the story unfolded. It was the show where Robert's family (the Barrones) meets Amy's family (the McDougals) for the first

---

[2]Season 8, Episode 9, available on YouTube.com

time. Amy's family is super-religious, and Robert's family is not. Amy's family has come from Pennsylvania to try to prevent Robert and Amy's marriage.

The clip ended, and Sara paused the laptop. "What did you think about that?" she asked. "Did you notice any stereotypes being portrayed?"

"I did," said Annie. "They were showing Amy's dad as being really judgmental. With the whole prayer issue, he basically told Robert's family that their prayers weren't real, and they were just using their prayers to further their own agenda. So he was clearly evaluating the spirituality of the Barrones by how they acted and what they looked like. And he thought he had the right to do that and to pass judgment about it based on his superior spirituality."

Alex said, "And, of course, they portrayed Amy's family as naive and weird. Like the mom is so soft-spoken; she appears really weak, so that things others would consider normal, like living together before you're married, are shocking to her. And then Amy's brother still lives at home, at like 28. And he seems to want Amy to come home and live with them too. It's like a cult!"

"Okay, good. Keep those things in mind, and let's watch the next clip." Sara turned again to YouTube, and showed a clip from the *West Wing*.[2]

---

[2]West Wing - Dr. Laura Parody -
http://www.youtube.com/watch?v=rPUNooNrwLw

The clip was right after a campaign for the presidency during the results party of election day. The president was giving a speech, but he was distracted by the presence of a conservative "doctor" who had a radio show. The president finally gave up trying to give his own speech and called this doctor out. He first berated her for calling herself "doctor" on the air when she had only a PhD in literature. He confronted her with the fact that listeners probably thought that she was a medical doctor or a psychologist because they called her for all kinds of advice.

Then he confronted her stated views that homosexuality is wrong. He used passages from Exodus and Leviticus–rules about stoning someone who plants two types of crops side by side or burning someone wearing clothes made out of two different types of material. He asked whether she followed those rules too. She was speechless to refute him.

Sara again stopped the clip. "And how about that one? Did you see any stereotypes here?"

Alex replied, "Well, it was like the fundamentalist was dumb. Dumb for believing in these moral values. And dumb because it was inconsistent for the lady to follow the rule about homosexuality and not all the other rules from the Bible. It's like the president was implying that the lady was a hypocrite."

"I think you're right, Alex. The president was definitely trying to point out the woman's hypocrisy–first by confronting her about her degree and then by pointing out what he thought were inconsistencies in her system of belief. How did that make you feel?"

"I felt attacked," said Annie. "I know it wasn't directed at me, but there was a lot of negative feeling on that screen, and it came through. It's like I was personally being ridiculed for my beliefs. But at the same time, I understand. I mean, I think the way that Christians treat homosexuals is horrible. Why shouldn't they be able to love people and have relationships like everyone else? I don't think we need to draw such black and white lines. Times have changed. The world has changed. And God loves people, doesn't he? I mean, isn't that the overriding point of the Bible?" Annie shrugged. "That's what I think, anyway."

"Annie, those are interesting observations. I want to come back to this, but I want to watch one more clip first. Hang on."

Sara flipped to another screen and pulled up an animated clip.[3] This wasn't part of a TV show. Annie and Alex watched as the little animated character spoke with a British accent and made fun of an email exchange he'd supposedly had with a Christian who was trying to tell him about Jesus. The guy challenged the belief in hell and said that he expected more from God–basically that God should

---

[3]www.youtube.com/watch?v=-2bpc7LSRZc

be big enough to love people unconditionally.

Annie and Alex sat in silence as Sara shut down the laptop. After a minute, Annie said, "Wow."

Alex said, "You know, that's exactly how I feel about my conversations with Drew. Like, I have these things that I want to say, but he doesn't understand. He takes them personally, and he gets offended. And I don't really know how to explain. How do you answer that whole 'Jesus is his own dad' thing? And then I just end up feeling like a jerk. Because I don't think he even really wants an answer. This guy certainly doesn't." Alex retreated into the back of the couch.

"There's a lot of tension, isn't there, in talking about faith and spirituality? Or there can be," Sara said. "So we've seen these three clips. We've seen some of the ways that Christians are portrayed in the media and the broader culture. Do you think these characterizations are fair?"

Annie said, "I kind of agree with them sometimes. I think Christians are really judgmental and shouldn't be. I think maybe we should just shut up. I mean, I see a lot of hypocrisy in the church, and I think until we get that straightened out, what do we really have to say to the world?"

"But Annie, we've got to tell the story of God." Alex said. "We've got to confront sin and tell the story of reconciliation. That's part of the mission we talked about last week. Isn't it?" Alex and Annie looked to Sara.

"You guys have hit on a very major tension here. Annie, I do want you to know that we do have something to offer to the world, even though we aren't perfect. The beauty of the story of reconciliation is that, even if it's not perfect, even if the church is as broken as the human beings in it, God can still use it. God can still use us to share his love and his story of hope and redemption with the world."

She looked at Alex. "And Alex, you are also at least partially right. There is sin in the world that is damaging to people–both the people sinning and the people around who are hurt by the sin. It's in everyone's best interest that the sin is confronted and surrendered to God."

Annie noticed Alex giving a self-satisfied smile.

Sara went on. "But there's a real fine line to walk with helping someone submit herself to God and calling her out in a judgmental way about all the bad things that you notice she does. It's not your job to judge people; it's your job to be a minister of reconciliation and bear the message of reconciliation. You do that by living out of a place of surrender to God and out of loving God and your neighbors. Sometimes that love demands that you gently confront the sin in someone's life. But that should usually only happen when you've laid a lot of groundwork in loving that person as a human being and walking alongside her as a friend, and it should never happen before someone has made a commitment to a life of faith."

107

Annie wondered what Alex was thinking. She wasn't sure that gentle was even a part of his vocabulary. She glanced over and saw that he looked pretty peaceful. She thought he might try to argue about what Sara meant by "judgmental."

"Let's look for a minute at this idea of hostility," Sara said. "We saw how hostile the media can be toward Christian beliefs and faith. What about in your own life? Have you seen hostility there?"

Alex replied, "I have. Definitely. Drew is a prime example. I tried to bring up God again, and he was just cold and hard and cynical. It was like he didn't want to hear anything about it at all. But Sara, I think he's dying. He needs to be told." Then he shrugged. "But I guess it's his loss if he doesn't want to listen."

Sara asked, "Alex, what do you think might be behind this hostility?"

"It seems to be connected to his family. He's told me a few times how his dad is pretty involved in church but also that his dad always lectures him about how Drew is going to hell because of his homosexuality. I think Drew's two younger brothers won't even talk to him. His mom does, but I guess she doesn't stand up to his dad. So maybe all that rejection is associated in his mind with God."

Alex frowned, and then continued, "But it doesn't make sense that he would hold that against God. He must

108

see that even if God hates his homosexuality, he doesn't hate Drew."

"Great thoughts, Alex. Before we discuss those issues, though, let's see if we can think of any more examples from our lives."

Annie responded, "I felt some hostility from my neighbor's daughter, Josie. She's sort of angry about a lot of things, so maybe it's just her attitude. But she did seem especially cynical about the music on my iPod when she saw that it was religious. It seems like she might have some hostility. She actually said the pastor was kind of a dweeb, and she made it sound like she thought he was just after money so that he didn't have to work at a 'real' job."

"That's a great example. I'm going to say that I think my grad assistant Daniel is somewhat hostile. He's pretty passionate about what he calls 'walking what you talk.' He has been pretty critical before of Christians, and he seemed to focus on the fact that many Christians aren't kind to their neighbors or to the environment. It seems like that's something that he uses to measure what kind of person you are and that he despises anyone who lives inconsistently with her beliefs."

Sara folded her hands in her lap. "So let's go back to the question of what to do about it. It seems like there's a lot of hostility out there in the world toward Christians. As Annie pointed out, some of it is legitimate criticism for the hypocrisy that exists in the church. And as in Drew's case, some of it comes out of very real hurts that are associated with God or with people who claim to follow God. This hostility is a very real barrier toward being able to hear or sense anything from God. Is there something that we can do to help others walk through the hostility?"

They thought for a minute, and then Annie said, "Well, with Josie this week, I sort of pushed through her hostility toward me, and she came to my house. And then I ignored her hostility toward church and just let her spend some time in my apartment. When she left, she wasn't warm, but she wasn't cold. It seemed like maybe I'd taken a step forward with her."

"I think you probably did, Annie. And I think that you're right. One of the first steps is just to treat a hostile person with love and compassion. When a person's objections to God come out of a place of hostility, it's rarely worthwhile to confront the hostility head on. But you can love the person and be kind to the person and pray for the person, and over time, the person may not be as hostile."

"And what's really interesting is that it seems like one of the first steps to someone overcoming hostility toward God is for a person to trust a Christian. So we have a very real opportunity to be a mirror image of God in our world. If people can learn to trust us, who are walking through life trying to follow God, then maybe they will conclude that the God we are following does not deserve the kind of hostility they have toward him."

110

Annie said, "I can see that. I certainly know that people who claim to be Christians can add to someone's hostility toward God."

"That's true," Alex said. "If we don't live what the Bible says, then people can become very cynical. Or if, like Drew's dad, we're overly judgmental about a person to the extent that we can't communicate love, that could alienate someone."

Annie said quietly, "And I think maybe if we say the wrong thing at the wrong time, we can make people more hostile. Like if I had answered back to Josie in a mean way, criticized her lack of faith, or kicked her out of my apartment, she would have chalked me up like every other Christian she knows. But by just being kind to her, I left the door open for her to come again and for us to talk again."

"Great thinking, you guys. As we live this week, I want us to think and pray about the hostility that we've seen coming from the people around us. What can we do to show love even to the hostile people?"

Sara prayed, and Annie left shortly thereafter.

Alex stayed sitting on the love seat for a couple of minutes, chatting with Sara. On his way out the door, he asked, "Sara, do you think that Annie's learning anything here?"

Sara smiled. "She is, Alex. She definitely is. But

what about you? Are you being challenged in anything?"

Alex shrugged, shivering a little at the cold. "I feel like we're not really covering anything new for me yet, Sara. I mean, this is the type of stuff that I've been trying to say to Annie for months now. I'm glad that we're finally getting it out there."

"Alex," Sara said, "think this week about showing love, okay? And I want you to try to do it without any words at all. Particularly with Drew. Is there anything you can do for him that would communicate love and acceptance without words? Just give it a try, ok?"

"Okay, Sara. Whatever you say." Alex stepped off the porch and headed to his car. Sara closed the door behind him, again uneasy at how he'd left. She was concerned that Alex didn't seem to be open to learning anything but was just using what they were talking about to reinforce what he already thought he knew.

Coffee and Convos

Alex awoke the next morning to a snowstorm. Work would probably be slow that day, he thought, as he prepared to leave the house. Alex lived about ten minutes outside of town, in an older suburb that had become more of a blue-collar neighborhood. He was renting a house here, and he shared it with a couple of other guys. They barely ever saw each other; they worked different shifts. Mostly when Alex was home in the evening, he was alone, and when he woke up in the morning, the other guys were still asleep. The house was a ranch set back on a tree-lined road. Alex had the lease, so he had the master suite with his own bathroom and a huge bedroom. He had the usual bed and dresser, but he also had a little sitting area with an easy chair and a small TV. As he showered and shaved, he tried to pray and prepare for the day to come. He thought that Drew would be in, so he was hoping for an opportunity to talk with him.

As he thought about Drew, he remembered Sara's challenge from the night before, that he try to show Drew God's love without using any words. Alex thought about that for a minute. It didn't sound totally right to him. How was Drew supposed to know that God loved him if he, Alex, didn't tell him? Drew's dad certainly didn't tell him. Drew was under the impression that God wanted to send him to hell. Didn't Alex need to confront that wrong belief before it was too late? He supposed there was nothing wrong with loving actions, but he thought they surely should be accompanied by some kind of communication. So he decided that he would try both, if he had the chance.

That problem solved, Alex watched a little news in his bedroom, and then left the house a little early for work. He made his way through town on the icy roads and was surprised to see how many people were out and about. And then he remembered it was the Christmas rush. He figured they might have more customers than he'd been expecting.

Sure enough, when he arrived at the shop, business was already hopping. Every minute or two the sound of the jingle bell went off as the door to the store opened or closed. There was quite a line for coffee when he got up to the counter, so he went right to work. Omar was also working the café that day, so he thought it would be fairly pleasant. Omar was a very nice guy–way more serious than Alex, but nice. They'd had one or two conversations. Omar was still fascinated by American culture. He would always ask questions about popular sitcoms or jokes he'd seen on Comedy Central. They didn't always make sense to him, so he'd try to get Alex or one of the other staff members to explain the jokes to him. Today, Omar was wearing his usual jeans with a tight designer t-shirt that showed off his tall, muscular build. He was working hard to take orders and make the drinks, so Alex took over the

114

cash register.

It started storming again mid-morning, so traffic started to slow down. Soon there were just a couple of people browsing the shelves, looking for books, and there was no one in the café. Omar sat down for a minute to catch his breath.

"Whew," he said with a slight accent. "What a busy morning! I would like to take a–ah, how do you say it–a stack off?"

Alex said, "A stack off? A stack off what?" Alex thought for a second, "Oh, you mean a load. You want to take a load off, Omar."

"Ah, that's right. What a strange language you have."

"What language do you speak, Omar?"

"I speak many languages, my friend. Arabic, English, and French, to start."

"What country are you from, again? I'm not so good with geography."

"I come from Qatar. It is a very small country, but very wealthy. I come for my studies. My father thought it would be a good idea to learn in English and be exposed to American business practices while I studied Engineering."

"That's right, Omar. I remember now. Is it very different here from your home?"

"Of course it is. People here seem very free–free with their money, free with their mouths, free with their thoughts. We are a much more indirect people. And you have so many seasons here in the north! It is cold! My home is mostly arid. We certainly do not see snow."

"What religion are you, Omar?"

"Why Alex, I am a Muslim, of course. It is not just a religion though, it is also my culture. My father is a very strong Muslim. He exhorts me to attend the mosque each week and pray five times daily toward Mecca."

"Why Mecca?"

"Mecca is the holy city, where Allah appeared to Muhammad. Allah is the God of Jacob and of Abraham and Muhammad."

"Wait a minute—are you talking about the Abraham and Jacob from the Christian religion?"

"Yes, and Jewish too. Allah is the God of all." Omar shook his head and then stretched. "I suppose I should get back to work. I'll wipe down these tables.

One of the customers wandered over to the counter to examine the baked goods, so Alex moved back behind the counter to assist her. He was disappointed that their conversation had been cut short before he'd been able to disagree with Omar. He'd have to come back to it later. He couldn't let Omar wander around thinking that Allah was the same God as Jesus.

But a steady trickle of customers remained, so he didn't have a chance to talk with Omar again that day. As there weren't that many people, he left Omar to tend to the counter himself and went up to the office to get a head start on his order sheets for the next day. He was relieved to see the office was empty. He still hadn't thought of anything to do for Drew, and things had been really tense between them since their conversation last Friday. If Drew was a girl, he could send flowers or a card. But seriously, what was he supposed to do? He couldn't even think of anything that Drew liked to do. Hmm . . . . Maybe he could set up a prank for Drew's enjoyment. They used to do pranks all the time. Maybe he could set one up for tomorrow.

The next day came and went, and Drew was nowhere to be seen. Alex wondered if something had happened to him. He didn't have Drew's home number or anything, so he couldn't even call to check. He worried that the cancer had already taken Drew and that now it was too late for Drew to get right with God. He fretted about this all weekend–he'd had to work both Saturday and Sunday.

Finally, on Tuesday, Drew turned up, looking only a little worse for wear. When he came in the front door, Alex looked up and noticed it was him. As quickly as he could get away, Alex went up to the office to check on him.

"Drew," he said as he entered, "how are you? Where have you been?"

"I've just been home, Alex. I had to spend a couple of days laying down after my last chemo treatment. It knocked me out! But I'm feeling a bit better now–at least well enough to be here." He looked around their cluttered office, "I see nothing much has changed."

"I was really worried about you, Drew. I would have done something, if I'd known. I could have brought you some food or something."

"I was a little too sick for food, Alex. But I'll try to remember to call in to your voicemail next time I'm hanging my head over a toilet bowl."

"I don't mean that, Drew. I was just concerned, okay?"

"Concerned my mortal soul was rotting in hell, and you too far away to do anything, you mean? Come on, Alex. Just lay off. I'm not in the mood for this."

"That's not what I said. It's just . . . ." And then Alex couldn't think of what to say. He had been concerned about Drew's mortal soul. That had been all he was concerned about. Not about food, not about how Drew was doing, just about whether he knew he was going to heaven or not. So Alex said, "I hope you feel better, Drew." Drew turned to his work, and Alex went back down to the café.

That evening, Annie got together with Oliver to play tennis. They did this once or twice a month after work when they both had the same shift. Today they played at Oliver's health club. They both preferred the outdoors, but of course, it was way too cold for that. Christmas was just a week away. Annie couldn't wait. Between lobs, Annie tried to carry on a conversation with Oliver.

Whack! "So, Oliver, what are you doing for Christmas?" Whack!

"Just hanging out with the family."

"Oh, will that be fun?"

"Well, my sister is coming back from Yale, (Whack!) where she teaches Asian literature courses. Mom and Dad will probably be all over me to do something more with my life, like Jane, the beautiful, wonderful sister who did everything right."

Oliver served. "But she's bringing home a boyfriend, so that could be interesting. (Whack!) Maybe that will take the pressure off."

Annie backhanded a shot and said, "That could be a good thing. My parents aren't really like that, thankfully. Course, I'm the baby of the family, so everyone loves me." She grinned and returned another serve. "It should be pretty nutso. All five of my brothers are going to be back, and all of them are bringing their current significant others. The house will be a zoo. My mom is all freaked out and demanding I come over this weekend to help her fix all the food. But I hate baking." She wrinkled her nose. "And I still haven't done any of my shopping. I have no idea what to get for anyone this year."

Conversation and play continued and Annie started

asking about Christmas traditions. "What kinds of things do you do every year for Christmas, Oliver?"

"Well, we always have my dad's whole family over on Christmas day. He is the oldest son, so the honor of hosting is his. We usually eat a pleasant mixture of American and traditional Korean foods. It's usually a pretty calm day. We open presents one at a time, so it kind of takes all day. But it's fun. It's the most fun to watch the little kids open their presents. My dad's baby sister has a couple of kids."

"That's cool. My mom always wants the whole family over on Christmas Eve. We usually go to church and then come home and open one gift. The rest we do on Christmas day, in the morning. My nieces and nephews want us to do it at like five in the morning. But we won't all be staying at the house this year, so I think we're going to get there around eight and then open presents after breakfast, if the little kids can wait that long."

"Oh, yeah. I forgot about Christmas Eve church. We used to go as a whole family, but now just my mom goes with whoever she can drag along. I suppose I'll probably go there too. It's not likely any of my friends will be getting together that night."

Annie knew Oliver was a pretty big drinker. Many of the days he came into work, he seemed a little blurry-eyed until he had some carbs and some coffee. He definitely tended to be a morning grump. She wasn't sure if this was a problem for him or how big of one. He often invited her to come out and drink with some other nurses that worked in the hospital. Most of the time she begged off. She wasn't much of a drinker and didn't like to drink and drive, though she would love to get to know some other nurses.

"Well, if you guys get together at all over the holidays, let me know. I might need a break in the insanity. Alex and I have to hit both of our family shindigs, and it's bound to be pretty crazy."

"What's Alex's family like?"

"They're a pretty tight-knit group. Alex has one younger sister. She's still in college, but she'll be home for the week. His parents are nice, but a bit straight-laced. I don't know how Alex came by his sense of humor because his family certainly doesn't have it. We tend to get into trouble when we're over there, and I'm afraid I instigate it. I just can't stand how stiff they are. I usually try to get him to leave as soon as it's polite. But I don't think he minds. I think he's been a bit of an odd duck out there."

"Okay, Annie. I'll give you a call if we go out." Oliver served an ace and said, "And that's game, set, and match. Good game, Annie."

Annie had beat Oliver just once at tennis. Usually he creamed her, as he had today. But she kept trying because she liked the exercise. And the challenge.

"Yeah right, Oliver. But it was fun. Thanks for

playing. Hey, what shifts do you work this week?"

"I work Thursday, Sunday, and Tuesday, day shift. How about you?"

"Saturday, Sunday, and Thursday. Also days. So I guess I'll see ya Sunday. Have a good one."

They parted ways then, Oliver to shower in the locker rooms, and Annie to bundle up to go home.

On the way home, Annie started thinking again about Christmas gifts. She was going through the list of who she had to buy for and what she wanted to get. She thought just then about Josie and Patti. Should she get them some kind of gift? Maybe something small? She hadn't really seen Josie around this week, and she hadn't stopped by. Maybe this would communicate love to those two in some small way. Yes, she would do it. But she'd better think carefully about what to get. She didn't want to cause any household arguments.

Annie did most of her Christmas shopping the next day. She got her parents a gift card to a nice local restaurant. She got Alex a designer watch he'd been eyeing for the past couple of months. She bought Sara a lovely candle for her living room. And she decided to just get Josie a gift card for the mall. That seemed like a pretty safe bet. At the last minute, she also found some luxurious lotion that she could give to Patti. Not a bad day's work, Annie thought. And then it was time to meet Alex for dinner before Sara's.

They met at Alex's and then drove over to an old-fashioned diner about ten minutes from Sara's. This was one of their favorite places. The food was greasy, but the dessert was great. Sometimes they only ate dessert. Tonight, though, Annie was ravenous after all her shopping, so she got a tuna melt and some onion rings. Alex ordered a taco salad.

"How can you eat that warm fish? It smells disgusting," Alex said when their food arrived. "Hmph," said Annie. "It tastes good. Here. Have an onion ring."

Their conversation moved on to the week they'd had. Alex was still trying to figure out what to do about Drew. "He's just so upset all the time. I was being really, really nice, and I didn't even say anything about God. I don't know why he acted like that."

He drank a swig of his soda. "Sure, I wanted to talk with him about God, but I didn't say that. I don't understand why he reacted the way he did."

"Do you think he maybe could feel that that's all you wanted to talk to him about? I mean, how many conversations have you had with Drew about other things since his partner left him?"

Alex thought for a minute. "Well, nothing really besides store business. We talk about that sometimes."

"Well, there's your answer, then. He thought that's what you wanted to talk about because that's what you've

123

been talking about. And anyway, what's the big deal? That is what you wanted to talk to him about."

"I don't know, Annie; he was so hostile. And he mocked me. I didn't like it." Alex scrunched his nose. "I'm just trying to help."

"Well, maybe he doesn't want to be helped, Alex. Did you ever think of that? Maybe he wants to be left alone. Maybe he wants to be treated as a person, not the object of someone's soapbox. How exactly do you think you're different than his dad, anyway?"

"Annie! I can't believe you said that. You can't really think I'm like his dad. I don't spend every conversation with Drew trying to make him feel bad about who he is and what he believes."

"I'm sure you don't mean to, Alex. But I kind of see where he's coming from. Can't you just treat him like a human being? Talk to him about something else. Talk to him about sports. Or about the weather. Something. Ask him what he misses about his partner or what he'll be doing for Christmas. Do you think he even has plans for the holiday? Is he welcome at his family's?"

"Religion and spirituality is very human, Annie, and I wouldn't be talking to him about it if I didn't care. He knows that. You should know that too."

"I do know that you care, Alex; that's not the point. The point is that maybe your conversations make him feel the same way as his dad's do, and maybe he doesn't want to be bombarded with that every day. Maybe he wants to feel loved and appreciated and accepted."

"But God doesn't accept sin, Annie. You know that. He's holy. He wants sin rooted out of our lives." He looked at Annie, waiting for her to respond.

"Look. I don't want to fight," she said. "But we don't have to be perfect to come to God. Isn't that what Jesus did for us? From everything you've told me about Drew, he seems to have no doubt in his own mind that he's not perfect. So I don't think I would personally want to be harping on him all the time."

"I don't harp on him, Annie. Gosh. I just try to tell him God loves him, and he bites my head off."

"Can we please change the subject? We've got to go to Sara's in a minute, and I'd rather not be in a bad mood."

They finished their dinner in near silence. Annie brought up their Christmas plans, and they got their schedules straight. But neither spoke from the heart. It was purely surface conversation until they left to go to Sara's.

In But Not Of

Sara greeted them at the door with her warm smile that lit up the room. She took their coats and led them into the living room, where she already had tea, hot cocoa, and Christmas cookies sitting. She noted that they seemed quiet and a little stiff, but she didn't let it affect her welcome.

"Help yourselves to the drinks and cookies, guys, whatever you want. I'll be back in just a second." Cups rattled and spoons clattered and then Sara was back, carrying a pile of index cards and some markers. She said, "I think this will help us visualize some things this evening."

"So, how was your week?" she asked. Annie and Alex both just said "fine" and looked at Sara.

Oh dear. Something was clearly amiss within their relationship. They weren't even sitting together on the love seat. Annie sat in an oversized chair instead. And they were barely looking at each other. Should she bring it up? Sara said a quiet prayer. She sensed that highlighting the tension between them would not be helpful tonight, so she turned to reviewing last week.

"So did you guys see any more hostility to faith or to God in your worlds this week?"

Alex answered, "Drew was out for most of the week, and when he got back, he was really hostile. I didn't say anything about God, and he was still rude and condescending about it. I think he's still taking stuff his dad has said to him out on me."

"Wow, honey. That's hard. How did you deal with it?" Sara asked.

"I just gave him his space. I didn't really try to respond or say anything. I just told him that I hoped he felt better soon. Did I tell you he's been diagnosed with cancer?" He shook his head. "He's pretty sick."

"Were you able to do anything concrete to show him love?" Sara asked.

"No. He was gone for most of the week. And I couldn't think of anything anyway. I didn't want to get him a card or flowers because that seemed really unnatural. So I didn't do anything."

"How about you, Annie. Did you experience any hostility or think of any ways to walk through that with someone?"

"I didn't see Josie around at all. But I did buy her and her mom gifts for Christmas. I'll find a time to drop them by their house when Jake is gone."

"That's great, you guys. Don't be discouraged if it takes some time to break through the hostility, though. I like to think in pictures, so I always think of it like we're preparing the soil for the story of God. When a farmer gets the field ready, there's a lot that he should do before he plants. One of those things is to pick up the rocks that will get in the way. It's tedious, difficult, and hot work, but someone has to do it. The hard thing is that there's no instant gratification. It's not like you can even tell that work has been done. But unless you get the rocks out of the way, there's no way for the seed to grow. I think that breaking through hostility is like that. It can take a long time, but it has to be done."

She glanced again at Annie and Alex. They were both tense. She could try to draw them out, but they didn't seem to want to say much tonight. Maybe she should just talk for a while to let them relax a little bit.

She smiled, "I'm sorry to say it, but I think I'm going to be doing most of the talking tonight. There's some information that I want to give you, and I'm not sure how to make it very interactive."

This had the immediate affect of allowing them both to get more comfortable. Alex relaxed against the love seat, and Annie tucked her feet up under her in her chair. Sara smiled and went on.

"So last week we talked a little bit about culture, particularly about how our culture views Christians. I want to talk now about a couple of different cultural ideas. The first is the idea of a Christian subculture. The second is the shift our broader culture has made from modern to postmodern. I think these are important concepts because they really affect how we share our stories and how we open our hearts up to those around us."

129

"I first really learned about culture when I was getting ready to go to China. I had to read some books on what they call 'culture shock.' Have you guys heard of that?"

Both shook their heads. "Well, it's the idea that we do things a certain way here in the U.S., and they do things entirely different in China. A simple example is how we all have cars here. A family could have three or four cars, depending on how many drivers they have. But in China, the vast majority of people have bicycles or mopeds. Another example is the kind of food we eat. Here, we'd never expect to eat rice for breakfast. But over there, that is what they'd always have for breakfast. So culture shock is when you move to a new place, and you have to get used to the new culture. You go through a process of hating the culture for a while before you get used to it and can appreciate it, even though it's different from your own."

"So anyway, I learned about culture to prepare myself to move to China. And culture itself is basically a sociological concept–it gives us a way to talk about the values and norms that a group of people holds in common. Something as small as a small town or city could have a distinctive culture. And something as big as a nation can have one culture. Then there are usually different subcultures broken down within a greater culture–groups of people who exist within a broader culture but have some special norms or values or traditions in common with each other that they don't share with the greater culture. So Christians form a broad subculture, and then there might be even smaller subcultures among Christians. But speaking generally about all Christians in the U.S., are there some values or distinctives that they have in common that maybe they don't share with other parts of the culture?"

Annie answered, "I know when I was growing up, the people in my church didn't do certain things that other people did. Like we couldn't go to movies. And we definitely didn't smoke or drink."

Alex shot a look at Annie, "Well, people at my church smoked, but no one 'took the Lord's name in vain.' And we didn't drink either."

"Exactly," said Sara. "Those are some examples of our Christian subculture. Now, can you think of deeper things?"

"What about divorce, Sara?" asked Annie. "The people in my church thought that getting divorced was really bad. When this one family divorced, they had to leave our church."

"That's another great example, Annie. So we can see that some of the things that form our subculture are more external choices–things we don't do or say. And then some go a little bit deeper about how we run our families and our homes. Now I know that not everyone fits in to these categories, and some of the things one group doesn't do, others do, like smoking. But generally you can see that

Christians are trying to live differently than everyone else. Where do you think that comes from?"

Alex was quick to reply. "God is holy, and he asked his people to be holy just like him. Holy means to be set apart. So a people who are set apart unto God are supposed to look different than the world. Jesus said we were to be 'in the world' but not 'of the world.'"

"And would you say that that's the basis for all those external rules that Christians are always trying to follow?"

"Yeah, I think so. I think it comes from a place of wanting to be holy and set apart for God."

"So that might be a cause of Christians having their own sort of subculture. But do you think that those are the things that are really important to God?"

Annie answered, "Maybe not, Sara. I mean, if you look at movies for example, there's nothing inherently wrong with them. But we have been encouraged to think only about good things. So if there's a movie that is full of bad stuff, stuff that will make us angry or upset or tempt us to do something wrong, maybe the movie isn't such a great idea." She caught Alex's eye and raised an eyebrow.

"Good, Annie. So where does the idea of holiness come from in the Bible?"

Alex answered, "I think probably the Old Testament. Maybe Deuteronomy?"

"Yep. Leviticus too. The concept of being a people

set apart unto God started out with the Israelites, who were called out to be God's people. But there was one really important distinction between them and the church today. Do you know what it is?"

Neither Annie nor Alex could answer, so Sara went on. "God had called Israel out to be his people, and he intended to be their king. He didn't want them to have a separate king rule over them. So he basically built a whole nation and laid down a whole law that the nation was supposed to follow. It was incredibly detailed. There were laws about justice; there were laws about cleanliness; there were laws about relationships. And the people needed them to be an organized nation. These laws created a whole culture that was distinct from the cultures around them. This gave Israel an identity that was separate. That separation was intended to help them stay spiritually pure and focused on serving and loving their God. How does the church differ from that?"

"Well," said Annie, "God isn't our king. I mean, maybe figuratively, he's supposed to be. But we're part of a nation. We have a president. It's a democracy." She shrugged. "We Christians don't have our own nation."

"That's exactly right. And when Jesus was here, he talked about what it meant to follow God, but he was much more concerned with the internal attitudes of people's hearts. Instead of being focused on the externals–don't eat pork, make sure to wash your hands before eating–he was

133

concerned with what was going on on the inside. The Sermon on the Mount is an excellent example of this."

Sara was momentarily distracted by the fact that Annie and Alex were now staring at each other. Neither seemed to be paying any attention, but there was an underlying frequency of tension humming between them. No, this did not appear to be a friendly stare-down.

Then Sara dropped her cup and saucer on the floor.

"Oh no!" she said. "My carpet!" Annie jumped up to get a dishcloth from the kitchen and Alex helped her pick up the broken teacup.

By the time they all sat back down, some of the tension had dissipated. Sara continued.

"Anyway, one thing that I've noticed is that the church has a tendency to focus on the ways that Christians can be different externally. Instead of realizing that Christians are meant to be different because of how they radically love others and love God, many times our churches still get caught up in defining our spirituality and our culture by what we do and don't do. Let's face it, that way, it's a much easier way to identify who's in and who's out. It's also so much easier to check things off a list of things to do or not do than to walk with God."

Sara sighed. "So what do you guys think? What effect do you think this subculture focused on externals has on our ability to share and live the story of God?"

They thought for a minute. Then Alex said, "It

contributes to the stereotypes that people have about Christians. Thinking back to that *Everybody Loves Raymond* clip that we watched, they made the family seem weird. Using your terms, they had their own culture that was totally different from normal."

"Definitely. What else?" Sara asked.

"It might also make it harder to connect with people," Annie said. "If I have only Christian friends, listen only to Christian music, and never watch any TV, it might be hard to think of things to talk about with people who don't share my values."

"I think it is. And that seems to be another reason Christians don't spend time with those outside their own subculture–they seem to like to spend time with only those who share their values. So now we're back to that all-important question. What can we do about it? Is there a way to bridge that cultural gap to build relationships with people who are different from us?"

Alex said, "Well, we don't want to go to bars or start swearing just to be like everyone else."

"Well, then what can you do?"

Alex and Annie remained silent. Perhaps now was a good time to tell Barry's story. She looked at Alex and Annie. They were still sitting separately, but they had loosened up considerably.

"Let me tell you a story, then. My husband Barry was a really shy, quiet man. It was amazing he ever worked up the courage to ask me out." Sara smiled, remembering. "But that's another story for another day. Anyway, shortly after we were married, we started talking about how much we wanted to be a part of God's work in the world. Barry had this deep desire to be used by God. But he was painfully shy. He hated talking to strangers. He barely ever left the house. He went to work; he came home; and he was happiest just hanging out alone or with a small group of people."

"He used to wonder how God could use him. He didn't even really know anyone outside of the people he worked with. So we had lots of conversations about how God made us each to be who we are and that he can use us just the way we are."

"We started talking about the things that Barry liked to do. He liked to watch the History channel; he liked to read old war novels; he liked to bum around used bookshops. Well, one day, we were at this bookshop, and there was a flyer for this civil war reenactment group. If you can imagine, my shy Barry signed up. And out of his love of history, he started forming relationships with people outside of his natural habitat. He started leaving home more often to spend time having coffee with people. It was beautiful to see."

"See, these civil war reenactment people are not the type of people I would be drawn to. Well, all except Barry, of course. But it would be a ton of work for me to try to find something in common with them, to find something to talk about, to build any kind of natural relationship. But Barry, he really became the center of that little social circle."

Sara smiled again, tears coming to her eyes. "What's so amazing is that God doesn't ask us to become different in personality to walk with him and to share our stories and his story. He uniquely gifted and created Barry to reach out and love his friends. Someone like me or you, well, we just wouldn't have been able to connect in the same way."

She wiped away a tear. "Hey guys. Let's take a short break. I'll get some more tea."

So Sara refilled the provisions and topped off the drinks. When she returned she said, "So I want to spend the next few minutes brainstorming some ideas of what we can do over Christmas break to build relationships outside of our Christian subculture."

She passed out the index cards. "I want you to try to think of five ideas and then write them down on these cards."

She then sat down to write her own list. After about five minutes had passed, she said, "All right. Let's share our lists. I'll go first. (1) Take my grad assistant out for holiday coffee; (2) Take my neighbors some Christmas cookies; (3) Go and visit Clyde, and make sure he has somewhere to go for Christmas dinner; (4) Look up the book clubs that are starting this January out of the bookstore; (5) Sign up for a photography class I've been wanting to take. Who's next?"

"I'll go," Annie said. "Here are mine: (1) Go out with Oliver and his friends over the holiday week; (2) Take a Christmas gift to Josie and Patti; (3) Invite Josie and Patti over for Christmas tea; (4) See if there are any women's indoor soccer clubs nearby. I couldn't think of a fifth one. How about you, Alex?"

"Well. I couldn't come up with very many, actually. First, I could ask Drew to go out for coffee. I don't think he'd go, but I can try. Second, I could see if Omar wants to play racquetball sometime at the gym. Third, well, I don't think I have a third. It's too early in the season to start training for sports."

"Alex, what kinds of things do you like to do in your spare time?" Sara asked.

"Well, I hang out with Annie. I work out at the gym. I sometimes do sports, but not many in the winter. I don't know. Play video games. Do you think there's a video game club I could join or something? But I'm not that into gaming."

"That's a good thought, Alex. Just remember that God made you who you are on purpose. Look to build connections out of who you naturally are and what you enjoy. It's there that you'll meet people you have things in common with, and relationships there will tend to be more natural."

Sarah noticed Annie was yawning, and she was feeling pretty tired herself. "It's getting kind of late, you guys. I had more I wanted to cover tonight, but I think we'd better wait until next time. We can skip a couple of weeks and get together the day after New Year's. Will that work for you both?"

Everyone agreed, so they prayed together. Sara challenged them to try to put at least one or two of the things they'd thought of into practice over the holidays, and she encouraged them to keep praying for ideas of how to share life and their stories with people outside of their natural subculture.

Alex's animosity had dissipated by the time they left, so he chattered on the ride home about inviting Drew and Omar over for dinner around Christmas time. "I don't know if Drew will come, but Omar might. It would be nice to have you there, Annie. You're so good with people."

He noticed Annie wasn't really paying attention, so he asked, "Hey, you're not still mad, are you, Annie girl?"

She sighed. "I'm not mad, Alex. Just thinking."

"Oh. What about?"

She bit her lip and turned her face toward the window. "Nothing, really. Sure I'll come to dinner with you guys."

Alex shrugged and drove home.

Christmas Spirit

"Oh, hi Oliver. How are you doing today?" Annie asked. It was Sunday morning and they were both in the locker room, getting ready for the day's shift.

"I'm doing okay, Annie. How about you? Did you get all your shopping done?"

"Yeah, I did. I'm pretty well ready for Christmas now. Is your sister back in town yet?"

"Nah, she'll be flying in tomorrow. Nothing like waiting 'til the last minute. But the flights are cheaper, and anyway, she had to turn her grades in today. Hey, there's a group of us going out tonight after work, if you want to come. Some nurses from the heart center and the oncology unit. There's that little place right around the corner."

"Sure, Oliver. I'd love to come. It'll give me an excuse not to go bake with my mom." Annie winked. "I'll see you around, but for sure let me know when you're about to leave."

The day passed in a blur because the season's first fake Santa came through the peds ward. Every year, they'd have several Santas, one right after another. The kids thought it was a blast, of course, and the Santas usually came with a group of people and some presents. The holiday sure did make people want to be giving. So halfway through her shift, Annie changed into a little green elf suit. Her favorite part was the jaunty green hat with the jingle bell. For the rest of the day, she jingled from room to room and made the kids sing her a Christmas carol while she checked on them. All in all, it was a great day for Annie.

Around 8 p.m., Annie and Oliver left for the pub. Annie had changed out of the elf suit but kept the hat. "I'm not going to be able to stay too long, Oliver. I've got a pretty big day tomorrow. Mom wants me over as soon as I can get up. She'd like it to be 7 a.m., but there's no way I'm getting up that early on a day off."

"No worries, Annie. Stay as long as you like. You know I'll be there 'til the bar closes." Oliver smiled and led the way.

The pub was a little place around the corner from the hospital. It was a throwback British pub that served a mixture of English and Indian fare. As soon as Annie walked in, she was suddenly starving. She ordered a curry rice dish and a vodka lemonade. She rarely drank, but she felt like it would be weird if she didn't here. Her one drink was odd enough, compared to the amount that everyone else was drinking.

Conversation revolved first around hospital politics, doctors' bad attitudes, and frustrating patients. After about half an hour, conversation moved on to Christmas plans. As they talked, Oliver downed six beers, and he showed no signs of stopping. After another 20 minutes, Annie checked that Oliver would have a ride home and then made her way out.

She left a little disturbed by Oliver's drinking. She knew he drank a lot, but tonight he seemed to be drinking to forget something. Not much of a drinker herself, she wasn't really sure how much was too much and how to recognize a problem. She knew Oliver's break-up with Heather had been devastating to him, so maybe that was the cause. She tucked those thoughts in the back of her mind and made it home safely by 10 pm.

When she got home, she returned a call she'd missed from Alex. Alex reported that Omar would be coming over on Wednesday, but he didn't think that Drew would make it.

"I don't think that Drew actually has any plans at all for Christmas. He does have friends and a sort of community here, but I think they all have families they're still close to. He's not planning to go home, I can tell you that. He wouldn't be welcome there. You should come in sometime to meet him; that might make him feel more comfortable."

"I'd be happy to do that, Alex. But I'm not going to make it before Wednesday. Mom has me baking all day tomorrow. Sometimes it's tough being the only girl. Are you still planning on Christmas Eve church with us?"

"Sure, Annie. And then your house in the morning, and my house in the afternoon, right?"

"Yeah. Hey, listen, Alex. I went out with Oliver and his friends tonight, and I'm really concerned about him. He drank a lot. And I was only there for about an hour. I don't know how much he drank after I left."

"Did you say anything to him?"

"It didn't seem like the appropriate place or time. There were a bunch of people around, and I didn't want to embarrass him. I just made sure he had a ride home before I left."

"Well, you have to say something, Annie. Drinking that much is really dangerous to his health."

"I know. I just don't want to sound judgmental. I mean, he doesn't criticize me for my bad habits. I really like him, you know? I really feel like he's becoming a friend. I don't want to ruin that by butting in where I haven't been invited."

"Annie, I really think you need to say something. It's important. Do you even know if he's a Christian?"

"I guess his mom goes to church, but it sounds like he doesn't. We haven't really talked about spiritual things much. It hasn't come up."

"Don't you think you should bring it up on purpose?"

"Maybe. But not if it doesn't happen naturally. I really don't want to offend him. I don't know how he feels about religion, and I don't want to make him uncomfortable. The thought makes me uncomfortable too.

144

Why should I try to impose my beliefs or my sense of right and wrong on someone else?"

"Annie! Your sense of right and wrong? Don't you believe that there is one right and wrong–and that the Bible tells you what it is?"

"Oh Alex, I don't know. Yes, I think there's right and wrong. Sometimes I think that it's really clear. But I think there are a lot of gray areas. I mean, I think there are a lot of things that don't fall in the absolutely right or absolutely wrong category. There are things that are wise, and things that aren't so wise. There are times when things might be okay, and times when you have to respect those around you and not cause them temptation, so you have to refrain. What I can tell you for sure is that I'm not always absolutely sure that I have the right answers or know where all those lines are."

"Sometimes you scare me, Annie. How do you know where to draw the line, then? If things aren't for sure, how do you make decisions?"

"I don't know, Alex. That's what I'm trying to figure out, actually."

"Well," Annie continued, "I'm going to head to bed, Alex. I've got an early morning tomorrow. I'll see you tomorrow night."

Christmas passed uneventfully, with very little tension between Annie and Alex. They made their normal jibes about the other's family, and Annie somehow set a potholder on fire at Alex's family's house. She would never live that one down. She grinned. Somehow she always brought a little bit of excitement wherever she went, either intentionally or unintentionally.

Annie was a little relieved that Alex had not proposed to her for Christmas. She'd wondered if he would, given where their conversations had been going in the last couple of months. On one hand, they did seem to be talking more about things, even things they disagreed about, without fighting.

But they didn't seem to be on the same page. Maybe he sensed that too. Maybe he just wasn't ready. Whatever the reason, Annie was glad she didn't have to make such a big decision just now. She honestly wasn't sure what she would say. She loved Alex. But she was seeing some things that made her uncomfortable. And the more that she tried to work out where God fit in her own life, the more she sensed they might be heading in different directions.

Wednesday dawned bright and snowy, and Annie saw Jake Conrads, Patti's husband, leaving the apartment fairly early that morning. As soon as she'd had some coffee and spent a little time praying, she went and knocked on the Conrads' door. A minute passed, and then Josie opened it.

"Hey Josie. Merry Christmas. Is your mom

around?"

Josie said, "It's Jo, remember?" She rolled her eyes. "I can check if my mom's here, but she may not want to talk to you. She doesn't talk to other people much you know."

Annie smiled. "I've noticed. Will you give it a try though? I have something for her." Annie held up a little gift bag.

The door closed, and Annie stood in the hallway, tapping her foot. This should be interesting. A minute or two passed, and then the door opened.

It was Josie again. "Mom said to say she's not here right now. Sorry. Can I take that for her?"

"Actually, I've got two things. This gift bag is for your mom. And this envelope is for you. I just wanted to say Merry Christmas. And I wanted to invite you and your mom over for tea. Sometime this week maybe? Can you tell her? We've been neighbors all this time, and I'd really like to get to know you guys a little."

"I'll tell her. Thanks," Josie said with a little frown. She seemed more confused than angry. So Annie just smiled and said, "Have a good day." She went back to her apartment, praying as she went. At least Josie didn't seem to hate her right now. It was going to be really hard to break through to Patti, though, if she would never come out of her apartment.

That evening, Omar and Alex came over to Annie's for a "Christmas" dinner. Annie had baked a chicken, made baked potatoes, and baked a green bean casserole. She'd enlisted Alex to make a cheesecake, his specialty, for dessert. She had a friend from the Middle East, so she knew that Middle Easterners sometimes had special diet requirements based on their religion. She'd looked diet restrictions up on the internet, and she thought what she was serving would be okay.

When the guys arrived, the apartment was dimly lit except for the candles on the table and the Christmas lights hanging from the ceiling. Annie's tree was beautifully decorated, and she'd decorated the bar with garland and the ceiling with lights. It made for a sort of reverent festivity.

"Welcome, welcome you guys. Come on in and make yourselves at home. I've got some sparkling cider chilling in the fridge and I'm just pulling everything out of the oven now. Alex, if you want to get the drinks, we can eat in just a minute."

She took the cheesecake from him and placed it on the bar next to Herman's bowl. She quickly placed the food in serving dishes and set them on the table. Meanwhile, Alex poured the drinks. Omar just stood there.

"Oh, Omar. I'm sorry!" Annie said. "I didn't introduce myself. I'm Annie, Alex's girlfriend. But I'm sure you'd figured that out." She smiled as she set the last plate of food down. "Here, why don't you have a seat. You can sit anywhere, we don't have any special seats."

"Why thank you Annie. Your hospitality is very much appreciated."

"Did you go anywhere for Christmas, Omar? Were you able to celebrate with anyone?"

"Yes, one of my friends from school invited me over for his family's Christmas dinner. It was very interesting to observe. I am fascinated by the way you do things here. It is so different from home. And yet, everyone seems to have the same needs and desires at the core of their being, do they not?" Omar nodded. Annie and Alex sat down.

Alex said, "Hey Omar, we usually pray before we eat. Do you mind if we do that now?" Omar shook his head. "That is fine, Alex." So Alex prayed and they began to eat.

After a moment, Annie asked, "So Omar, does your family celebrate Christmas at home?"

"Not really. It is a holiday that we know about, and I was once invited to a Christmas party by some foreigners. A lot of our stores have Christmas trees. But it is not a public holiday because it is Christian."

"So what do you think of Christmas here?" Annie asked.

"Well, I find it interesting that it is not so much of a religious holiday. It seems much more to be about the giving and receiving of gifts than about celebrating religion. I do not know if there are religious traditions associated with the holiday here?"

Alex said, "Yes, there are. Annie and I went to church on Christmas Eve, to a candlelight service with her family. It is a time to remember the birth of Jesus."

"Ah yes," Omar responded, "the birth of Jesus. He claimed to be God, did he not?"

Annie nodded while Alex answered. "Yes, he was God. It's a very interesting reality actually, if you think about it. To imagine that God became man."

"Yes, I have been talking with some of the other college students about this. I am very interested in American culture and religion. But tell me, what do you say will happen to all those who do not believe in your Jesus?"

Annie shifted uncomfortably in her seat, while Alex answered, "They'll go to hell and be eternally separated from God. This is not what God wants, you understand. But it is what must happen because God can't be in the presence of sin."

"So you believe that my family will end up in hell then? And me, unless I believe in Jesus?"

Again, Annie squirmed, while Alex answered with no hesitation. "Yes. That's what the Bible says."

"Isn't that interesting." Omar commented. He shifted the conversation then to ask Annie about her family. He was most interested in her five brothers and what their lives were like growing up.

After dinner they played a card game, and then Omar had to leave because he had the early shift at the café the next morning. "Thank you for inviting me into your home, Annie." He smiled warmly. "See you at work, Alex," he said as he opened the door and left.

Annie and Alex set about to clean up the kitchen and put the leftovers in the fridge. "Alex," Annie asked, "why do you think Omar was asking all those questions about religion?"

"He seemed curious about what we believe, Annie. Like maybe he was trying to get all the facts straight."

"I don't know, Alex. It seemed kind of important to him to know what would happen to his family if they didn't believe. He asked you such a specific question about that."

"I thought he was just sort of taking inventory of the beliefs, Annie, and how they differed from his own."

"Maybe. But I got the sense that there was something more." Annie shrugged. "I don't know. It's so hard to know what to say or do in that situation. I mean, you didn't even really have time to explain the whole story. It seems like there are more important parts of the story than just what happens to people who don't believe when they die. Like we didn't have a chance to say anything at all about reconciliation, or changed lives, or hope for the future. It seems like maybe he got an incomplete picture."

"We answered his questions, though, Annie. I think that's enough. He can ask more if he is still wondering about things. I work with him, so he can always ask more."

Annie pondered this as they finished the dishes quietly. She really did think that there was more to his questions than just comparing the facts. He had seemed really interested. But what if that was all he ever knew about Jesus? She felt that maybe they'd lost an opportunity to share more of the story of God, but thinking about it, she couldn't imagine what she would do differently next time.

After the kitchen was clean, Alex and Annie went to the living room and talked quietly for a while. Annie snuggled up to Alex, and he asked, "So how have you been doing, Annie girl? I feel like we haven't really talked for a while. The craziness of the holidays and all."

Annie stared across the living room at Herman on the bar and answered, "I'm all right, Alex. There's just so much to think about. Where are we going? What are we doing? What is my life going to look like in five years? I don't know."

Alex was puzzled. What could be wrong? He squeezed her hand. "But we're doing okay."

"Are we, Alex?" Annie asked, looking up at him.

"Of course, we are. I think you're finally beginning to see what I've been talking about, and that makes it so much easier. We haven't really fought in I don't know how long. Sure, we still disagree. But it's nothing like it was." That should comfort her.

Annie was silent for a moment. "And I'm still a little worried about Oliver. And I went to my neighbor's today. Patti wouldn't even come out to talk to me. But I gave the gifts to Josie and invited them over for tea. I hope they'll come."

"That's great, Annie. I hope that you have lots of opportunities to talk to them."

Annie sat up, "But don't you see, Alex. I'm not sure what to say. I'm not sure how much to say. And I'm not sure how to treat them in a way that they will feel like they are people and not some project that I'm trying to do. I just don't want to do it wrong. I don't want to ruin any chance that God has to work in people's hearts. I'm just afraid."

Alex frowned. "But don't you think that God will use anything you say, Annie? It is up to him to draw people to himself."

"I think that ultimately you're right, Alex. But I do think that we can do a lot of damage, unintentionally, to the work that God is trying to do in people's hearts. I'm not saying that we can necessarily screw up everything, but I think we can make it much harder for him to get through. And I really don't want to do that. I want to be a part of making it easier for God to get through. You know?"

"I think so, Annie." Alex checked out his watch. "Hey, I'd better get home. Thanks for having us over tonight. It was so good to have some time with Omar outside of work. He's a nice guy."

"Sure, Alex. It was fun." Annie walked him to the door. "Call me tomorrow?"

"Of course, Annie girl. Sleep well."

Accidental Pressure

A few days later, Annie ran into Josie in the hallway again. "Hey Jo. How's the Christmas holiday been for you?"

Josie looked up from her phone, "Fine, Annie."

"Did you talk with your mom about coming over for tea?"

"Yeah." Josie hesitated. "I think she might be willing to come if you ask her again. Go to the door sometime today between now and five, when my dad gets off work. If she answers it and you invite her, she might say yes. She really liked the lotion and has been putting it on every night."

"Will do. Thanks, Jo. Have a great day."

Josie nodded and went back to messaging.

An hour or two later, Annie brought some Christmas cookies over to Patti's house and knocked on the door. She waited a minute, but she didn't hear anything, so she knocked again. This time, she heard quiet steps coming toward the door and then a pause. She thought Patti might be looking out the peephole. Finally, the door inched open and Patti peered out around it.

"Hello?" Patti said.

"Hi Patti! How are you doing today?" Annie immediately noted that her exuberance might be too much, so she toned it down a little and handed over the cookies. "I was actually wondering if you and Josie might want to come over to my house for tea sometime."

"Well," said Patti quietly, "I don't see why not. When would you like us to come?"

"How about Friday? I don't have to work, and I think Josie is still out of school. Would that work?"

"Okay. We could do that. What time?"

"Two p.m.?"

"Okay. Please don't mention this to my husband." With that, Patti shut the door. She didn't even say goodbye. Annie shook her head. That was kind of strange, but at least she'd agreed to come. Now she had to figure out how to entertain them. She had no idea whether she had anything in common with Patti. She already knew that Josie didn't like her music. She was used to being the life of the party, but it was hard to have a party by yourself. You needed atmosphere. And at the very least you needed people who wanted to be entertained.

Annie remembered what Sara had said about living out of who you were. It was an interesting concept, really. To imagine that God had created her as Annie for a purpose, and that maybe there were people that she could connect with that even Sara would have a hard time with.

So if she was being herself, who would she be? She supposed that she would want the apartment to be bright and friendly. She already had a modern-style sofa with

156

bright throw pillows and blankets. But she could maybe get some festive plates and cups from a dollar store. And she could try to find a cake with Christmas-style fondant. She was always watching those cake decorating shows on TV, and she was dying to taste one of those cakes. This could be good. Maybe she could even find a Christmas tree cake.

Excited now, Annie went overboard on her planning. She had to go to a special store for the ingredients she wanted, but she thought it would be perfect. Friday could not come around soon enough!

And come, it did. By 2 p.m. on Friday, everything was perfectly decorated. She had set three places at the table. She had talked her mom into baking a Christmas tree cake for her, one covered with green fondant. Annie had then piped some regular buttercream frosting on the top in different colors to represent the lights and the ornaments. It looked fantastic, if she did say so herself. She was just heating up water for tea when she heard a knock on her door.

She opened the door, and Patti and Josie filed in. She was a little surprised that both showed up. She thought that maybe if Patti came, Josie wouldn't want to. But there they both were. Patti was looking well-kept in a plain brown dress. Her hair was newly brushed and hung to her waist. Her features were nondescript, but she smiled a little as she came in the door. Meanwhile, Josie was looking cool in her dark clothes and very dark eyeliner. She had an ear bud in one ear; the other hung down the front of her sweatshirt.

"I see you brought your own tunes," Annie said, nodding toward the earphones. She smiled. Josie rolled her eyes and said, "Yep."

So that was the way she was going to be. This could get interesting. As Patti had never said more than a sentence to her, Annie imagined she could easily be the only one talking.

Annie led the pair over to the dining room, which was really just a table in the small alcove off the galley kitchen. She sat them down and asked if they wanted tea or cocoa. Josie's eyes lit up when she saw the cake, though she tried to hide it. Patti just said quietly, "Tea please." Josie wanted cocoa.

Annie brought the hot water and a selection of teas over to the table. There were already plates and cups there. "Well, help yourself, you guys. Let me cut this cake, but you can help yourself to the tea and cocoa." They spent a few minutes getting drinks and cake situated, Annie chatting all the while. She told them about her Christmas. She told them about begging her mom to make the cake. She even told them about Herman. After about five minutes, she thought she might venture a question.

"So, what did you guys do for Christmas?" She

waited an awkward moment while no one answered. Then Patti said, "Well, we just had a normal Christmas dinner at home." Hmm . . . . Okay.

"Did you guys decorate a Christmas tree?" Again a pause.

Patti answered, "Yes. We have a fake one we get out every year." Then all was silent, so Annie thought she might try to change to a different subject.

"So what do you like to do in your spare time, Patti?"

"I don't have a lot of spare time right now. I spend most of the time cleaning the apartment and doing laundry and taking care of Jake and Josie. I guess when I do have spare time I like to read."

"Oh. What do you like to read?"

"I like to read mysteries," Patti said with a small smile.

"What do you like about them?"

Patti gave a nearly imperceptible shrug. "Well, I guess they just keep me entertained. They're always exciting."

Annie thought it was interesting that someone so bland would like to read about murders–that she would find them so interesting. Perhaps there was hope for their friendship after all.

"What else do you find exciting, Patti?" asked Annie.

Patti sat forward a little in her chair. "Well, hmm, I like to watch travel shows on TV. It all looks so interesting. But I especially think that Asia is fascinating. It's so different from here! What would it be like to travel there?"

"Really? That's really neat." Annie said. Then she had to pinch her thigh to keep from laughing. *Really neat.* What kind of comment was that?

"My boyfriend, Alex, went to the Philippines once, when he was in high school. You'll have to ask him about it if you ever meet him."

"Oh, wow!" Patti said, "I've seen some documentaries on the Philippines. It does look interesting. But where I'd really like to go, if I could go anywhere, is the Great Wall of China. It looks magnificent." Patti's normally pale cheeks were now flushed. This was going great. If only Annie could think of something else to keep her going.

"Have you ever traveled anywhere out of the country?" Annie asked.

Patti's face fell. "No," she replied.

Oh dear.

"Me neither, actually. But I dream of traveling. Where I'd like to go is Greece. I hear that the sea is beautiful, the people are kind, and the food is great. I do love Greek food."

Patti nodded her head. She looked over at Josie, who was now just moving some cake and frosting around

160

on her plate with her fork. Patti said, "Did Josie tell you that she's a great artist?" There was pride in her voice. Josie scarcely moved, but a smile played around the corners of her mouth.

"Oh, really?" Annie said. "What kind of stuff does she do?"

Josie answered without looking up from her plate, "Chalk and charcoal, mostly. I like to do people–portraits. Maybe I could do yours."

"Sure. I would love that. When can you come?"

Josie looked up, "Seriously?"

"Yeah, seriously. I would love to have my portrait done. I could give it to my parents as a gift or something. They would love it."

Josie shrugged. "I could come by some time while I'm still off of school. Or maybe some afternoon." So they arranged a time for Josie to come and they finished up their cake and their drinks. Soon Patti and Josie made noises about leaving, and Annie showed them out. As she closed the door, she gave a big sigh.

As she cleaned up the kitchen, she tried to evaluate how the afternoon went. It was touch and go there for a while, but now she knew a couple more things about what these women were passionate about. And she was strangely drawn to Patti. She seemed so quiet, and yet there seemed to be some deep longings there. The way she lit up about traveling and then closed down again when she thought of reality. It really did sound like she had a dull life, always just cleaning and taking care of the others in her world. It seemed like maybe she wanted more out of life but didn't know how to get it. That would be something to pray about.

And she was excited that Josie would do her portrait. It would be a great time to spend with her and to get to know her a little bit. She had seemed so angry and distant at first, but Annie was beginning to think it was mostly an act. There may be some hot button issues that lit her up, including religion and God, but ultimately, she seemed like a pretty good-natured kid who totally brightened when someone took an honest interest in her. She would have to keep pursuing them. Maybe she could invite them over for tea again soon.

Every year, Annie planned a New Year's Eve scavenger hunt around the city. They would split into teams of three to five people and have to find and take pictures of themselves with different things. The last stop was always Annie's parents' house out in the suburbs, where the teams would watch the ball drop and then prizes would be awarded. Usually they just invited their small group or people from their church. This year, Annie and Alex agreed to invite some of their friends outside that circle. They weren't sure how the two crowds would mix or if anyone other than their regular attenders would come, but they thought it was worth a try. Omar was busy, and Drew couldn't come. Annie didn't even ask Patti.

But at the last minute, Oliver decided to come. He was all set to go to a party with his group of friends when he found out that Heather would be there, and he couldn't stand the thought of facing her. Annie was pumped. Here was a great opportunity for Oliver to get to know some of her Christian friends a little better, and maybe some doors would open to some spiritual conversation.

She thought hard about which group to put him in. She couldn't be in a group because she'd written all the questions, but she wanted Oliver to have fun. There were a couple of other medical people that went to their church, so she put Oliver with them. She thought they might have some things in common.

After the scavenger hunt, Oliver's team was the third to arrive to her parents' house. Annie and Alex greeted everyone with an exuberant "Happy New Year's" and handed out little "Happy New Year" headbands and noisemakers. Annie noted that Oliver seemed more reserved than usual. In the best of times in a group, he was not usually the center of attention. He was much better one-on-one. But he seemed quieter than usual.

As soon as possible, Annie pulled him aside. "Hey Oliver, how was the scavenger hunt?" she asked.

"It was okay." He shrugged and gave a halfhearted smile.

"Are you sure, Oliver? You don't seem like yourself."

"Yeah, Annie. It was fine. I think I'm going to take off though. I got a text from some friends, and I think I'm going to celebrate with them for a while. Thanks for the invitation, Annie."

"Sure, Oliver. No problem. I'll see you at work."

Now Annie was really uncomfortable. Something was obviously wrong, but Oliver was not going to say anything. So she tracked down Dawn, who'd been in his group.

"Hey Dawn. How was Oliver? Did you guys get a chance to talk with him?"

"Oh, yeah. He was great, Annie. We had some great conversations. I know you mentioned that he wasn't a believer, so we tried to take some time to share our spiritual stories and how important it is to decide to follow Jesus. I think it went really well. He was really positive about it. I mean, he didn't really say much himself, but he didn't seem to be upset that we were talking about it. And he agreed with almost everything we said."

Oh no! Annie knew that Oliver would not have wanted to make anyone uncomfortable and that he rarely challenged anyone's claims or statements to their face. He was like that at the hospital. If he disagreed with something, you'd never know it while you were talking in a group. Even if he was uncomfortable, he'd never challenge you to your face in front of anyone else. At most, he would wait until there was a time when you were alone together, and then he might very indirectly say something.

This was not at all what Annie had been hoping would happen. She loved Dawn, Amy, and Mike, but she had no idea if they had any sensitivity to people about their belief systems. As far as Annie knew, none of them really had relationships with people outside of their church circle except some casual acquaintances from work. She had no idea if they were overbearing, black and white, or just completely off the mark for where Oliver was. Annie hadn't even determined yet whether Oliver had any openness to spiritual things.

She quickly prayed that God would salvage whatever of her relationship with Oliver that had been damaged by the events of tonight. She wasn't sure that there was damage, but Oliver was certainly more distant than normal as he was leaving. She knew that he knew her as an individual, but she felt somewhat responsible for what her friends had said to him. And she wasn't sure whether she'd have to undo it or if she'd be able to build on it.

Maybe inviting him to a mostly Christian event hadn't been such a great idea. She just hoped she'd be able to fix whatever had been broken.

The ball dropped; the party dispersed; and Annie shared her concerns about Oliver with Alex. It spurred a bit of an argument because Alex couldn't see the problem with the carload's comments to Oliver. Annie couldn't make him see that perhaps this wasn't the appropriate time or way to share with Oliver. And she couldn't really back up her nebulous fears with proof because she still hadn't gotten to the point of true spiritual conversation with Oliver. When they left for their respective homes, the tension was back in the air.

The Peace Child

Alex still felt a little bit of tension between them as they made their way to Sara's on Wednesday. As they got settled in on Sara's living room love seat, the three talked about how their Christmas and New Year's holidays had gone. Sara had hosted a dinner party with some of the single folks from her church and a few of her neighbors. Apparently, it had been a smashing success, and they were still raving about the food. Sara was a little self-conscious about it, but she seemed pleased.

Sara checked in with Annie and Alex about whether they'd been able to adjust their lives to accommodate some more time with people outside the Christian subculture. They reported on their different activities over the holidays, and Annie expressed her concern about Oliver and what had happened with her friends in the car.

"Ah, Annie, you've hit on a very difficult thing. One of the challenges of being a minister of reconciliation in a church culture that sees things in black and white is that you have to be wise about how you connect your Christian friends with your other friends. Sometimes, bringing a person into a church culture, particularly a modern church culture where your friend is more postmodern, might well damage that person in a way that takes a long time to undo. So you have to know your church friends and your other friends very well and prayerfully decide whether to invite them to mix or not."

"What do you mean about modern and postmodern culture, Sara?" Annie asked. "Is that anything like the cultural differences we talked about last time?"

"Mostly I'm referring to a shift in culture that we have seen in the last few decades. We've moved from a thinking, scientific-method based culture to a feeling, experiential culture. But I'd like to talk about that in a couple of minutes."

Alex thought Annie looked a little confused. To tell the truth, he was too. He'd heard the words postmodern and modern before, but he wasn't sure he could tell the difference. He was just about to ask a question when Sara continued.

"Before we get to that though, I want to tell you why I think culture is so important. You guys know that I went to China several years back. We had to work really hard to learn culture and language to be able to communicate with our friends there. Some of the things that we did and thought were normal, like walking around with shoes on in the house, were really offensive there. So we tried to learn about what was appropriate there and do that. We didn't want to offend anyone."

"Just like it was so important for us to study the culture and learn about what was acceptable there, I think it's important to do that here. Part of that is because the shift of culture I just mentioned. But the other part is because many times we're so sequestered in our own church culture that we totally miss what's going on around us. But in order to build relationships with the people around us and really share our stories, we have to know how to communicate it effectively."

Now Alex had to say something. "But Sara, how can there be more than one way to communicate truth? Either something is true or it's not. Why should it matter how you frame it?"

"Well, Alex, say I was living in rural China and I wanted to share something with a neighbor. If I walked into her house with my shoes on and tucked my feet up on the couch underneath me, she would be so offended by my breach of etiquette she wouldn't be able to hear a word I said. Taking off my shoes wouldn't hurt what I was trying to say, but it would allow my neighbor to hear me."

"I get that, but I'm not sure the analogy totally translates to how we talk about God. I know there's a huge value of tolerance in our culture today. But to tiptoe around that value, I'd have to allow that there is more than one way to get to heaven. And that's not true."

"Would you really, though? What if you just allowed everyone to hold their own beliefs without trying to change them and just shared your own story from your own experience? What is the worst that would happen?"

"They would think that I agreed with them. They might never know that the only way to be saved is to believe on the name of Jesus."

"I don't think that's true, Alex, and I'll tell you why. Treating another person's beliefs with respect shows that you respect him. If you respect him, you are able to have a relationship with him. If he gets to know you well, he will certainly learn all about your beliefs. There are a lot of opportunities and a lot of ways to share what you think and feel with those around you. You don't have to attack someone's ideas and beliefs in order to share your own."

Sara's comments cut Alex to the core. They went against everything he'd ever been taught. How could he just sit by and allow someone to have wrong thoughts or ideas, unchecked. He knew he couldn't control what anyone thought, but at least he could engage the things that were wrong so that people could have an opportunity to see the truth.

"Look, Alex," Sara continued. "Surrender is a journey, and it's a lifelong process. The value of tolerance simply provides you with an opportunity to share out of your own experience. If you frame what you share out of a value of diversity of thought and tolerance, it's been my experience that people tend to be very open to talking about spirituality and what it looks like for you. In these types of discussions, much of the truth of God's story can be shared. If framed in terms of experience, the barriers to authoritarian claims of truth are down, and the Spirit is able to take those truths and use them in a person's life.

Does that make sense?"

Alex was uncomfortable. "I understand what you're saying. But it doesn't sound like anything I've heard Pastor say."

"I know, Alex. I know. I think the way that I have made my way through that discomfort is to trust in the fact that God is a being who wants a relationship with people. People have to get to know him, as a being, in order to have a relationship with him. If people are really getting to know God, then their understanding of God will be inherently limited by the bounds of who he actually is. It's his job to reveal himself, his character, and his actions, not mine, and he's capable of defending himself."

Sara paused to take a drink. "I can speak from my experience and my understanding, but it's always going to be limited, whether I'm making claims about truth or sharing my own experiences. I believe that God can use both to reach the hearts of other people. But I know that sharing the story of my experience is much more likely to resonate with someone in this culture than sharing claims about truth or about belief."

Alex shrugged. He was not convinced, but he didn't really want to make a scene. He looked over at Annie. She'd been silent throughout their exchange, but she was scribbling furiously in her little notebook. He wondered what she was writing down. Hopefully she wasn't just accepting everything Sara said as true.

Sara said, "So, assuming for the sake of argument that it's a good thing to become students of our own culture to be able to better-frame our own stories and the story of God, what other things do you know about what our culture values or appreciates?"

Annie said, "Well, we seem to like our media: texting, messaging, and social networking. But what does that have to do with anything?"

"What do you think? How does it change the way you might tell your story if you know that people like to use media?"

Annie's eyes widened. "You're not suggesting that we make a presentation using powerpoint or something, are you? That would be awkward."

Sara laughed. "No, I'm not. But it does seem like people want interaction rather than teaching. You guys even–your eyes cross anytime I talk for more than a minute or two at once."

Annie said, "Oh, so you're saying that presenting something or giving a lecture or a speech wouldn't be a good idea. But maybe having discussions where there's some give and take would be a good approach."

"Sure. So what other things do you notice about your culture?"

Alex thought for a minute. What could he say about Drew and the culture there? Was it possible that his approach to Drew had been wrong because he'd violated some cultural value without even knowing it? But what might it be?

Alex shook his head, as if to clear it, and asked, "What about the desire to learn and discover for yourself rather than being told what to believe?" Maybe this is why Drew responded so badly whenever Alex tried to tell him that he was doing something wrong.

"I think you're right, Alex. My parents' generation learned from other people and gave a great deal of deference to what an expert or authority figure thought. But our culture has access to so much information at our fingertips that everyone can be an expert. We're much more prone to credit our own experience than someone else's claims about truth."

"A few other things I've noticed are that we've moved from a more linear way of thinking to a story-based culture. So speaking about ideas in narrative form seems to be much more effective than making claims. Also, we've moved from a thinking, rational-based culture to a more intuitive, feeling-based culture. All of these things can and should affect how we frame our stories. If we want to communicate effectively, we have to take all of these things into account.

Sara looked at her watch. "We're getting a little low on time, but I do want to talk about one more thing. When we think about talking about the story of God within the context of different cultures, some people have talked about finding redemptive analogies in these cultures."

"What's that?" Annie asked.

"Let me answer that with a story. It's the story of a man and his wife who moved to a cannibalistic culture in New Guinea in the 1960s. The man, Don Richardson, wrote a book called *The Peace Child*[4] that tells the story. Basically, he and his wife moved to the jungles of New Guinea. They lived among the Sawi people, who were cannibals. They spent a long time learning the language and the culture of the people. They really wanted to be able to share the story of God with this people."

"As they were getting to know the people, they discovered one value that horrified them: the people delighted in violence and betrayal. One of the things that the Sawi people valued the most was when a person was super-friendly and kind to someone else for a time and then turned around and betrayed that person. So when the people heard the story of Judas's betrayal of Jesus, they saw Judas as the hero of the story, and Jesus wasn't interesting at all."

"Wow." Annie said.

"Yeah, I know," Sara said. "This made Mr. Richardson very sad. He could not see how the gospel could penetrate this culture, where the values of love and self-sacrifice were disregarded and the values of betrayal

---

[4]Don Richardson, *Peace Child* (Regal Books 1975)

and killing were held in high esteem. He and his wife started praying that God would reveal to them the key to sharing the story of Christ in a meaningful way. But none was forthcoming, so Mr. Richardson started talking with the Sawi people about leaving.

"Wait–why didn't he just tell them that they were wrong about the point of the story?" Alex asked.

"He couldn't explain it to them. They simply didn't have a value system that would allow Jesus to be the hero of the story and Judas to be the villain."

"So Mr. Richardson felt he had to leave because, when he came to live with them, he had forced them to live in closer communities than they were used to. They were fighting a lot and the different family groups were killing each other. He believed that his presence and their continued close community would lead to more violence and the eventual annihilation of the culture."

"When the Sawi people learned that he was going to leave, they talked and talked among the different tribes, and then they agreed to make peace. Mr. Richardson watched as the tribes exchanged a 'peace child.' One family from each tribe chose a child and exchanged that child for the other. For as long as the peace child lived in a tribe, the child served to enforce the promise that they would not go to war against the other tribe."

"Mr. Richardson then spent several months trying to understand how the peace child worked and how it played out in keeping the peace between the tribes. After some time, he was able to use the peace child as an analogy of how Jesus was sent as a peace child, an eternal peace child, to bring peace between God and mankind. This analogy ultimately paved the way for many Sawi to come to have a relationship with God."

"That's really interesting," said Annie. "Did they stop killing each other?"

"Not entirely. But many of them began to rely on Jesus to make peace between the tribes and to make peace between them and God."

Sara stopped for a moment and looked at Annie and then at Alex. "So what was the point of my story?" she asked.

"Are you saying that we should be looking for those kinds of stories within our own culture? Obviously, we don't have peace children here." Annie said.

"I'd like to encourage us to do just that. As we study the culture around us, I would like for us to look for those places where there are already stories or ideas that illustrate God's great story."

Alex said, "I see how that worked in the jungle, Sara. But is it really a biblical idea?"

"It seems to be. The apostle Paul did something similar. In Acts 17:22-31, Paul teaches the people of Athens about their 'unknown God.' They had altars to lots of gods, and just to be on the safe side, they had an altar to make sacrifices to any god they may have missed. When Paul went to talk with them, he used this altar as an entry point. He found a place in the culture, and he said, 'This is where God comes in. I know this God, and this is what he is like.' It's especially interesting to me that he didn't start by telling them that there were no other gods. He didn't try to correct their thinking. He found the place in the culture that provided a starting point for spiritual discussion, and then he went from there."

"So the question for us this week is whether there are similar places for spiritual discussion in our own worlds. And I'd also encourage us to try to identify the cultural values that are all around us."

Uncomfortable Boundaries

The next morning, Alex woke with a vague sense of discomfort about the things they'd discussed last night. From what he could see, all that Sara had brought up about postmodern culture and sharing faith with postmodern people was amorphous. It didn't have any boundaries. And it didn't seem to have the same inherent checks and balances as what he was used to hearing.

Growing up, he had learned to analyze a person's faith based on the beliefs the person ascribed to. There was a nice concreteness to that. You could know whether someone did or did not have the right beliefs. What Sara was saying seemed so much less measurable because it was simply based on stories rather than beliefs. How can you measure the truth of a story? And how do you know whether you've told the right story in the right way?

And Sara didn't really seem concerned about identifying whether a person was actually saved or not. If faith is a journey, as she seemed to think, then how do you measure where the journey starts and where it stops? How do you know when you passed the point of "not saved" and rose to the point of "saved and going to heaven"? Alex didn't have answers to these questions.

And he felt it would weaken the power of the gospel to talk about faith based on his own experience. The gospel story should be able to stand out there, on its own, without help from his story. It seemed to take away the deity and "otherness" of the gospel to claim only that "this is my story" rather than "this is THE story."

Sara somehow seemed content to rely on the power of the Spirit to take hold of the story in a person's heart, but Alex didn't exactly know what she meant. He supposed that, as a premise, he could agree that it is the Spirit who transforms lives. But wasn't it his job to make sure that the story got told properly, and all the parts were told, so that people could be confronted with the truth? What they did with it was up to them, but he still needed to present it right.

Alex sighed. This was all so difficult. His own life had been transformed by God. He had met God in the hospital room, and before that, on the trip he took so many years ago to the Philippines. He knew that God was real, and powerful, and loving, and good. And he so badly wanted his friends to know that too. He wanted his friends to encounter the living God. So surely he and Sara agreed on that.

But she was proposing a method of sharing that has really undefined limits. What would happen if, say, Alex's interpretation of God's hand in his life was incorrect? And he was going along, sharing his story with a friend, and giving out incorrect information about God? That was what made him the most uncomfortable, out of all the rest. He could certainly accept the need for redemptive

180

analogies. He could even understand that cultural shifts made a change in communication style necessary. But he couldn't accept the seeming lack of boundaries. She'd said something about the inherent limitations of the character of God last night, but he had no idea what she was talking about.

In case he was misunderstanding what Sara had said, Alex called her. She wasn't home, so he just left a message on her machine. For some reason, Sara didn't seem to have a cell phone. Alex asked Sara to clarify how, based on experience, one could share about God and have any certainty that what was being shared was actually true. Maybe he could get on the same page with Sara if he could understand that.

Alex and Omar were working in the café that morning, so he went to work hoping that they would have a chance to talk a little bit. A lull in traffic happened right around 10 a.m., so he and Omar sat down for a minute to chat.

"So how did you enjoy our Christmas dinner, Omar?" Alex asked.

"Oh, it was very nice, Alex. Thank you for inviting me. I enjoyed meeting Annie. She is a very good cook!" Omar smiled.

Alex laughed. "Yes, she is. She's kind enough to feed me sometimes. Living in a house with other guys doesn't lend itself to a great diet, otherwise."

"You are dating her seriously?"

"Yes. I expect we'll get married soon. The accident threw a wrench in our plans, and now we are working out some differences in opinion about things."

"What kind of things do you disagree about?"

Alex paused before answering. How in the world could he describe this? "Well, I believe that, as a Christian, I am called to evangelize nonbelievers. I think I am meant to give my life to this purpose. I don't think she exactly agrees."

"Oh. I see. Do all Christians not agree with you about proselytizing? I have been led to believe that that value is shared among the Christian religion."

"I think it's valued as an idea, but maybe not in practice. And actually, I think Annie might agree with the idea, but maybe not the method. I think she thinks I am too straightforward."

"Ah, I see," Omar said. "It is an interesting problem, how seriously to take the words of Allah. My family is very devout, and I suppose I am still undecided about how devout to be. I am not currently practicing all the prayers and other requirements. I only sometimes attend the mosque. But it is very important to my father." Omar sighed, "But it has been very interesting for me to discuss with Americans the ideals and ideas of Christianity. I have enjoyed that immensely. It seems that we are not so far apart, Islam just having the additional Prophet

Muhammad."

"Oh," Alex said, "We have a very different way of looking at things, actually. I think that we probably differ on the deity of Christ. You don't believe that Jesus was God, do you?"

"No, we do not. And it really does not make sense that he could be. How could God be born a man? Even your own Scriptures call him a man, no?"

"That's right. It is believed to be a miracle, that he was born a man."

"But the biggest problem that we see with your religion is the amount of errors that have crept into the Christian Scriptures. We, in Islam, have worked very hard to keep the Qur'an pure. Many people have memorized it and other checks and balances exist to be sure that what we have today is exactly the same as what existed before. Your book is not similarly trustworthy, I understand."

Alex didn't know what to say. He was totally out of his element here. He remembered his pastor doing a series on apologetics about three years ago, but he couldn't remember a single thing. "Well, we do believe the Bible is inspired, and many do believe that it is without error."

"But what do you do about the contradictions in the book? Even the four gospel accounts do not agree on every detail. How can you trust a book like that?"

Alex thought there was something to be said about the difference between inspiration and what Omar was referring to, but he could not remember. "I don't know, Omar. I'm not really an expert. But I could find out for you, if you like."

"That's okay, Alex. I have talked to some religious leaders here, and they have not been able to satisfy my questions either."

Conversation moved on to Second Story's management and corporate changes that were coming. Soon customers began to arrive for the lunch time rush. Alex and Omar returned to work. It was only as he was mindlessly filling coffee and lunch orders that Alex wondered what might have been different if he had taken a more "postmodern" approach to that conversation. He wondered if he could have told a story of transformation from his own life that would have engaged Omar's curiosity on a different level. He shrugged to himself and thought he might try it the next time, if there was a next time.

Sara arrived at Second Story at 2 p.m. on Friday to meet with Alex. She'd been praying for this conversation all the way over to the store. When she arrived, Alex bought her a cup of tea and then led her over to their original table.

He spent a couple of minutes tracing his thoughts and reactions to their discussion on Wednesday, and he concluded with, "So I just don't know, Sara. I hear what

184

you're saying on a lot of levels. It just seems that it would be easy to lose sight of what is true using your method, and I was wondering if I was missing something."

"Alex, I'm so glad that you called," Sara answered. "I knew I was rushing through on Wednesday, but it seemed like we only had time for an overview. But let me see if I can answer some of your questions. I do think there are some boundaries that we have that will provide some external checks on the experience-based idea."

"The first boundary I see relates to the whole story of God. We're going to talk in a few weeks about helping people to get to know God through using the whole story that's available in Scripture. And I think that, unless your story of God's interaction with you is subjected to the way God interacts with all mankind in the whole story of God, you're absolutely right–you can end up so far out in left field there's no returning. So one boundary is making sure that what you're claiming as experience fits within that broad narrative."

"Maybe a subset of that boundary is actually the character of God himself. The whole story of God can lead you to understand who God is and what his character is like. If your experience with God does not fit what you know about his character from the story of God (the Bible), then your experience is not something that should be shared because it is not something that can be trusted."

"Another boundary we have been given is the

185

broad orthodoxy of faith communities throughout time and space. This is not the first time in history since the story of God began that the world has gone through a cultural shift. Assuming that we're around for a while longer, it will probably not be the last. But over time and culture, the church as a whole body of believers has said certain things about God and about a life of faith. Everyone does not always agree, so there's room for interpretation within the bounds of orthodoxy. But the outer limits of what is considered orthodox can provide a boundary for testing your experience."

"Finally, I would suggest that the fruit of the experience could be a way to test it. Jesus told us that we could know his followers by the way that they live. If your spiritual experience did not produce the fruit of the Spirit, then you know to question whether it was actually from God or whether you interpreted the experience correctly."

"There's a lot there, Alex. There's a lot to provide boundary and checks and balances. But we were never intended to live only by rational thinking or only by experience. The recent cultural shift has illuminated a great divide between the two, but those walking in the Spirit should be using both–both to reach out to those around them in love and both to learn more about and experience more of God."

Alex gave a small nod. "I see what you're saying. I can see that it's not quite so undefined as I'd originally thought." He paused. "But it's so uncomfortable. I'm going to have to think about this some more."

"That's fine, honey. Take your time. It's a process. This is where I am at and how I have made sense of the things around me. I'm not sure that I'm totally right. But I am growing in my understanding day by day, and God-willing, I am able to effectively communicate from my experience to those around me without leading them astray."

They sat for a few moments in silence. Sara was never in a hurry, and she wanted to give Alex time to ask more questions, if necessary. Finally, Alex shook is head as if to clear it, and then he explained he had to get back to work. They parted ways, Sara quietly praying for him in her heart.

Alex and Annie talked over the weekend about Alex's questions and Sara's answers. Annie seemed content to rely on the boundaries Sara had mentioned. But Alex was still not sure. He spoke often of his sense of discomfort, and Annie suspected that it felt to him like a loss of control. As much as Alex enjoyed the excitement of a game or a prank or a joke, he was much more comfortable with the world around him defined than not. They talked over and over about it, and Alex could not seem to move on. One problem she thought he had was that he kept focusing on experience versus authority rather than on the

187

need for both.

Finally exasperated, Annie said to him on Sunday afternoon, "Alex! I don't think that's what Sara was saying. One of the boundaries she mentioned to you was Scripture–so there is authority there. I think it's more a method of communication than a serious difference in the way she perceives reality. I don't think that she thinks that your experience is valid or "true" just because it's what you perceived happened. But she sees experience, subject to the boundaries, as something that can be another part of the story of God's interaction with mankind. I don't think she's saying that experience is the only way to measure truth. But there can be truth in experience. We just have to find it!"

She continued. "Now can we please talk about something else? I am getting so tired of this conversation. Let's go do something fun." So they went bowling, and, provided they weren't talking about spiritual things, they had a great time.

The next day at lunch, Annie was glad to see Oliver sitting in the lunch room. She hadn't seen him since her party, but it had been a relaxed day on the floor, so she actually had time to sit down and eat for once. When she arrived, she saw Oliver sitting at the little round table in the corner. He was not doing the crossword puzzle as he normally would. Annie bounced into the seat beside him.

"Hey Oliver!" she said. "How's it going today?"

His eyes on the table, Oliver murmured something unintelligible. He started rooting around in his lunch bag for something, but he didn't look her in the eye.

"What's wrong, Oliver? Are you okay?"

Oliver sighed. "What did you tell your friends about me? You know, the ones at the party?"

"Oh, that." She grimaced. "Oliver, I'm really, really sorry about that. I wasn't sure what they would be like. I know that group of people from church, and they usually just hang out together. I mean, we rarely have anyone come to anything that doesn't go to the church. So talk about spiritual things happens a lot of the time. I didn't want them to make you uncomfortable, so I just mentioned that I didn't think you went to church anywhere and that I didn't know what you believed. What did they say to you?"

"Well, basically they spent the whole time trying to convert me. One guy even had this little booklet of information about questions God might ask me at the gates of heaven. I got the impression they were waiting for me to make some sort of decision or proclamation that I agreed with them. I didn't want to argue, so I was just as positive as I could be."

"Oh, Oliver. I'm so sorry!" Annie said. "That's not at all what I wanted to happen. I think they really mean well, but I didn't invite you because I wanted you to be lectured by a bunch of people. I was hoping that they would find some other things to talk about besides religion."

"Well, it's not that I'm not a Christian, Annie. I believe in God. I know my life isn't perfect, but I'm working on it." He got a little heated. "And I have questions. I have questions about God and the church. I don't think the church should be able to tell me what to do, about who I have sex with, or how much I drink. Anyway, I'm still trying to find a balance of my own with that stuff. Maybe when I do, I'll go back to church again."

"I'm sorry, Oliver. I really am. I just hope you know I didn't mean for that to happen."

"Well, it sort of surprised me, given the fact that that's not how our relationship has gone. I know you're a Christian, but it's not like it overtakes your whole life, you know?"

Annie was quiet for a minute, "You know, Oliver, I kind of want it to, though. That's one thing that I've been learning this year–about how being a Christian means following God with all my heart, soul, mind, and strength. I am sure that I haven't been doing that, and maybe that's why you don't know how important it is to me. But it's becoming the most important thing in my life."

Oliver looked at Annie a minute and then shrugged. "Okay. Well, at any rate, you haven't made me feel bad about myself, which is more than I can say for your friends."

Oliver quickly changed the subject, and Annie thought it best to let the matter drop. She'd been praying for Oliver every day since this had happened, and she hoped this wouldn't affect her relationship with him long term. She was also disappointed that he didn't know, based on her life and her attitude, that she was serious about following God. But it had only been a few weeks since she really had been trying to be surrendered to God every day. So maybe it wasn't showing yet.

Emotional Barriers

On Wednesday, Sara, Alex, and Annie gathered again in Sara's living room. Alex noticed that they were sitting in the same seats they always chose. He'd have to mix it up a little next time. After they'd settled in, Sara asked them to take a few minutes to pray together for themselves and for the people they'd been praying for over the past weeks.

"I know that we haven't been so focused on prayer during our talks, but I can't say how important it is to rely on the Spirit to lead us. I really had the sense tonight that we needed to pray for those in our world. So let's take a couple of moments to pray." Annie had shared briefly about Oliver, so they spent some extra time praying for him and that Annie's relationship with him would not be significantly damaged by what had happened.

After prayer, Sara asked if they had any nagging questions from before. Though Alex still wasn't totally comfortable, he didn't bring anything up because he didn't think he'd get new information. He just had the same questions he'd had before, and he expected the same answers. Annie said she was fine and they could move on to a new topic.

Sara said, "I want to shift now to talk about some of the things that keep people from walking with God in faith. Let's refer to those things as barriers. So what do you think? What are some of the thoughts, ideas, or feelings that people you know have when they think about faith?"

"There's sin, of course," said Alex.

"Okay. Our sin does separate us from God. But conviction of sin comes from the Holy Spirit, not from us. So what are some specific thoughts or ideas or feelings that we can interact with that might keep people from seeking God?"

Annie said, "What about what Oliver said to me this week? I couldn't really tell, but he seems to want to wait until he has his life together to go back to church."

"And where do you think that desire to go to church only when you have your life together comes from?"

Annie said, "Well, I don't know about Oliver, but there are lots of times when I feel bad at church about who I am. There's this expectation that only perfect people show up. And I don't always measure up, so I sometimes don't want to go at all."

"Great, Annie. I heard you use the word 'feel' in there. Do you think we could call this barrier an emotional one?"

"I guess so. I'm not sure exactly what you mean, but I guess it is my emotions that would prevent me from going to church at those times."

"What about God? Do you think people have a similar thought about measuring up to God's standards?"

"Sure," said Alex. "The Bible says that no one measures up to God's standards–'there are none righteous, no not one' and all that."

Sara nodded. "This is one barrier that everyone faces on the way to faith. It's something that we could call a spiritual barrier. We all have pride, going all the way back to the garden of Eden, where we want to be like God. We want to be good enough to come to God on our own. We don't want to have to admit that, without him, we would not be able to make our own way. But I think it also has emotional components. I feel bad about myself when I don't measure up to God's standards, and I want to feel good about myself." Sara shook her head.

"Anyway, do you think we can respond to or interact with these spiritual barriers?"

Annie said, "I'm not sure that we can fix them or convince people to leave them behind, can we? I mean, if it's something within our spirits, I'm not sure that anything outside us can really help with. It's almost like it's something that has to be surrendered to God."

"But what about confronting this issue, or at least bringing it up?" said Alex. "There must be times when someone isn't aware of the barrier that's there and needs someone to tell him."

"I can't say that would never be appropriate," said Sara. "There are certainly times within relationships that we need to confront one another in love. But I think the operative words there are 'relationship' and 'love.' Outside of those two things, confrontation can make it much harder for a person to walk forward in faith."

Alex noticed that Annie was nodding intently. He could understand the need for love in confrontation, but he also knew how many times in his own life where someone confronting him and challenging his thinking had helped him to grow. Even though it didn't feel that great, the end result had been good. So why not do the same thing for others? That was exactly what he had been trying to do for Drew all this time. Even though it hadn't produced any outward results, how could he know that it hadn't made a difference in Drew's inner life?

Sara said, "So here's another example of barriers. I had this friend at the university who teaches history. She grew up a fundamentalist Christian, so she had incredibly strong beliefs about the literalness of the Bible. She believed that every word was literally true. But when she started studying history, she learned a system for evaluating whether documents or books are actually true. This system is based on probabilities. She eventually concluded that, based on this system of evaluation, the Bible wasn't totally literally true. Her faith in God was totally shaken."

"We used to meet for lunch every once in a while, and we talked about God sometimes. She was always looking for and asking for something that would give her proof that the Bible was true using the system of historical evaluation that she used. As far as I know, she never found it. So what barriers to faith might have been present in her life?"

"Well, there's the obvious barrier of there not being enough 'proof' for her," Alex said.

"Sure. That's one. That's a barrier based on rational reasons, right? But can you see any emotional barriers there?"

Annie said, "Well, what about how it must have felt for her whole system of belief to be shattered? If she learned about something that she began to trust more than the Bible itself, it seems like that would be really hard to take. It would make you question the foundations of anything you ever believed."

Sara said, "I think so. But I always wondered too if there wasn't an element of identity wrapped up in it. The woman had gone so far with that historical evaluation system that, if she allowed herself to question it, she would have been questioning her identity. But she had become an historian, and she couldn't give that up. So faith in the Bible and in God had become incompatible with her identity." She smiled sadly. "I always wished there was something I could have said to her that would have broken through all that. But I never found it."

"Anyway," she continued, "one of the most difficult things about barriers to faith is that they have many layers to them. There may be a layer that is a spiritual barrier that only the Holy Spirit can break through. There may be a layer that is a rational argument against faith. And there may be a layer that is totally emotional. There are lots of great resources out there that address rational questions about faith. But I don't see anything out there that talks about how to identify and speak to emotional barriers."

She continued. "And one of the difficult things is that it's sometimes really hard to get behind the rational questions people are asking to discover what their emotional barriers are. Take the issue of homosexuality for example. Remember that speech by the president in the *West Wing* clip we watched?" Annie and Alex nodded.

"Well, they were arguing about the rightness and wrongness of the idea of or actions related to homosexuality based on the verses in the Bible. But people's reactions to the question are rarely just rational. There's usually an emotional component to it."

"I don't really understand what you're asking, Sara," said Alex. "What could be emotional about that? Either homosexuality is right or wrong, and people who I talk to about homosexuality want to talk about whether it's right or wrong. At least that's what Drew always wanted."

Annie said, "But Alex, you've told me before that Drew has said that he hates himself for being a homosexual. Don't you think that he really believes it's wrong? That's the impression I got from what you've said before."

"Okay, Annie," said Sara. "That's an example of what I'm talking about. So when Drew is trying to discuss the idea of homosexuality with Alex, we can infer from what he says that he believes that it's wrong. If that's true, then what do you think he's really asking for when he talks about the issue? What do you think he's wondering about?"

Annie scrunched up her nose as she thought. "Maybe he's really wondering if God loves him. I mean, we know that he grew up hearing about God—his dad is a leader in the church. But from what Alex said, his dad is really judgmental and has basically thrown him out of the family. I bet he wonders whether God could still love him." Annie paused. "That's it, isn't it, Sara?"

"I don't know that we can ever know for sure what's going on in people's hearts, but that's the kind of thinking I'm talking about."

"But wait a minute," interrupted Alex. "Whenever he brings it up, he wants to talk about the verses. He tries to argue about what the Bible says about it, about whether we're reading it right, about whether that was just a cultural rule. He doesn't ever say anything about God's love."

"That's the tough thing, Alex. And that's what I want you to see. There are the things people say, and then there are the deeper questions of the heart behind those things that we say. Hmm . . . . Let me see if I can put this in another way." She tapped her finger against her lips.

"Okay. When I used to have arguments with my husband, it would often be about how we chose to complete a task. We always did everything differently. So when he would ask me why I was doing something one way, I would get defensive. Instead of just answering the question, we would get into a huge argument about the pros and cons of doing it one way versus the other. But in the end, all I really wanted was to know the way that I was doing it was okay. I was never really sure of myself, you see?"

"But talking about things on that level is hard. It's much easier to have an argument about how to put the toilet paper roll on the holder than to actually ask my husband to validate my feelings of insecurity. It took us about ten years to figure out that's what I needed. And when we did, I got better at asking the question I really meant to ask, and he got better at reading behind my statements for the questions that were too difficult to ask. I think it's similar in other areas of life too."

"For Drew, it's too big a question to come out and ask whether God still loves him. It's too big a question to risk being vulnerable with God, even, to ask God if he's still there. So Drew keeps his questions on a safer, more rational level."

Alex struggled to understand. Why would Drew

not say what he meant? It didn't make sense. If a person has a question, he should just ask it, not beat around the bush asking questions and debating things he doesn't care about. How could he even begin to think about how to engage people in meaningful conversation if this was true? He shook his head.

Sara continued. "But when you engage Drew on the surface, you never get to answer the questions that he's really asking on the inside."

Alex said, "But Sara, how can we ever know what to talk with people about then? How are we supposed to figure out what the real issues are?"

Sara answered, "Well, that's one of the reasons that we pray for our friends. Human beings are really, really good at masking heart issues. We're rarely close enough to people to actually open up to our most vulnerable level."

"But we can also look really closely at what people react to. If someone responds to an idea with a lot of emotion, or if someone avoids talking about something entirely, those might be clues that there's something deeper going on inside. We can learn to watch for the clues and then try to hear what's not being said."

Sara paused for a minute and all was quiet. Alex didn't say anything because he didn't know what to say.

"I've also noticed that the same emotional barriers seem to come up for a lot of different people. For example, people might have a hard time with the idea of hell. I've known some people who struggle to come to faith in Christ because their mom or dad just passed away not knowing him. If they accept the story of Christ as true, then that means their relative is in hell. Another one is that a lot of people feel that they aren't worth or good enough for God's love. Can you think of any others?"

Annie answered, "Well, I've heard several people talking about how bad the church is or how hypocritical people in the church are. Is that one?"

"Sure, Annie. What else?"

Annie said, "What about the problem of evil? Like–how can bad things happen if God is real and God supposedly is in control?"

"Ah, that's a great one. A lot of people struggle with that question. Really, the list can go on."

Alex sat, puzzled. He could recognize these issues that people had. "But Sara," he said, "I've had discussions before with people about the problem of evil in the world. But we talk about evil as an idea, and we talk about how it is possible that it can exist alongside God. We don't talk about feelings."

"I understand that. But I do wonder why people care about that issue. Is it really a logical issue they have? Do they really believe it's logically impossible that God and evil could coexist? I don't think so. I think what most people really want to know is whether God is good and how a good God can allow evil to be in the world. At its heart, that question comes out of an emotional reaction to the idea of God allowing bad things to exist in the world."

Sara looked at Annie and Alex. "So let's talk for a minute about the friends that we've been praying for. With Oliver, for example, we might have identified a spiritual issue. From looking at his life and your conversations with him, can you identify any other possible barriers?"

Annie thought for a minute. "Here's one that you didn't mention. But I know that he has a nominally religious upbringing, so he probably has this idea of a list of rules he'd have to follow to be a Christian. I also know that he drinks a lot, and I suspect that he might be an alcoholic. Do you think that it's possible that to him, choosing to follow Christ will eventually be a choice between his drinking and Jesus?"

"Well, that's certainly a possibility. And it is true that we can become really attached to the ways that we have to cope with life. If a person sees that he might have to give up one of those coping strategies to walk with God, it's very possible that could create an intense emotional barrier."

"How about Omar, Alex? Can you think of any possible barriers he might face?"

"Well, we talked about hell when he was over for dinner. It was a really rational discussion though, so I think it could be a rational barrier."

"Wait, though," Annie said. "Do you remember

how he was asking about his family? Maybe he was asking that because he knew they would never become Christians. We don't really know where he's at in his journey, but he's been talking with other people about Christianity. Maybe he's been considering what it would mean for him to follow."

"You're definitely getting the idea. This is great." Sara smiled. "I think we should wrap up here, but I want to leave you with this thought. It often takes a lot of work and a lot of prayer to be able to see clearly what another person's barriers are. When we do, then we have to figure out how to engage those barriers. As I mentioned, it's tough to see many emotional barriers because they are presented as if they're rational barriers. What I'd like to focus on this week is just trying to see the emotional barriers around you. Consider them in the context of your relationships with your friends. You could also look at some more media–TV or movies–and see if there are specific barriers that are presented with why faith in God doesn't work or isn't right."

"I'll try," said Alex. Annie nodded and said, "Me too." The three wrapped up their conversation and prayed that God would help them to see the emotional barriers of the people around them.

On the ride home, Alex looked over at Annie. He thought she seemed excited because she was tapping her foot and talking fast. But he wasn't sold on the whole idea of emotional barriers to faith. He could see the possibility that there were emotional barriers out there, but he was having a hard time identifying them.

When he pulled up to her apartment, he simply said, "Have a good night. Sleep well, Annie girl." He kissed her cheek, and she jumped out of the car. He watched her as she walked up the sidewalk and opened the apartment door. She turned and waved, and Alex went home.

A Portrait of the Lady

Friday, Josie came over to do Annie's portrait. She'd come in carrying a gigantic piece of paper and an easel. She set it up in Annie's living room and pulled over a dining room chair. She ordered Annie to sit with her face toward the light coming from the sliding glass window in the living room. She immediately got to work, charcoal in hand.

After about five minutes, Annie started to squirm. "Do you really need me to sit here this whole time?" She moved as if she was going to get up off the chair.

"Wait! Don't move." Josie commanded. "You have to stay there."

"For how long?"

"Until I'm done. Or at least until I have the basic form and facial expression down."

Annie stopped moving and sat there for a minute, biting her lip.

"Don't bite your lip. It screws up your facial expression."

"Then what can I do?"

"Just sit there."

Annie surreptitiously drummed her fingers against the chair she was sitting on. "So, can I talk?"

"If you try not to move your lips."

Annie rolled her eyes. Yeah right. How was she

going to do that? "So how was school today?"

"What is it with adults and school? Nothing ever happens there. It's pointless to talk about." Josie was drawing intently.

O–kay. Hmm . . . . "When did you start drawing?"

"When I was like five or something. I don't know. I've been doing it a long time."

"Did you ever take any classes?"

"Just some art classes in school. Nothing much. Mostly I just learned myself."

"That's really impressive."

"You haven't even seen any of my stuff yet."

"Yeah, but just knowing that you can do it and that you taught yourself to–that's pretty impressive."

"Ok. Whatever. Listen, if we're going to talk, you need to do most of the talking. It's really hard for me to talk and draw at the same time. Unless you want this to take like ten hours or something."

Annie didn't think she could sit still for an hour, let alone ten. "Well, what do you want to know about me?"

"Tell me about Alex. How did you meet him? Why are you dating him? What's he like?"

"Ah, so you want to know about Alex." Her eyes sparkled. "Well, he's a great guy really. He's really sweet. He likes doing things to surprise me. He likes to play practical jokes. We met at college, in biology class. He just had this great sense of humor. We dated for about three years in college, and we were talking about getting married. But then he had this motorcycle accident." Annie's voice drifted off.

"Hey, stop making that face."

"What face?"

"Your forehead is wrinkling."

"I'll try. So anyway, Alex kind of changed then. I mean, he was still himself, but he was much more serious. It was like the accident made him think a lot about life and death. Now he always wants to talk about what life means and what we're doing to make a difference in the world. But he seems more uptight too. I'm not sure why. It's like he can't just let things be anymore. He has to do something to fix them or to challenge them or to change them. Sometimes it makes me feel really uncomfortable. I think it's important to walk alongside people, to be a friend, to listen to them. But he seems to think it's important to speak strongly into their lives."

"What do you mean?"

Why was she telling all this to a 14-year old kid? Weird. She guessed that she hadn't really talked about Alex much with anyone, except her mom. But her mom didn't really offer much beyond the basic, "He seems like a really nice guy." She wasn't sure what insight she thought she'd get from Josie, but it was kind of nice to just talk about it.

"I don't know. It's like he wants to confront

people's beliefs that don't match up with his own. It's almost like he believes he's right on everything, and when people don't agree, he thinks it's his job to change their mind. He never did that before the accident." She shrugged. "He was always a strong personality. He was always opinionated. But it was more like he loved to debate than that he really tried to get people to follow his way of thinking. Now it's like he's invested in the result."

"Oh, I don't know." Annie shook her head. "It's such a mess."

"Do you love him?" Josie stopped drawing and looked at Annie.

"Yes, of course. I love him a lot." She paused, biting her lip again. "But I don't know if I like him anymore."

This admission brought tears to her eyes. Was that really true? Did she no longer like Alex? How could that be?

She jumped up and started pacing. She needed to see him. Right now.

"Hey. You've got to sit down."

"I don't think I can right now. Can we stop? Do you want to go to the bookstore to see Alex? Maybe get a cup of hot cocoa?"

Josie looked at her picture. "I guess I can finish up later. Sure, we can go get some cocoa. Let me just put this stuff away."

When they arrived at the bookstore, Annie was a little apprehensive. Why did she drag Josie here anyway? What was she hoping to see?

When they entered the store, Annie immediately looked behind the counter. There he was. His reddish hair was spiked as usual. And his features were animated as he explained the different types of drinks they offered to a little old woman. She had probably never been to a café like this before. Annie smiled. She hovered near the door.

"Well, come on. What are we waiting for?" Josie asked. So Annie followed Josie to the counter.

Annie knew the second Alex saw them. He smiled a huge smile and gave an exuberant wave. "I'll be right with you guys."

He finally got the old lady to order, and then she went to wait for her drink. Annie and Josie stepped up to the counter.

"What are you guys doing here?" Alex asked.

Annie smiled. "I just wanted to see you."

"Well, what can I get you?"

"I think we both want hot cocoa with lots of whipped cream."

"Coming right up. Why don't you go sit down? I'll bring it to you. I can take a little break."

Annie found a table, and Josie wandered off to look at the books. Alex arrived a minute later with the drinks.

"Who's the kid?"

"It's Josie, my neighbor's daughter. She's really pretty sweet."

"What is she wearing?" He raised an eyebrow.

She smacked his arm. "Come on Alex. Don't be mean. She's just a kid. She's trying to express her individuality or something. It's not a big deal. Actually, she's pretty cool. She was just working on drawing my portrait for me."

"So what are you up to this evening?" Alex asked.

"Not much. Have some laundry and stuff."

"Should we rent a movie? I could bring it over. You could cook for me." He grinned. "You know I'd just waste away without you."

"Sure, that's fine. Just come on over after work. I'll be there."

Josie slid into the seat beside Annie. "Great art section." She took a sip of her cocoa. "So. You must be Alex." She looked him over. "I've heard a lot about you. Sweet, charming, mischievous. Anything else I should know?" She raised her eyebrows.

"Ah, not that I know of."

"You're not, like, a total jerk or anything, are you?"

"No–" Alex answered as Annie said "Josie! What are you saying?"

Josie looked at Annie. "I was just checking. Sometimes women are stupid. Friends need to look out for each other." She hopped up. "I'll be over in the travel section."

Annie watched her walk away. "That was weird. She used to barely talk to me. I thought she was shy." She shook her head and then turned back to Alex. "So how's work today?"

"It's okay, nothing too exciting. Drew's out sick again." He shrugged. "But I should get back. It looks like we're about to get busy." He nodded over at the counter.

Annie collected Josie, and they headed out to the car. "So, what did you think of Alex?" Annie was curious. Her own feelings were mixed after seeing him. He was the same old Alex. Nothing had really changed between them. Yet she wasn't really comfortable. She'd been holding her breath when he was talking to Josie, praying that he wouldn't open his mouth and say something dumb. That had been kind of stressful.

"Decent. He didn't really know what to do with me, but that's pretty normal. I don't think he'd intentionally hurt anyone. So that's good."

Annie looked over at Josie. Her jaw was clenched and she looked straight ahead. "Why did you feel like you needed to protect me?"

"Like I said. Some women are dumb. We've got to look out for each other."

Alex had a busy afternoon, but at about 4 p.m., things slowed down. He and Omar cleaned up the café and finished all their little jobs. Finally, they sat down for a break.

"So, Alex, how has your week been going?"

"Not too bad. Not too bad. What have you been up to?"

"Nothing special. I did speak with my father this week. He has instructed me that I should prepare to return home after this semester. I will not be returning to the university next year."

"Really? Wow. Are you happy to be going home?"

"I am. I do love my country. But I do believe that there is so much more that I could learn here. I wonder why my father would like to cut my stay short." He shook his head. "But he must have his reasons."

"Will you go to school when you get home?"

"Yes. I will transfer my credits there."

"Can I ask you a question?" said Alex.

"Of course."

"Have you ever considered becoming a Christian? I mean, what would it take for you to leave Islam and become a Christian?"

Omar toyed with a paper napkin on the table. "Well, I have investigated the Christian religion while I have lived here. I have asked a lot of questions. But I just do not see how it is possible." He stopped.

"But why? How could it be impossible?"

"Well, to give up Islam would be to give up my

home, my family, and my culture." He shook his head. "No, I could not do that."

"Would you want to? I mean, if you could?"

"I do not know, Alex. I do not know."

Alex approached Annie's door that evening with anticipation. It seemed like forever since he and Annie had just had time to relax together. The holidays were always stressful for everyone, he knew. But it seemed like this year was especially so. He was looking forward to a quiet evening in her apartment.

He knocked on her door, and Josie answered. "Oh, hi Josie. How are you?" Gosh. He hoped the kid wouldn't stick around too long.

"It's Jo." She held open the door. "Come on in, then."

He entered to see Annie laying on the couch with an ice pack on her ankle.

"What happened? Are you okay?"

"Oh, I went for a jog and tripped over an uneven sidewalk. I landed wrong on my ankle. Jo was kind enough to come over to make sure I was okay. But we're going to have to order a pizza or something."

Josie said, "Well, I'll be off then." She turned to Alex. "Take good care of her."

Alex looked at Annie and rolled his eyes. Annie

said, "See you Jo. Thanks."

So Alex ordered some pizza, and he fanned out the movies he'd brought. "Action? Comedy? Drama? I've even got a chick flick here."

Annie smiled. "You can choose, Alex. I'm just glad you're here." Her face looked strained, but he supposed that was her injury.

So he picked the comedy and they settled in to watch the movie. Eventually, he felt Annie snuggle up beside him, and he was content.

One Story at a Time

By Wednesday afternoon, Annie's ankle was feeling much better. She'd arranged to have Josie and Patti over for tea. But 2 p.m. came and went, and they never came by. Annie started to worry. The night before, she'd heard some disturbing noises coming from their apartment. She thought she'd heard yelling and maybe a crash or two. She was really concerned. But then it was time to go to Sara's, so she didn't have a chance to find out if everyone was okay.

Annie was excited about their conversation that night because she really wanted to know how to interact with the barriers she was sensing all around her. It was obviously possible to create additional barriers to faith instead of walking through them with people, and she didn't want to do that.

After opening with prayer, Sara led them to jump right back in to the discussion where they'd left off.

"I meant to say last week that one thing I've noticed is that engaging barriers on the rational level tends to lead to arguments. Very often, those arguments lead to a breakdown of relationships. I think this is because, most of the time, we're not coming from the same foundational assumptions as those we're arguing with. And when you're arguing rationally, if you don't start from the same assumptions, neither side will ever be convinced to move to

217

the other's point of view."

"But engaging the heart issue in an open way can create dialogue rather than squelch it. It can increase understanding and build relationship. And that's really the goal. If you can treat this like dialogue that you're having with a friend rather than a kernel of truth you're trying to pass on to someone who's clueless, people are more likely to feel valued and understood or like they are human beings who have hearts and souls and minds that you care to know because that's how you're treating them."

"Anyway, I want to talk some more about barriers tonight and how we can respond to the deeper emotional barriers we sense in others. So let's start where we left off, with Drew's barrier related to his homosexuality: how might you be able to engage the question behind his objection to the condemnation of homosexuality in the Bible?"

Alex and Annie thought, so it was quiet a couple of minutes. Then Annie thought out loud, "Well, it might be hard to just say 'Hey Drew, God loves you.' I think Alex's done that anyway, and he tends to respond really negatively. So I don't know."

Alex didn't respond. So Sara said, "One thing that I've found to be really effective in responding to an emotional barrier is being able to tell a part of the story of God in response to the deep issue. Jesus did this sort of thing in his parables. So is there a story from the Bible that you can think of that might answer what we think might be Drew's deeper question?"

Annie and Alex thought some more but remained quiet. So Sara asked, "When you think of sin, what do you think might be the worst sin someone could commit?"

Alex answered, "Well, probably something from the Ten Commandments. Those seem to be the most important moral principles. So I'd probably say murder."

"Going with that," Sara said, "can you think of any stories that relate to how God related to or viewed a murderer in the Bible?"

"Sure," Alex said, "King David. He murdered Bathsheba's husband so he could marry her. There's probably nothing that's worse than that."

"Okay, Alex, so tell me that story."

Alex straightened his shoulders and sat up on the couch–this he could do. "So there was this guy, David, and he was the king of Israel. And he was a really special king because God had chosen him to be king out of all the people of Israel. God looked at the hearts of all the people in the nation, and he saw something about David that he liked. So he made David king. Actually, David had a really hard time with the prior king, and it took several years. So anyway, David was a really, really wealthy guy. And in the time when kings usually went to war, David stayed home one year. So he's outside on his roof one night, at the palace, and he looks over at another roof and sees a beautiful woman there, bathing on the roof. He's immediately taken with her, and he wants her. So he goes and sleeps with her. And she gets pregnant. So, trying to cover it up, he gets the husband to come home from war, hopefully to sleep with her, so the baby will look like his rather than David's. But the guy is so honorable that he refuses to take any comfort while the rest of the men are out fighting. So he never sleeps with his wife. And David doesn't know what to do until he has the brilliant idea to send the husband to the front lines to hopefully get killed in battle. And he totally succeeded. The guy died, and David took Bathsheba as his wife."

"Great, Alex. Now how might that story answer Drew's question about whether God loves him?"

Annie answered, "Don't we kind of need the end of the story too? God eventually gave David and Bathsheba a son named Solomon, who became the next king and built God's temple. So even though this happened in such a terrible way, and there were terrible consequences, God still used David. He still loved David. He even sent a prophet to David to confront him with what he did wrong."

"I think you do need the end of the story, Annie. So if Alex ever had the chance, he could tell Drew this story. And he could point out that no matter what we've done, God still loves and pursues and can use us. And at the end of the day, we know from other places in Scripture that everyone has sinned and falls short of God's perfection. But, Jesus is able to make a way to the Father for us, no matter what we've done."

"Wow," Annie said. "That's cool. I mean, I can kind of see how this might work. It might be a little bit awkward at first, to all of a sudden burst out with this story from the Bible. But if a person is wrestling with spiritual truth, maybe it won't be so difficult."

"And depending on who you're talking to," Sara said, "you may sometimes want to frame this as a story from your spiritual tradition. Or sometimes you can just say something like, 'Wow, I've struggled with that same thing too. But there's a story from the Bible that really helped me with those feelings. Do you mind if I share it with you?' You'd be surprised at how many times people are actually open to hearing."

"Ok, Sara," said Annie. "So what about Oliver? What about his reliance on drinking? I can't really think of a story that goes with that."

"You've got to look deeper, Annie. Why is he drinking?"

Annie shrugged, "It's not like he's told me or anything. It's just something he does, and does a lot."

"I understand," said Sara, "but still, why do you think, in general, that people have addictions to substances or other coping mechanisms? Specifically, have you seen or heard anything with Oliver that might give you a hint to why he's drinking?"

Alex answered, "I think people are trying to fill up something inside that they feel is not right. Or maybe they're trying to escape from the overwhelming brokenness of the world. I know that I do that too, sometimes. Many of the sins I struggle with are ways that I try to cope with reality instead of bringing it to God."

"Okay, Alex. So if there's a deep hunger there, and you think God might be able to fill it, is there a story that you can think of that might fit with that?"

Annie and Alex were silent again. Sara said, "What about Jesus with the woman at the well? Do you remember that story?" They nodded. "Annie, can you tell that story for us?"

"Um, I think I remember it. Jesus was traveling on the road with his disciples, and they left him alone for some reason at this well. And they were in Samaritan country. So this Samaritan woman comes up to the well and starts getting water, and Jesus asked her for some. She was shocked he was talking to her, because he was a Jew and she was a Samaritan, and the two groups hated each other. So she asked him why he was talking to her, and he said something like, 'If you knew who I am, you would ask me for water that would never run dry.' And I heard a pastor explain one time that this woman was so immoral that going to the well however many times a day she needed to was probably torture because the whole community

222

probably knew about how she basically slept with every guy that walked by. So anyway, Jesus said something to her about this water that would never run dry, and she immediately wanted it. And then somehow he got to telling her that he was the Messiah. But he also told her that he knew that she didn't have a husband and she was living with some guy that wasn't her husband."

"Good, Annie. So do you see any spiritual parallels that you could draw from that story?"

Alex jumped in, "Yeah. It sounds like Jesus saw the need in her life and said it was he who could meet it."

"I think so, Alex. And this is where the second step comes in. When you're helping people work through barriers, telling a story that illustrates a spiritual truth is a first step. But there are some times when you can also think of a way to challenge that person to take a next step in faith and trust in God. So if the person isn't really ready to admit that there's any kind of hunger, challenge him to go for a week without drinking—to really feel the hunger he may be experiencing and to try to identify it. Then, when it was being experienced, the challenge is to bring the hunger to God instead of trying to fill it."

Sara continued, "One of the most amazing things that I have seen in my life is the fact that the principles of the Bible can be lived out before people actually believe that they are true. So challenging someone to take a step toward faith and trying things out can illustrate the need for God's presence and help in life, but it can also illustrate that God's ways are good."

Annie was still confused, "Sara, I see the idea, but I'm so confused about how to bring these things up. First of all, it feels like such a risk. It's bringing spirituality into a conversation where maybe someone doesn't want it. Second, if we're just going along, talking about drinking, and I'm actually able to identify there's an emotional barrier there, how do I actually transition to telling the story? Doesn't it seem a little jarring? 'Hey, so we went to the bar the other night and you were trashed. Let me tell you a story.' I don't know, it seems weird."

Sara laughed. "You're right. It would be weird if you did it that way. So one bridge to the story might be telling part of your own story, 'You know, I used to get trashed like that, and I found that I was doing it because I was really hurting. And I found some help in this story I read. Do you mind if I share it with you?' That would be more natural."

Sara continued, "But if you don't share the experience with the person, then it might be a harder transition. I might start transitioning using questions about why he thinks he drinks. Does it make him feel better? Those things might bring up a natural opening to talk about a story and then challenge a person to some sort of action."

Alex asked, "So, you mentioned challenging a

person to go without drinking or something. But what other things might you challenge people to do as a step toward faith?"

Sara answered, "Well, I might show them another story in the Bible that they could read. I might challenge them to pray to God. It really depends on the situation. So it's really important to know the stories of God and the story of God, and it's also important to be praying as you're talking. The Spirit is able to bring the right things to mind at the right time."

Annie asked, "Do you know of a good way to learn the stories of God? I know some things about the Bible. But I'd never be able to know enough of these stories to tell to other people. I don't really remember what I learned in Sunday school."

"One thing I would definitely recommend is the idea of a storying group. There's an author who has written some stories that are available for free on his website, echothestory.com. There are about 21 stories that go through the overview of the whole story of God. I would really recommend that you start there. Talking through the stories of God and walking inside them in community is a really powerful thing. And honestly, getting a children's Bible story book is another idea. You can at least absorb the arc of the stories that way. And God can illuminate the spiritual truths that those stories are meant to convey."

Annie nodded her head, and Alex actually looked grudgingly accepting. Sara continued to answer questions and they threw out some more spiritual barriers and potential stories. They talked about the problem of evil in the world and how that was often a barrier to faith. They discussed the possibility of telling the story about the Israelites' 400 years of slavery and exodus as a story to illustrate the truth that judgment is coming. They also talked about the story of Jonah and how that illustrates that God uses people to bring the message of repentance and redemption. And if people aren't doing it, it's not getting done. They also discussed the importance of talking about how Jesus is with a person who is suffering, so they could tell the story of Jesus, Mary, and Martha as it relates to the death of Lazarus.

They talked about the barrier of trust and how hard it is to trust a God who you don't know anything about. They thought about the possibility of telling the story of Abraham and Sarah and how their trust in God ebbed and flowed in their journey toward having a child.

Finally, Sara wound things up, and Annie and Alex prepared to go. Annie gave Sara a quick hug and thanked her for the night. On the way home, Annie and Alex continued the discussion about possible barriers and possible stories to respond to those barriers. That night, Annie went to sleep praying for Patti and Oliver and what tomorrow might bring.

Becoming Storytellers

The next morning, Annie got up to go for her regular run. As she tied her shoes and pulled her curly hair back into a short ponytail, she prayed for the things the day might hold. She asked God to help her to see the barriers of the people around her and also prayed that she would have wisdom to know if there was a story that she could tell.

She had a glorious run in the snowy cold–it was exhilarating to feel the cold wind whipping by her as she propelled herself down the sidewalk. She loved these early morning times to run and think, and now to pray.

As she slowed to a walk and then approached her apartment, she noticed Josie's familiar form sitting on the doorstep. Annie breathed a quick prayer and then sat down beside her.

"Hey Josie. How's it going?" She asked.

Josie barely acknowledged her presence and barely nodded her head in response to the question. She looked worried. Her ear buds were in her ears, but Annie couldn't tell if there was any music playing or not. Annie pushed on.

"Is anything wrong, Josie?" She waited.

Josie slowly removed the ear buds. She said simply, "Mom's in the hospital."

"Can you tell me which one?"

"Mercy General. She's supposed to come home

tomorrow."

Annie nodded. She sat some more. Then she asked, "Josie, do you mind if I pray with you, for your mom?" In that moment, Josie exploded. She jumped up, threw her iPod across the parking lot, and screamed, "I do NOT want you to pray, I do NOT want to hear another thing about God. That's how she got into this mess in the first place. You and your stupid religion. No. I don't want to hear another word out of your mouth." With that, she stalked away.

Annie stared after Josie for a moment, not moving. Then she shivered and came to herself, shaking her head. Should she go after Josie? What had happened to Patti? And what did Josie mean about religion causing her injuries? She prayed for the Spirit to give her the eyes to see, and she knew that she needed to go visit Patti. Now.

She raced inside, took a quick shower, and then made her way to the hospital. When she arrived at the hospital, she was directed to the tenth floor. She located Patti's room and walked up to the door as a female police officer was leaving.

Annie took that in and then gently knocked on the door. She didn't hear an answer, so she peeked her head in and said quietly, "Hello?"

Patti looked over, and Annie saw that her arm was in a cast and her face was black and blue. "Oh, Patti," Annie said, "I'm so sorry." At that, Patti turned away and looked out the window.

Annie stepped into the room silently and quietly closed the door. She sat down in the visitor's chair a couple of feet from the bed, opposite the window. Questions were flying through her mind, but she was quite sure that now wasn't the right time to pump Patti for information. So she sat quietly until Patti turned and looked back at her.

"Thanks for coming," Patti said in a near whisper.

"Of course," Annie replied. "I ran into Josie this morning, and she told me where you were." Annie paused. "Patti, what happened? Are you okay?"

Patti looked away again. "It was an accident," she said to the window. "Bike. I fell off my bike. I had a concussion and some internal bleeding, so they had to keep me for a couple of days. But I'm going home tomorrow." It sounded robotic.

Annie hesitated. This didn't exactly seem to match what Josie had said. How could a bike accident have been caused by religion? No, there must be something more to it. But Annie wasn't sure how far to push. She didn't know Patti all that well, and Patti was still looking out the window. She seemed really hesitant to say anything more.

Annie glanced around the room and noticed a simple bouquet sitting by the telephone. "Those flowers are nice," she said, "are those from Jake?"

Patti was silent so long, Annie wondered if she'd fallen asleep. Finally, Patti turned back. A look of pain flitted across her face, but it was immediately replaced by a mask of calm. "No. They're from some women at the church we go to."

Annie hesitated and then asked, "Patti, Josie told me that God was the cause of all this. She seemed pretty mad about it. What did she mean?"

Patti's face darkened, her whole body stiffened, and she looked away again. Annie sat there, trying to read the emotions that played across her face.

Annie wanted to speak–to say something. This inaction was killing her. But she didn't know enough about what was going on. She tapped her foot on the floor, up and down, up and down. It made a little tapping noise.

Finally Patti turned back again, her face a mask of calm. Her voice was all ice. "The man who did this to me claimed to do it in the name of Jesus. Now please go. And ask the nurse to bring me some more pain medication."

Annie was sickened. Jake. Her heart was breaking as she stood up to leave. At the door, she paused and turned back and said, "I'm so sorry Patti. Please let me know if there's anything I can do for you or Josie." She closed the door behind her and quickly went to see the nurse about the medication.

As she headed home, she called Sara. "Sara, Annie. I've got a huge problem." She explained what had happened, and she asked Sara what to do.

"Is Jake going to be there when she comes home

tomorrow?"

"I don't know. I don't know anything. Maybe I should see if I can find Josie. But I'm not sure either of them really want my help right now. They know I'm a Christian, and they really don't want anything to do with that. I don't want to add to any of the emotional barriers that Jake has caused them."

Sara answered, "You don't have to worry about hurting them by loving and pursuing them. They might not want your help, but they might need it more than they think right now. I've got the number to a domestic violence shelter. Even if they've got a place to stay, the shelter has a lot of resources. Let me track that down for you and call you back."

When Annie got back to the apartment, she knocked on the Conrads' door, but no one was there. She would just have to wait to see if Josie came home from school.

Afternoon came and went, and there was still no Josie. Annie went over about 15 times that afternoon. She had called Alex and asked him to pray for her and for the two women. Finally, she heard loud music blaring from the speakers next door.

She headed over, and to her surprise, Josie opened the door. She wore a fierce look on her face, but her eyes looked haunted.

"Can I come in?" Annie asked quietly. Josie opened the door a little wider in response, so Annie entered. She glanced around at an apartment that had the same basic layout as hers, only it had an additional bedroom. The apartment was obviously normally kept immaculately, but there were two days' worth of fast food containers strewn about the kitchen and dining area. Josie showed Annie over to the oversized couch in front of a widescreen plasma TV. Wow. They certainly had enough electronics in here to stock a Best Buy.

Annie and Josie sat down and looked at each other. Josie's look was wary, so Annie supposed that she would have to direct the conversation. "I went to see your mom today. She looked okay. She said she's coming home tomorrow." Annie watched Josie for some sign that she had heard what Annie said. Then she asked, "Josie, is your dad coming home tonight?"

And then Josie was crying. She started sniffling, and then her eyes watered. Annie watched as she desperately tried to maintain control and then suddenly broke down. Annie grabbed some tissues and scooted down to Josie's side of the couch. Annie put her arm around Josie and let her cry. As she hugged the girl, she tried to think of a spiritual story that could bring hope and a measure of healing in such a difficult situation. And what could she say that would not incite the hostility that she'd already brought out this morning?

About five minutes passed this way, and then the tears subsided. "Do you want to talk about it?" Annie asked. Josie just shook her head. "Okay. Here's what we're going to do. I'm going to call your mom at the hospital, and then you're going to come over to my house tonight to stay with me. The couch is pretty comfortable, and you'll be safe there."

Again, to her surprise, both Patti and Josie complied. Josie grabbed a couple of things, and then they headed back to Annie's place. Annie set Josie up with some tea and gave her the TV remote and then sat down beside her until she fell asleep.

She didn't know if she'd done the right thing by not saying anything. She knew that Alex would have jumped in with some kind of statement about how much God loved them. And she wanted them to know that. But right now their trust was so fragile, and they clearly didn't have anyone else. She didn't want to alienate them. She thought that maybe now was not the time to have a spiritual conversation. Maybe there would be time to process it with Josie and Patti later, but right now, it seemed like what they needed was to see an actual Christian acting like a Christian instead of spreading hate and evil.

When Annie awoke the next morning, Josie was already up and dressed and making scrambled eggs at the stove. She seemed reserved but a little less vulnerable than the night before. Annie grabbed some cereal and then sat down at the table.

"Josie, can you tell me what happened?"

Josie threw her a quick glance and then sighed. "Dad and Mom got in a huge argument and Dad got more violent than he ever had before. I finally got him out of the house and took my mom to the hospital. I haven't seen him since. But Mom said she talked to the police and she wants to press charges. I don't know if he's been at work or not."

Annie nodded. "Okay. How do you normally get to school?"

"My friend picks me up. She'll be here in a couple of minutes."

"Does your mom have a way home?" Josie shrugged, so Annie said, "I'll make sure she gets home safe, okay?"

When Annie brought Patti home later that afternoon, she made sure that Patti was able to get comfortable on the sofa. She offered to bring dinner over later. Patti thanked her for helping out, especially with Josie. She seemed a little softer today, but there was a steely glint in her eyes that Annie had never seen before. Something had shifted in her, and she was going to fight. Annie was glad for that–no one should remain in such a horrible situation. But she also sensed that Patti could be tempted to throw the baby out with the bath water. Because Jake had used the name of God to justify his

234

abusive behavior, she didn't know if Patti would be able to separate it. As Annie left, she remembered to hand over the telephone number of the domestic violence shelter, just in case.

As Annie prepared dinner that night, she wracked her brain for stories or other information in the Bible that could give Patti hope in such a horrible time without alienating her. The only thing she could think of was one of Jesus's parables about the wheat and the weeds growing together. So if she had a chance, maybe she'd say something about that. And there was that one place where Jesus said something about lots of people calling him "Lord, Lord," but not really belonging to him. But she couldn't really remember what that story was about.

When dinner was prepared, she knocked on the Conrads' door, and Josie answered it. She opened the door to Annie. As Annie walked in to put the food on the table, she saw that Patti was just sitting on the couch, looking out the sliding glass window. She abandoned the table idea, and just helped Josie put some food on a couple of plates. She brought Patti her dinner along with a soda and then sat for a moment in a reclining chair. Patti didn't acknowledge her at all.

Annie sat still for a moment and prayed. She really felt that she needed to say something–not just for Patti but also for Josie. They needed to know that not everyone who claimed to follow Jesus was like Jake. She bit her lip and then said to an unmoving Patti, "Patti, I know that you know that I'm a Christian. And I know that Jake claimed to be, and did so many terrible things to you, and probably to Josie, and claimed that he had a right to because of the Bible. But I want you to know that he was wrong. He was wrong to do that to you, and he was wrong about what the Bible says. Jesus, when he was here on earth, told his disciples that there would be lots of people walking around, claiming to be his followers, who really weren't. And he told them a story about wheat and weeds that look almost exactly like wheat–so much so that you can't tell the difference until they're adult, when they bear their fruit. Jesus said his followers would be known by their fruit–things like love, joy, peace, patience, and kindness. Jake's abusiveness, that didn't come from God. I just want you to know that. I want you to hear that."

Annie rose to leave. Patti didn't move, didn't respond, and didn't give any clue whether she'd heard or not. As Annie left, she said, "I'm right next door. If you need anything, please let me know."

Josie closed and locked the door after her, and Annie returned to her apartment. She was sad and horrified at the brokenness that one person had created. She sat up for several hours praying for Josie and for Patti.

The next Monday, Drew and Alex were both working together at Second Story. Their conversation, as always, was fairly minimal. Alex just had not been able to handle the negativity that Drew spewed at him whenever he opened his mouth, so for the last few weeks, Alex had said barely two words. But Drew had come in that morning with a bit of pep in his step, so Alex ventured some small talk when they were both in the office. Drew was almost pleasant. Alex commented on it and learned that he'd met someone new over the weekend.

Alex was immediately shocked and repulsed. It was one thing to know that Drew was gay. It was another to picture him dating a guy. Alex just couldn't stand it. And he longed to engage Drew in another discussion about the morality of his sexual orientation. He longed to. He couldn't contain it. So he somehow finagled the conversation toward spiritual things.

Drew was either a little more open than usual or not really paying attention, and Alex launched into the story of David and Bathsheba. Drew didn't really interact with the story, but he didn't object to it either, so Alex plunged on.

At the end of the story, Alex remembered that he was supposed to give some sort of challenge to Drew. A challenge to him to take a step forward in faith or something like that. So when he reached the end, he asked Drew, "If the prophet Nathan were to come to you, what kinds of things do you think he might say?"

Drew's face turned beet red and his muscles tensed, but he did not respond. Instead, he picked up his papers and left the office, not even glancing at Alex on his way out.

Alex sat, confused. What had gone wrong? He thought he'd told the story right. The transition into the story could have been a little smoother. But this was a biblical story. And it was a valid question. As he considered it, he remembered that, at Sara's, they'd discussed this story as a way to communicate with someone that even though he felt self-loathing for sin or weakness, God still loved him and could use him. Admittedly, Alex's goal of sharing the story had been different. But couldn't using stories to illuminate sin work in the same way? He thought about it some more, and thought that yes, sometimes that was necessary. There was no way to repent without recognizing your sin.

Alex nodded to himself. He felt satisfied with his performance, even though he didn't know what its effect had been. He would just trust that God would use his words and his own Word in the story to speak to Drew's heart.

For Annie, the beginning of that week was crazy. She worked Saturday, Sunday, and Monday, and barely had time to speak with anyone. Each day, she thoughtfully brought over food or something else to Patti and Josie. Each day, Josie would greet her at the door and take whatever Annie had and shake her head about whether Patti wanted any visitors. Every time she saw Josie, Annie made sure to tell her that she was always welcome at Annie's house. But Josie had stepped into the role of her mother's caretaker, and she never wanted to leave Patti's side. Annie kept praying.

The Gospel Message

Wednesday night rolled around, and Annie and Alex had to drive separately again. Alex was working late at the bookstore. Because of everything with Patti, they hadn't really had time to talk at all that week. They both arrived at about the same time, so they entered Sara's house together. Everyone quickly settled in for another discussion. Annie and Alex were both excited to share how they had used the things they'd been talking about. Sara was excited for their conversation that evening, and she invited them to share about their week.

Annie shared first and mentioned her thought processes throughout the week. She shared about how she still wasn't sure that she should have said what she did to Patti and Josie but that she'd really sensed from the Spirit that it needed to be said. She explained how she had continued to pursue Patti and Josie, and how she still wasn't sure what was going on with Jake. She asked that they take some time that night to pray for the Conrads.

When Alex's turn came to share, he was especially animated. He seemed excited to be able to share that he and Drew had a decent conversation, and that he'd been able to share the story of David and Bathsheba. He explained about Drew's new love interest and said, "I had to change the point of the story a bit. Instead of focusing on how God still loved, pursued, and used a murderer, I focused in more on Nathan's parable to David and how he had confronted David for his sin. And then, as the challenge part, I asked Drew what he thought Nathan might say to him, if he were here today."

Annie looked horrified. She sat there, her jaw hanging slightly open. Sara did a better job containing her reaction. Inside, she too was horrified. How could Alex have so totally missed the point of their conversation the last week? How could he still be talking about only one thing with other people–God's judgment? But she simply asked, "And how did Drew respond?"

Alex answered, "Well, it was kind of weird. He turned a little red in the face and then left the office. I haven't really seen him since." Alex shrugged. "But I told the story. So I did what we've been talking about, right?"

Sara didn't answer immediately. She quieted her own spirit and prayed that God would speak through her. Rather than answer directly, she asked a question.

"What's the heart of the gospel, Alex? What is the point?"

He thought for a moment and then said, "Well, people are broken and need a Savior–their relationship with God is broken and they need a way to come to know him."

"Where does judgment come into that reality?"

"Well, those who don't believe in the name of Jesus will be judged at the end of this age."

242

"Why did you focus on judgment with Drew?"

"Because. Well, if he doesn't place his faith in Jesus, he's going to be judged."

"Do you think that people are motivated to true faith and relationship with God based on a fear of what will happen in the future?"

Alex shrugged as his face tightened. "Maybe some of them."

"Do you think that fear of what will happen creates love?"

Alex thought for a minute, "The Bible says that perfect love drives out fear. So I guess not."

"So if the calling of a follower of Christ is to love God with all his heart, soul, mind, and strength, how is that love produced? Where does it come from? How does it begin?"

Alex pursed his lips. He answered, "Probably not from an understanding of judgment."

Sara nodded. "Yeah, probably not. So the issue remains then, how do people come to love God?"

Annie said, "I think they would have to know him first, you know? You can't love someone you don't really know. So they would have to come to know his story."

"Yes! That's exactly right. The story of God that God has chosen to tell us is in the Bible. And it's a huge story–it spans thousands of years. It's impossible to really understand parts of the story without understanding how the whole thing fits together."

"Theologians have pulled from the story several essential themes or pieces of the story that are necessary to truly understand what it means to walk with God. The arc of the story runs that we and the world were created for good, but that we were damaged by evil, that Jesus came to bring restoration and healing, and that we can be healed and sent out to help others find the same kind of healing. To really understand Jesus, to be able to put faith in Jesus and hear from Jesus, a person has to understand the parts of this story."

"So creation–what do we need to know about creation?"

Alex answered, "Well, God created the world in seven days–the earth and everything in it, birds, fish, animals, plants, moon and stars, sun, and people. And then he rested."

"Hmm," Sara said, "What if a person believes in evolution? Does that mean that she can't know or follow God?"

Alex was nodding. But Annie answered, "Well, the Bible seems pretty clear about God being the creator, right? I mean, there's the Genesis story, but then there are all these other places where God is called the creator. It seems like if you take that away, you're missing some awfully important information about who God is."

"That's true. God as creator does seem to be a really

important characteristic that's revealed in the Bible. But there are Christians who believe in some kinds of evolution. And this goes back to the argument about whether the Bible is absolutely literal in every story or whether there are metaphors. There's a lot of tension about this. But this may be one of those places where orthodoxy could help us to find the appropriate boundaries. It could be that creation happened in a literal seven days–God could do that because God could do anything. It could also be that God used evolutionary processes to create the world and the beings in it. We weren't there, so we can't really know. And the Bible wasn't written as a scientific text, so it doesn't really tell us how that all occurred. But what we do know is that God was the origin of life. Although the belief in evolution is probably more of a rational or modern barrier to belief, it still can come up now and again. But I would encourage you not to get caught up on it."

Alex was shaking his head. He had tensed up again and he looked as though he was trying to say something, but nothing was coming out. Finally he said, "But Sara, how can you just sweep the whole seven-day creation thing under the rug? Don't people have to believe and understand certain things, including creation, to come to know God?"

"I hear what you're saying, Alex, but I have known people who have genuine relationships with the living God, who walk with God and love God and actually live out the calling he has placed on their lives, who believe in evolution. What is common is that they do believe that God was the origin of life. Seven-day creation and evolution seem to be mutually exclusive, but they may not be with God. And even if one camp or the other is wrong, it doesn't change the ultimate message of the gospel. I'm not going to say it doesn't matter, but I will say it doesn't have to be a stumbling block to following God."

Sara continued, "So in order to be the foundation for understanding the big story of God, is there anything else that a person needs to understand about creation?"

Annie thought for a moment. Sara noted that it looked like she'd lost Alex completely. Annie answered, "I think it would be important to know that what God created was good. It was perfect."

"Exactly right, Annie. So when you're telling the gospel story, the big picture of God's interaction with us, it's really important to tell the part where God looked around and said 'This is very good.' There's one more important aspect of creation, and it's that Adam and Eve were God's special creation. Why were they different from all of the other parts of creation?"

"Because they were made in God's image." Annie replied.

"That's right," said Sara. "People were created to be image-bearers or reflections of God. We bear his image in that we are relational beings. We also have a will to choose how we're going to live our lives and why. That makes us different from other parts of creation. And at the beginning, our relationship with God was perfect. There was nothing to separate us from walking and talking with him."

Sara asked for the second part of the story. Alex explained that man's perfect relationship with God was disrupted when Adam and Eve chose to disobey God's direct instructions. Sara asked, "And what was the heart of the disobedience? Where did that come from?"

Annie answered, "They wanted to be like God. They wanted to know the difference between good and evil."

Sara asked, "So what was the consequence of their disobedience?"

Alex answered, "Well, they were thrown out of the garden and there were relational consequences. Adam and Eve's relationship was screwed up. There was also more work they would have to do and more pain in the world. And their relationship with the earth was changed."

Sara continued, "Okay. Then the third part of the story is the part where God sends Jesus to die on the cross to cover the sin of the people and restore relationship with God. But he didn't stay dead, he rose again and triumphed over death and is working to bring healing to all those broken relationships."

"Finally, those who believe in Jesus and trust that

he is their way to God have been called to be part of bringing healing to the world. We kind of talked about this calling the second time we got together–the calling to love God with all our hearts, souls, minds, and strength. We are also called to love our neighbors and our enemies. We want to see relationships with God and with creation and with ourselves restored."

"So the story starts with a perfect creation broken. And that's a great starting point for entering this discussion because there's no question that the world is not perfect. War, famine, AIDS, abuse, crime–these things show how broken a world we live in. And Jesus came as the hope to restore relationships, and ultimately, to restore creation. And we have something bigger to live for than ourselves or our own happiness–we can live to love God and others and to bring reconciliation and restoration."

"So Sara," Annie said, "do you have like a little tract or anything that we could use? I know that we used to get those at church and stuff. That might help me to remember."

"Well, I'm sure that we could make one up, but I'm not sure that it would really help. This kind of storytelling is interactive. You may not always want to start at the beginning, for example, maybe you have someone who's really passionate about living for something. Like my grad assistant this year. He's hyped up about doing a lot of great things with his life. If I wanted to enter a conversation about the gospel with him, I might start by sharing what I'm living for–the mission that I've been given. And then eventually I'd want to backtrack and tell the rest of the story. But story is flexible, and you want to keep it that way."

"One thing that I think you could do is create some pictures or symbols that help you remember each part of the story. This is another great thing available on that echothestory.com website. They actually have symbols for most of the parts of the story that we mentioned today. If you could draw those on a napkin while you're talking to someone, that might help visualize the progression of the story. But you could make up your own symbols too."

Alex had been quiet for quite a long time. At this point, he got up and said, "Hey, I've got to run. I'll see you guys soon." With that, he got up and left. He barely glanced at Annie or Sara–he just picked up his coat and left.

Sara was about to get up and head out the door after him, but Annie said, "What do you think is going on with him, Sara?" She looked lost and confused and uncertain, so Sara stayed.

"Well, the things we've been talking about for the past couple of weeks have really shaken his belief system. He's struggling to accommodate all the uncertainties that come with postmodernism. It's been my experience that uncertainty is accepted as a matter of course among postmoderns, and they are fairly comfortable walking in that. But making the shift from holding tightly to a set of certain propositions to walking in uncertainties whose only foundation is a relationship with God is tough. And not everyone can make the jump."

Sara paused for a minute, wondering whether to share part of her story. She thought it may help and comfort Annie, so she went ahead. "I was very much like Alex at one time. I had very strict lines that I drew that I thought separated truth from untruth. But when I went overseas, that really shifted for me. I was confronted with whole new belief systems, whole new cultural systems, and whole new ideas. They really forced me to challenge those lines. It was a really painful process, Annie. On this side of it, I feel like I'm much better able to love people. I know the things that I think are important to hold onto, and the rest of the things I'm willing to hold loosely. It was a huge struggle though."

"What will happen to Alex, do you think?"

"I don't know, Annie. God can certainly use him, and he clearly has a heart to reach out to people. But I think he's going to find it increasingly difficult to do that within the postmodern culture unless he is able to reevaluate the things in his world that are cultural versus those things that are truly biblical. To some extent, in today's world, to effectively communicate the story of God, you've either got to be postmodern yourself or have the ability to be bicultural. I don't know if Alex's going to get there."

Annie sighed. "That's what I'm afraid of. Sara, I'm horrified about what he said to Drew. I'm horrified that all Drew knows of God is judgmentalism. I'm horrified that he doesn't know the love of God. I want to tell him. But I have no relationship with him, so I realize it wouldn't really accomplish anything."

She shook her head and sighed again. "I don't know if we're going to make it, Sara. This has opened up such huge things in my life–if Alex had never brought me here, I might never have really surrendered my life to Christ. But now the chasm between me and Alex seems even wider than it was before."

Sara sat with Annie for a few more minutes, and then they prayed. They prayed for Alex and Drew and Oliver and Patti and Josie. They prayed for Annie.

Shifting Ground

As Alex had sat in Sara's living room that evening, his mind had been whirling. At an emotional level, he felt like everything he'd been setting his faith on had been pulled out from under him. And he was resisting it. He wanted to hold on to those pillars of belief. He did believe in a literal seven-day creation. He believed an actual Adam and an actual Eve had been tempted in the garden. He believed an actual serpent had spoken to them. And he thought it was important for other people to believe that too.

Alex considered his own faith journey. He remembered in church, growing up, he was taught the "Romans Road" to salvation. "All have sinned and fall short of the glory of God." Romans 3:23. "For the wages of sin is death, but the gift of God is eternal life in Christ Jesus our Lord." Romans 6:23. "That if you confess with your mouth that Jesus is Lord, and believe in your heart that God raised him from the dead, you will be saved."[5] He couldn't remember the reference for that one. But it was so familiar. Walking from one belief to the next. First, you have to know that you're a sinner. Then you have to know the penalty for sin. Then you have to know how to trust Jesus. What could be more simple than that? How could

---

[5]Romans 10:9

that have changed?

It couldn't have. If that was the way to salvation at one time, it must be the way to salvation for all time.

Yet he thought back to what the pronouncements of sin and judgment had wrought in other people's lives. He couldn't think of one time that he had challenged someone personally where this information led to a transformed life. Not one. And, in fact, his message seemed to alienate him from others.

But wasn't that predictable? Isn't it true that the cross of Christ is foolishness and offensive to people? Didn't his pastor always tell him that he would be scorned and persecuted for his faith?

Finally, when he couldn't take it anymore, he had gotten up and left. He knew it was abrupt, but he couldn't bear to have Sara try to tell him why he was wrong or confront his belief system any more tonight. He felt like it was something he really needed to decide on his own. So he left. On the way home, he avoided a call from Annie and didn't call her back.

He struggled to sleep that night. He prayed and thought, and eventually, he pulled down his Bible from the shelf. When was the last time he'd read it? He'd been so caught up the last few months with this mission. So he went back to the 2 Corinthians passage.

The message and the ministry of reconciliation. What was that message? It certainly didn't stop at judgment. Reconciliation is a restored relationship, a right relationship. So was he missing the point?

But how do you restore a relationship that you don't know is broken? Don't you have to know how you've hurt someone to make it right? Alex prayed, and then he slept.

The next day, Alex was surprised to see Annie show up at Second Story. He shouldn't be, he supposed. Usually he would have called her back. She must be really worried about him. When he saw her come in, he told Omar he'd be taking a break from the counter. He came to meet her and they found a secluded table in a small alcove of the café area.

Alex gave her a quick hug and kissed her cheek, and then they sat down. Annie spent some time arranging her coat and purse on the back of her chair. Her face looked a little guarded. Alex just waited, taking in the way her soft brown curls bobbed slightly as she moved.

Finally, Annie looked up and spoke. "Alex. I'm really concerned. What's going on?"

He just shook his head. He couldn't answer. He didn't have any answers.

Annie continued softly. "You just left last night and didn't call me back. I was really worried about you."

"I'm sorry, Annie. I wasn't trying to ignore you. I'm just not sure what to think of all this stuff Sara has been saying. I needed some time to think. I've got all these voices in my head, and I don't know which of them is right."

Annie grabbed his hand. "What can I do?" she asked.

Alex shook his head again. "I don't know, Annie. I think I need some time to make my way through. I'm just not sure that I can accept these things. I can't deal with the lack of certainty. How can it not matter whether God created the world or whether there was evolution?"

Annie squeezed his hand. "That's not exactly what Sara said, Alex. She didn't say it doesn't matter, just that we can't be sure what exactly it all looked like."

"But don't you see, Annie. That means the same thing to me. If I can't be sure of what's in the Bible, if I can't know that everything in there is literally true, then how do I know that there's truth there at all?"

"Oh, Alex. I don't know." She looked down at their hands.

"It's okay, Annie. It's just something I have to work through, okay? I have to figure it out."

They sat quietly for a few minutes, Annie unusually still. Finally, Alex stood up and explained he had to get back to work. "Thanks for dropping by, Annie girl." He gave her another hug and then went back to work.

Annie sat for a few minutes, watching him. He

returned to the counter and then greeted the next customer with his usual warmth and humor. Even from the alcove, Annie could see his eyes dancing and sparkling. Oh, how she missed the times when the dance and sparkle was all she ever saw. But there was a heaviness now to each of them and their relationship to one another. She wasn't sure that they would recover.

On Sunday, Annie returned from church for a quiet afternoon at home before she had to go in for a night shift at the hospital. She usually worked days, but she picked up some overtime this week, so she was taking a night. She had just sat down to put her feet up for a second when she heard someone knocking at her door.

She opened the door to see Josie standing outside. "Hey Jo. What's up?" she asked.

"Can I come in?" Josie replied.

"Of course," said Annie. "Can I get you something to drink?"

Josie waved away the offer and went to sit on the couch. But she didn't flop down, as she normally did. She just sat on the edge of the couch, not at all at ease.

"What's going on, Josie?" Annie asked, worried now.

Awkwardly, Josie blurted out, "I need you to tell me more about how God didn't want my mom to get beat up."

Oh dear, oh dear, oh dear. What did Josie need to

hear right now? Annie tried to remember back to what she'd said to Patti and lots of stories flowed through her mind. Would one of those work? Abraham and Hagar? Probably not, because God sent Hagar back to a horrible situation, saying he'd protect her. Um . . . .

"Oh, honey. Abuse is horrible, horrible stuff. I don't know what your dad might have said to try to justify his actions. But whatever it was, it was wrong." Oh, that's right. She'd talked about the wheat and the weeds.

Annie sat down in the recliner, facing the couch. "Look, honey, abuse is part of the brokenness of our world. It's wrong. It hurts people. It creates pain. But God didn't intend the world to be that way. Have you heard about the story of creation?"

Josie nodded, so Annie continued, "So you know that God created the world, and when he did, he looked around at everything he'd made, and he said it was really, really good. And his people, Adam and Eve, well, they were specially created in his image. And they had a really special relationship with God, where he would come and talk with them every day. There was no abuse; there was no hatred; there was no evil. Everything was good."

"But then something happened. Adam and Eve were tempted to make themselves like God. They didn't want to follow his instructions anymore; they wanted to know what he knew. So they disobeyed God. And this caused great harm. Their relationship would never be the same."

"But there's hope, Josie. There's hope. It's God's desire to restore everything that was broken. God loves people, and he wants to help fix what is broken in our own lives, in our own relationships, and in our relationship with him and with the earth. So he sent Jesus to come and show us who God actually is. But the people here didn't really recognize him, so they killed him. And God allowed Jesus's death to pay the penalty for all that sin–to cover all that wrongdoing and to redeem it. That doesn't mean that your dad's abuse was okay. But it does mean that God wants to bring healing to your life and your mom's life. He wants you to know that you are deeply loved."

"But how?" Josie asked. "My dad is gone. My mom isn't really talking. She just sits there. What am I going to do?" Josie buried her face in her hands and cried. Annie crossed over to the couch and sat down with her, putting her arm around her. She prayed out loud, "God, Josie is hurting so deeply right now. And so is Patti. But I pray that you would walk with them through this horrible, horrible time. I pray that your Spirit would be present with them, comforting them. And I pray especially for Josie, that she would come to know how deeply you love her."

"Josie," Annie said, "I know this is so hard. And I'm afraid that God doesn't promise to change the circumstances of your life. But he promises to walk through them with us. If you ask him to, he will walk with you. You can talk to him like you would to a friend, and you can ask him to comfort you. He will hear you."

She looked at Josie. Her face was still buried in her hands, but her sobs had stilled and she seemed to be listening.

"I had a really hard time in my life, about six months ago, when Alex was in a really bad accident. We didn't know if he would survive. He had to have emergency surgery, and we didn't know if he'd make it through. And then, even when he did, he had to spend several weeks in the hospital. I couldn't pray to God to change the situation–to make the accident not happen. It already had. But I could pray for God to be with Alex, to bring him healing, and to walk with me."

"And he did, Josie. He really did. He met me in that really, really hard time, and he helped me."

Josie sniffled. "But how did he help you?"

"I sensed his presence. And I prayed to him to help me love Alex and keep putting one foot in front of the other. And I felt his comfort, and I was able to keep going, even though it was hard."

"Okay." Josie whispered. A few minutes later, Josie went home. Annie wondered if she'd said enough or said the right things.

Monday, Alex and Annie met for dinner at the diner near Sara's. The red vinyl seats and the checkerboard floors made them feel right at home. Annie decided to skip dinner and just have dessert. Alex had a Belgian waffle with strawberries and whipped cream.

As they ate, they caught up on the week. Alex mentioned that he and Omar had some time to chat about the story of Jesus. Omar showed a great deal of curiosity about Jesus. But Alex couldn't figure out what his actual beliefs were or what his motivations were for all these questions. Annie talked about Patti and Josie. Josie had come back for another chat at Annie's earlier in the day, and Annie was about ready to start teaching her the story of God.

"I really feel like she needs to know the whole story, you know? Like Sara was talking about. I don't think she knows enough about who God is to really trust him or to put her trust in Jesus. But she's open to hearing about spiritual things, and she really wants to believe that God is good, I think. She is looking for something to hold onto. I was thinking about looking into that storying stuff that Sara mentioned. It seems like she knows just bits and pieces of the story. What do you think about that?"

Alex shrugged and said, "Sure. That's a great idea." Annie noted his complete lack of enthusiasm and asked, "So how are you doing with things?"

"I don't know, Annie. This is all so foreign. I love telling stories." He grinned, "You know I like to be the center of attention. But I don't know. Stories are so hard to contain. They're hard to define. What if you tell it wrong? What if you emphasize something that's not meant to be emphasized?"

"But isn't that the point, Alex? Stories illustrate truth in a really powerful way. They give me something to hold onto. I can actually imagine what something means if I see it in story. I just bought this Bible story book, like Sara recommended. Alex, it's incredible the way that God, the living God, jumps off the page to me. I think that for so long, describing God and talking about him in the abstract almost gave me permission to contain him. I mean, I could have these rules and lines around who God is and what he did so that I could try to predict what he would do in the future. But I'm not sure that's right, Alex. C. S. Lewis said that Aslan was not a 'tame' lion, and I think that might be true of God too. I don't think we can contain him."

Alex thought about that as he polished off his waffle. "But how do I know that I'm right? If I'm relying on the story of God to convey the truth of God, how do I know that I have the right ideas or that my imagination is correct?"

"Don't we have to rely on the Spirit, Alex? I mean, even in biblical interpretation and systematic theology and all that other stuff, at the end of the day, aren't people relying on God to teach them and show them what was meant? And it goes back to this idea of how the Bible was written. It's the story of God and Abraham and Isaac and

Jacob and Jesus. It's not a textbook. It's written as literature. It's written as narrative."

"I guess so, Annie. But that's not how we've studied it in church my whole life."

"I know, Alex. But seeing it as a story–as the great story–is opening up so much life to me. It's amazing." Annie was impassioned. Her eyes were bright, and she was waving her hands around as she continued. "I really want to see it do that for you too, Alex. And I really want to be touched and transformed by the story and by the God behind the story. I don't want to just know about God, I want to know God."

Annie finished her shake, and Alex drank the last of his orange juice. He was quiet, and Annie just watched him. She had so much more to say, but she didn't want to push him. He had to move this direction of his own accord, or it would just be her belief system rather than a mutual one.

Tuesday morning Annie and Oliver met for tennis. She must have been distracted because she kept missing easy shots. Oliver started working really hard to give her shots she could return instead of trying to kill her like he normally did. But Annie barely noticed. As they packed up their gear, Oliver invited Annie to stop somewhere for breakfast.

So they went to a breakfast place near the highway.

As they sat and ate, Oliver asked Annie if anything was wrong.

Annie replied, "No, why?"

Oliver said, "Well, there was a bit of an issue at tennis this morning."

"Really? What was it?"

"You didn't notice?" When Annie shook her head, Oliver said, "Um, I was playing on your team for the second half of the morning. You still couldn't hit anything."

"Oh. No, I guess I didn't notice. I'm a little distracted. Alex and I are still having a hard time with some things."

"Do you want to talk about it? I did just break up with Heather, so I'm sort of an expert in these things."

Annie hesitated. What should she do? She really hated sharing deeply with people she didn't know very well. It was hard to be vulnerable like that. But he seemed really concerned. She wasn't sure that he would really understand, but she decided to go ahead. Maybe Oliver could give her some good advice.

"Well, you know we've been struggling since his accident, right? He sort of changed after that. He used to be super fun-loving and nothing stopped him. But then he became super-spiritual. Everything was spiritual. Everything was about God and the Bible and what we should be saying or doing. So it was really hard."

Oliver nodded sympathetically. "My mom's sort of like that. It can be really intense."

"Yeah, it was. So then we started meeting with this really nice lady. She started challenging us with some spiritual ideas and even about how to talk about spiritual things with other people. And, I don't know how to describe what happened, but it was pretty transforming for me. I was a Christian before, but now I really take it seriously. So I try to think about God and pray about things before I do them. I'm trying to learn to walk with God."

"So you're on the same page now then?"

"That's the really weird thing. I guess the best way I can describe it is those friends that you met at the party. They were so intent on the message, they didn't get to know you, you know? They spent all this time talking to you and sharing with you, but they never heard anything that you had to say. They never got to know what a great person you are, or how funny you are, or how smart. I feel like that devalued you as a human being. I'm afraid that Alex makes people feel that way too when he talks to them about spiritual things."

"Hmm . . . ." Oliver said. "Yeah, that would be a problem."

"It is. It really is to me. People are really important to me, Oliver. Relationships are important. It's important to me that the people I bring into my life feel loved and valued and appreciated for who they are. I don't know if I can always be around someone who doesn't have that value. No–that's not right. It's not that Alex doesn't value people. He really, really loves them. But he unintentionally makes them feel like crap."

"So I don't know. I'm worried that we're going to split up. And he's really struggling with all these ideas we've been talking about. I don't know where he's going to end up."

"Wow, Annie. That's really hard." Oliver paused, "I'm actually kind of impressed though. It sounds like you guys are really working hard on your relationship. You're trying to be respectful and loving in spite of your differences."

"Yeah, we do. We don't want to hurt each other."

"Man, that's really different than how things went down with Heather. She was really, really cold. She ruined my relationships with about half of the people I know–they won't even talk to me anymore. So I think it's really cool that you guys are working through it."

"I know. I know. Alex really is such a great guy."

The Works of God

Wednesday arrived, and it was unseasonably warm for the first week in February. Annie and Alex arrived at Sara's in just sweaters and gloves. Alex was dreading their discussion. The last few weeks, their discussions had led to complete chaos in his own life. If he didn't start getting some threads to hang on to, it seemed like his whole system of belief could unravel. So he was nervous about it. The turmoil was difficult to endure.

When they arrived, they made semi-awkward small talk until Alex finally said, "Hey Sara, I wanted to apologize for leaving so abruptly last week. I don't know what I was thinking. I just had to get out of here and get some mental space to think. But it was rude."

Sara responded graciously, and added, "Let me know if you want to talk about anything, Alex, okay? I wasn't sure whether I should call you this week or stop by the bookstore, but I wanted to give you some space. Just know I'm here if you need me."

Alex nodded.

So Sara got them started. They spent a little time reviewing the ideas they'd talked about the last few weeks. Then Sara said, "So we talked a couple of weeks ago about emotional barriers that people have to faith. We mentioned the idea of hypocrisy as one of the barriers. Have you seen any examples of this in your own lives?"

267

Annie immediately answered, "Yeah, I definitely have. Patti's husband claimed to be a Christian and misused biblical passages about submission to justify his abusive behavior."

"Okay," Sara nodded. "That's an extreme example. Do you have any that are more common?"

This time Alex answered, "I had this friend, he was a neighbor while I was in school, and he would always talk about how his pastor would say that they should tithe and give money to the church, but then he lived in this really expensive neighborhood and had a pool and stuff."

Annie added, "I do remember talking to Josie a couple of weeks ago–even before the Jake thing–and she was also saying how the church seemed like just a front to ask people for money."

Sara nodded. "Good. I have one too. I was talking with my neighbor Clyde the other day–the one who's always calling the city on me for my yard work–and he was going off about how the Christians he's known have been some of the most conniving, backstabbing people he's met. He was really frustrated. He could quote all these Bible verses and said he challenged them about how they were living. Well, you can imagine how that went down. They never talked to him again. He felt like all they wanted to do was preach to him, but they weren't willing to hear what he had to say."

"How about examples of the opposite? Do you

guys know any Christians whose activities actually make people think or feel good things about God or the church?"

"Hey, I have an example of that," said Alex. "I saw this interview on TV not too long ago. It's one of those regular evening shows, and the anchor was interviewing this famous woman about her efforts to relieve the AIDS epidemic in Africa. The woman told the story of how she met God when she was in Africa serving on a mission trip. She told how that meeting had changed her heart and her soul and gave her the passion and commitment to see the AIDS problem eradicated. And I've never seen a media person speechless in the way this reporter was. Instead of ridiculing the woman for her faith, the way the reporter clearly wanted to, she sat and listened as the woman poured out her experience with the gospel message and how it had changed her life. And the reporter couldn't be sarcastic. She couldn't ridicule. Because the woman was doing something."

"Wow," said Annie. "That's amazing. Especially considering how those sitcoms we watched portrayed Christians as naive idiots."

Sara nodded and said, "Jesus was so serious about this that when he talked about how he would identify those who knew him from those who didn't at the end of the age, he told his disciples that he would look at who fed the hungry, gave water to the thirsty, and visited those in prison."

"Prison. Can you imagine that?"

They all sat for a moment. Alex tried to picture himself visiting a prison, but he couldn't. What would he say to the prisoners? He imagined himself walking the catwalk and seeing all those arms hanging out of the bars, hearing the whistles and cat calls.

Sara went on, "The book of James in the Bible talks about this–it talks about how faith without works is dead. Do you remember what kinds of things James mentioned?"

"Wasn't it like helping the poor or something?"

"Sure, Annie, giving to those in need." Sara answered. "And there are other works we are called to do as well. We are called to love our enemies, to pray for those who persecute us, to care for the earth, to seek justice for the oppressed, to care for the widow and the orphan–basically, the lowliest people in our society."

Sara continued, "So what 'works of God' are we doing in our lives right now? Are we living in a way that shows the truth of the gospel?"

They all thought for a few seconds. Annie replied, "Well, I volunteer as a relief hospice worker once a month. Do you think that counts?"

"Sure. Sitting with the dying is a very difficult thing to do, especially when you don't have to. How about you, Alex? Are there things that you are doing that show what kind of God you serve?"

"Sometimes I volunteer building habitat houses. I

guess that would count." He shrugged, "I also volunteer at church, but I'm not sure if that's what you mean."

Sara responded, "I'm thinking more about what's going on in our communities. Who are the neglected populations? Over the history of the church, many amazing ministries have been established outside the walls of the church. Hospitals, charities, all kinds of things. These are often started by Christians who do it because they believe that God would want them to–because these things flow out of the heart and compassion of God."

Alex couldn't remember doing anything like this recently. He thought about his time in the hospital and how difficult that time had been for him. Maybe he could find a way to walk beside some other people who had been in traumatic accidents.

Sara said, "There's another reason I'm bringing this up though. Not only does this help show the truth in the story of God, but it also gives us an opportunity to invite others to join us and to build relationships around this service."

"Let me give you an example. I've been volunteering teaching reading to immigrant students at a local school for years. I remember moving to a new country, so I know how important learning language is. And I know how many ways our immigrants here get taken advantage of when they can't speak the language. So that's something that I'm really committed to. Well, I was talking with my grad assistant, Daniel, one day about how he's off to join the Peace Corps this summer. And we were talking about justice issues. So I was able to invite him to come with me. We were able to speak about why I'm doing what I'm doing and why I'm so committed. So I got to talk about my spirituality in a really natural way without having to force the conversation. I just got to share from my heart what's important to me."

"Another great example is of this dentist I know. He retired early from a really lucrative practice and is giving his time to help manage the dental practice in a community dental clinic. He could be making tons of money, but he's practically giving away his time. He spends lots of his time recruiting other people to give away their time too. He's had some great opportunities to share why he does what he does with both dentists and patients."

Annie asked, "Do you have other ideas of what we can do?"

"Well, I think you should do the works of God that draw you–the ones that flow from who you are and what you value. As you are continually remade in the image of God, those values and desires might lead you to some interesting places. But it's important to live authentically and to do the works of God out of who you are and out of your relationship to God. You don't want it to become a rule you have to follow. So hospice is great for you, Annie, because you're compassionate. And it really fits with your nursing skills." Sara paused.

"Another thing you might do is volunteer to run a sports camp during the summer in a low-income neighborhood. You guys are active and love sports. Just think about what you love and get to know the heart of God. You will find ways to walk with God into those places where his works are needed."

They threw out a couple more ideas, and then Sara wrapped it up. She challenged them to work this week on inviting someone to go along with them to a place where they were serving and doing the works of God already.

Invitations and Conversations

That weekend, Annie and Oliver were supposed to play tennis again at his health club. When she saw him in the hallway at work on Friday, she asked if she could bring Josie along.

"Who's Josie?" asked Oliver.

"She's this neighbor girl I've been helping out. Her mom and dad are going through a rough patch right now, and she's having a really hard time. I was trying to think of something I could do for her to give her a healthy way to work through some of her emotions. Exercise always works for me."

Annie smiled sweetly, "Anyway, you're a much better player than me. I was hoping you'd be willing to help me teach her."

Oliver was silent for a moment. "Okay," he finally said. "It's fine this time. But let's not make a habit of it. I like to cream you at tennis at least once a month." He grinned. "It's good for my ego."

Annie walked away thinking about Josie. She had no way of knowing how her stories or her words had affected Josie the other night in the apartment. But Josie was still hanging around, and she had lost some of her hostility toward any mention of religious things. She seemed now to be looking for help in whatever way she could find it. The poor girl was totally overwhelmed.

Annie's thoughts wandered to Patti. Patti had seemed a little more functional when Annie had dropped off dinner the night before. Her apartment was looking immaculate. Patti still wasn't talking about anything of consequence to Annie though. She had been polite, even thankful, when Annie had dropped off the meal, but she hadn't really wanted to talk. Annie would keep serving her though. It didn't seem like Patti had anyone else supporting her just now.

After work, Annie dropped by the Conrads' apartment. When Josie answered the door, Annie invited her over to bake some cookies later that evening.

"Why would I want to make cookies?" Josie asked. Annie wondered if she'd ever cooked before. She remembered all the fast food containers that had been in the apartment when Patti was in the hospital.

Annie smiled. "Well, there's this lady from my church who has five kids, and she just had surgery, and she's kind of laid up right now. So I thought maybe the kids would want some cookies around, you know, until she gets better."

Josie shook her head, "Do you always help everyone out?" She waited for an answer. Annie wasn't sure if this would cheapen what she'd done for Josie and Patti, or if it would help Josie to see how much she cared about other people.

Annie answered, "Well, I don't know. I try to look

out for how people need encouragement around me."

Josie shook her head again. "Whatever."

Not to be deterred, Annie said, "So you'll come."

Josie gave a dramatic sigh but then agreed. "What time?"

"How about right after dinner? Then you can go with me to drop them off."

"Sounds like a blast," Josie muttered as she closed the door. Annie just smiled.

Cookie delivery to the Bixly family went down without a hitch. Annie and Josie brought over a couple dozen oatmeal raisin and chocolate chip cookies. Jillian, the youngest, opened the door to a modest ranch style house. She was about five years old. As Annie explained why they'd come and Josie displayed their wares, Jillian's blue eyes widened and she opened the door. When they were inside, she raced into the kitchen, beckoning them to follow.

Annie and Josie made their way through a narrow hallway to a small kitchen, where the other four kids sat around a table. The older three were doing homework, and the youngest were meant to be reading from library books. Annie pointed to the counter, and Josie set down the cookies there. Annie then went over to the table and chatted with the kids about their homework and how their mom was doing.

Five minutes later, they were back in the car. All was silent for a few minutes, and then Josie asked, "So, you really do this often?"

Annie shrugged. "Sure. As much as I can."

After a minute of silence, Josie asked, "But why?"

Annie looked over through the dark at Josie and drove and considered how to answer the question. "Well, Josie, maybe I can explain it like this. When Alex was hurt and in the hospital, that was a really hard time for me. I was questioning everything, including God's care for me. Did he even care that my boyfriend nearly died? Was Alex going to get better? In really hard times, it's hard to feel that God is there. We know he is because he tells us. But we can feel it when his people reach out to us in love and care. Does that make sense?"

Josie said "a little" but sounded like she meant "no, not at all."

"Josie, God loves us into a mission and a purpose to love and reach out to the people around us. He loves us so much that he pursues us and Jesus came to earth to live and die for us. But he doesn't love us just for our own comfort. He loves us, and he calls us to walk with him. Part of that is walking with other people when they need something."

As they pulled up to the apartment, Annie invited Josie to play tennis the next day with her and Oliver. Josie protested halfheartedly that she didn't know how to play, but Annie begged her to come. In the end, Josie agreed.

278

Josie entered the apartment thinking about the evening. When they'd entered the Bixly house and Annie started talking to those kids, their eyes had lit up. They were so happy to see her. What would it be like to be able to have people actually be happy when you entered a room?

And there was a strange sort of comfort for Josie when she was hanging out with Annie. It wasn't that Annie had all the answers or even sounded certain about things all the time. But Annie had a sort of LIFE; she had a sort of purpose that moved her forward into things. Josie was trying so hard to sort everything out. Annie had this sort of confidence that even when things were awful, they would work out. Josie wanted to be around that.

Annie, Josie, and Oliver gathered the next morning to play tennis at Oliver's club. Oliver wasn't sure how this would go. For one thing, Josie was wearing totally unsuitable clothes–loose jeans and an oversized t-shirt. But she seemed ready to try anything, so Annie patiently instructed her about the rules and the strategy of the game. After a couple of minutes, he and Annie demonstrated different types of swings. Finally, they got Josie on the court, and he started to lob balls over to Annie and Josie. They played this way for about half an hour, and then they started a game.

Josie really got into it. She was as competitive as

Annie, and she was picking up the pattern of tennis pretty quickly. Oliver beat them, of course, but Josie had a couple of really good plays.

When they finished, Oliver watched as Annie showed Josie how to take care of the tennis equipment. Oliver couldn't see why Annie would want to spend time with Josie. She was just a kid, and one who didn't really have anything to offer, at that. She didn't seem extremely interesting or really all that different from any other teenager he'd see anywhere.

But, what did he know? These days he really only spent time with people when he felt like drinking. Otherwise he preferred to stay at home. Heather had done that to him. He just couldn't get himself to care about getting to know anyone new. It was too hard, too much trouble, and for what? So that eventually life would move on and they would move on? No thanks.

It was a wonder that he had friends at all. But he'd been working at the same place for a couple of years, and some of his friends had stuck with him through the Heather thing. Almost all of his non-work friends had been his-and-Heather's friends, and spending time with them now was just awkward. Most of them still saw Heather regularly.

Anyway. He looked back over at Annie and Josie and saw that they were packed up. They headed through the club and out to the parking lot. As they parted ways,

Oliver shook Josie's hand seriously, "You have some talent, there, Josie. You'll have to come back again." Now why had he said that?

Josie smiled a real smile. "Thanks," she said quietly. She and Annie got in the car, and Oliver was glad he'd complimented her.

Annie and Alex were together that night for dinner. Alex was cooking a rare meal at his house. Annie sat at the table in his kitchen while he finished up dinner.

The kitchen was a bit of a wreck. The guys struggled to get the dishes in the dishwasher on a normal day. But when Alex was cooking, all bets were off. He had piles of pots and pans and measuring cups surrounding him on the counter. Annie had set the table, and now she was just sitting, watching him complete his preparation.

Annie smiled to herself as she watched him. He was so intent on his task that he couldn't hold to a conversation. But he was humming quietly to himself.

Annie considered where they had come from and where they were going. They started out as two fun-loving friends. They'd enjoyed hanging out during college and causing a ruckus. She remembered back to the time they'd convinced everyone to bring in little travel alarm clocks to their biology class. Everyone got to class a little early and they set the alarms to go off in five-minute increments. By the end of the class, even the professor was laughing. That was one of their first practical jokes together.

Her mind flitted next to graduation, where they seemed to have so much promise for their future together. Alex was going to get a good job, she was going to work as a nurse for a couple of years, and then they were going to get married and start a family. The way had seemed so clear.

But it all had changed. Completely. Suddenly. And even when she'd gotten Alex back, she hadn't really. It was months before she understood what had changed. And now, now she understood.

But.

But he seemed to care more about the idea of sharing his faith than about the people he was sharing with. No, that wasn't quite right. She was sure that he cared about the people. But she thought back to his descriptions of his awful conversations with Drew. What had he accomplished other than making Drew less and less able to see the God who loved him so much? The whole process made her feel so uncomfortable. The need to express God's judgment and wrath in every conversation was something that she couldn't connect with. And, in fact, she had seen it damaging Alex's relationships.

Annie was called back to time and space as Alex set the main dish on the table with a flourish. "Chicken Parmesan," he said proudly. "What do you think?"

"Oh, Alex, it looks awesome," Annie said. They

settled in to eat and talk, but Annie seemed far away. Alex tried to draw her in with his stories of mischief at the bookstore. But Annie would not be drawn in. She couldn't shake the melancholy that had swept over her as Alex prepared dinner.

At church the next day, Alex saw old Mrs. Pruitt standing in the foyer looking forlorn after the service. When he asked her what was up, she told him her kitchen sink was leaking and she didn't know what to do about it. Her husband, Jerry, had died just a few months back, and the details of life seemed to be overwhelming her. Alex offered to come over that afternoon to take a look. But what he could do, he had no idea. He wasn't such a great plumber.

On the way to Mrs. Pruitt's house that afternoon, he had the brilliant idea of calling Omar to come over. Alex thought that he was some sort of engineer student–maybe even mechanical engineering. So he should know more than Alex, anyway. Omar agreed to come, so Alex waited out front of Mrs. Pruitt's door until Omar arrived.

They were greeted at the door by a very relieved Mrs. Pruitt. She showed them through the foyer to the kitchen in the back. The foyer had goldenrod wallpaper that looked to be from the 1970s. The kitchen was decorated during the same period, and it had a lovely, old cookstove that might have been an antique. Mrs. Pruitt offered them some tea or coffee and her fresh-baked muffins. The men declined drinks, but couldn't resist the smell of banana-nut-spice wafting around the kitchen. They devoured their muffins and then got to work.

"So what seems to be the problem, Mrs. P?" asked Alex.

She turned on the water to show them. The water was dripping out of the faucet connection. Alex looked at Omar. Omar turned it on and shut it off again. He looked below the sink and didn't see any water there. "Does it ever drip below, Mrs. Pruitt?" he asked.

"It never has, that I know of."

Omar nodded. "I think it is a bad washer. We can fix it, but we will need to buy a new one. We will come right back."

They ran to a nearby hardware store, and when they returned, it only took them about half an hour to get it fixed. Mrs. Pruitt was so thankful she was in tears.

Alex thanked Omar profusely on the way out the door.

"It is no problem, Alex. It was a simple issue, easily solved. Does she have no family?"

"Her husband died a few months ago," Alex explained. "She's been having a rough time, I think. It was really, really kind of you to come and help her."

Omar brushed this off, but he looked pleased. He asked, "But what about sons? Does she have no children to

284

take care of her?"

Alex thought for a second. "I think she has two daughters–one lives out west and one in New York City. I don't think they get home to help her out very much."

Omar shook his head, so Alex continued. "But that's what so great about being part of my church. We take care of each other. Like family. So even though her kids aren't here and her husband died, she still has family. We're her family–we call it the 'body of Christ.'" Alex went on to describe how his church had reached out to him and Annie when he'd been in the hospital.

Omar just shook his head again. "So you're saying that because you're part of this faith community, you treat each other like family?" When Alex nodded, Omar continued. "What about people outside the church? Do you treat them the same way? Like if I had a problem, would you get people from your church to come and help me?"

"Well, maybe. If you wanted us to. I don't know. I never have before. Do you need something?"

"No, no. I was just trying to understand. I don't think in my country we have quite the same associations with people who attend the same mosque."

Alex wasn't sure how to reply. And then the moment passed, and Omar took off. Alex pondered whether there was something else he could have said. Did he miss an opportunity to share something of value?

Loving for the Long Haul

The next day, Alex arrived for work to find Drew in an awful mood. Alex no sooner had entered the office when Drew got up and stalked out. In fact, when Alex walked by him in the history section during one of Alex's breaks, Drew wouldn't even look at him. He just had this huge scowl hanging like a thundercloud around his face. Alex didn't even try to say a thing. He just started praying–that he might have an opportunity to speak with Drew, that he might say the right thing.

Throughout the day, Alex tried to muster up the courage to approach Drew and ask him what was wrong. But he kept thinking back to the last time they'd talked and how that had turned out. Drew had yelled at him. Maybe it was better if Alex just left his nose out of things. But he felt like he should do something. He was really the only Christian he knew of in Drew's life, besides Drew's parents. And obviously that wasn't going so hot. But he just couldn't think of what to say.

Finally, when Alex went upstairs to get his coat and things from the office upstairs before leaving, Drew was there. Alex crept into the office, so as not to disturb Drew. But on his way out, he paused. What came out of his mouth was an invitation to come over for dinner on Friday night–with him and Annie. "And you can bring your boyfriend too, if you want to." Alex held his breath.

Slowly, Drew turned around and looked at Alex. He sort of sneered and said, "What's the catch? Is there some video preacher you want me to listen to while I'm there?" He turned back to his desk.

Alex froze in the doorway, his mind racing. Is that what Drew thought of him? His mind flew back through all the recent conversations he'd had with Drew. He tried desperately to find something there that wasn't preaching. But he couldn't. After about a minute, Drew turned his head slightly, "Are you still there?" he asked, and turned back to his work.

Alex dove in. "I'd really like for you to come. And not to listen to any video preachers or anything. I thought it might be fun to spend some time together outside of work. Think about it," he said. And before Drew could respond, he turned and left.

The next afternoon, Sara stopped by Second Story during Alex's lunch break. He had to work Wednesday night, so they weren't going to be able to meet together with Annie this week. Sara wanted to check in with both Alex and Annie though, and she thought one-on-ones would be just as good a way to do that.

When she got to the bookstore, she got a bite to eat and then made her way to the now-familiar table in the corner. Alex said he'd be right over. So Sara sat down and started to pray. She'd been pondering some tough things that Alex probably needed to hear, and she was praying about whether to share those now or at another time. She didn't wish to discourage him from reaching out to people around him, but she was just as concerned as Annie was about how damaging some of Alex's comments could be. So she nibbled on her sandwich and just prayed that God would guide her.

After a minute or two, Alex plunked his food on the table and sat down with a dramatic sigh.

"Tough day?" Sara asked.

"Are you kidding? Tough month." He settled in and then asked, "How about you? How are you doing, Sara?"

Sara smiled. "I'm doing just fine, honey. Really. Thanks for asking. So how did it go this week? Were you able to invite anyone in to the works of God with you?"

"Well, I did invite Omar to help me with this lady's sink from church. It seemed to go okay. Except I wasn't really sure what to say about it."

"What do you mean?"

"Well, Omar seemed to be trying to figure things out. But he was mostly concerned about the lady's kids and why they weren't helping her. So I talked to him about how the church is like a family. But I don't know if it really made sense to him, you know? And I wasn't sure–was I supposed to say more? Less? I have no idea what I'm doing, Sara."

Sara smiled. "Can I let you in on a little secret? No one really does." She continued, "Don't you find that's true in any relationship though? When you're trying to share your heart with someone, the reasons why you're doing or saying what you are–well, it's a process. You have to get to know the other person so that you can learn to communicate in ways he understands. But speaking from your experience, like you did, is one of the most powerful ways to share with someone."

They were silent for a few moments, as they ate and thought about this. Then Alex said, "I've always felt like belief is a giant puzzle, and that there are all these pieces, and maybe in some situations, just one missing piece. I feel a lot of responsibility for making sure that final piece is explained right. And I'm anxious about getting it wrong."

Sara thought for a moment. "Alex, tell me. When Jesus was on earth, how did he interact with people?"

"What do you mean, Sara?"

"Well, when people came to him with questions or needs, what did he do?"

"He answered them. Didn't he?"

"Why don't you spend some time with that question this week? See if you can see how Jesus interacted with people."

"Do you mean the stories, Sara? Like parables?"

"Well, that's one thing. But I know you like to know that things are biblical. So why don't you take some time and look at Jesus's interactions with people? I'd love to know what you notice about those interactions."

Alex shrugged. "Okay, Sara. I'll see what I can find." He smiled.

"I've got another question for you, Alex. What does it mean to love someone unconditionally?"

"To love them in spite of how they treat you, I think."

"Yeah, definitely. What does that look like for you?"

"For me it means being kind to people no matter what they do or say to me."

"Let's bring this right down to reality. What does it mean for you to love Drew unconditionally?"

"Funny you should ask that. We had kind of a strange interaction yesterday. He was really sarcastic with me, but I could see that something's going on with him. I prayed about what to do all day, and then when I was going to leave, I just invited him over for dinner on Friday. I don't know if he'll come."

"Interesting. How did you decide that that's what you wanted to say to him?"

"I didn't really decide. It just came out of my mouth. I didn't know what to say because of how things have been between us."

"This sounds a little different than your other interactions with him, Alex. Why the change?"

"Well, he was obviously upset, and everything I said to him before just made him more upset—like, it seemed to make him hate me more. Even though I think he needs to hear those things, maybe that wasn't the right time. Why? Do you think I should have said something different?"

"No, Alex. I think you did fine. I was just curious about why you shifted gears there. I think it's great. But what are you going to do if he doesn't come to dinner?"

"Well, I guess I'll just invite him again some other time. Seems like eventually, he'll cave." Alex grinned.

"Actually, Sara, do you know what he said to me? He asked if I wanted to have him over to watch some evangelist lecture him on TV. It kind of struck me that maybe the only thing he ever hears from me is religious stuff."

"Did that bother you?"

"Well, I mean, I think it's really important, so I spend lots of time talking about it. Even with Annie, that's what we spend a lot of time talking about. But at the same time, I got to thinking that we don't really have a friendship, Drew and I. I want to be his friend, but I don't really know him. And all he knows about me is what I think about God and what I think about homosexuality. And I'm not sure that's enough. It's not enough to really walk with him, you know? He's suffering a lot right now, and I think he needs people to walk with him. But I'm not sure that he has anyone."

"Wow, Alex. Those are some great insights. Do you think that will change your behavior toward Drew at all?"

Alex thought for a minute. "Maybe. Maybe I can focus more on just getting to know him for a while. We used to have a lot of fun together. I don't know."

Alex and Sara paused to finish up their sandwiches, and then Sara asked, "So tell me how things are going with Annie, Alex. Do you feel like she understands your passion now?"

"Sort of. I mean, she definitely gets the vision to reach out to people around her. Which is awesome. But I don't know. I still feel like we're not quite on the same page. All the stuff we've been talking about, all the stuff that's made me uncomfortable, well, she seems to be jumping right in with it. She doesn't seemed super concerned about how it all fits into the Bible."

"How are you working out those differences in your relationship?"

Alex grimaced. "I don't really know that we are, Sara. Some days she seems so far away." He trailed off.

Sara wanted to probe deeper, but she thought that she might have challenged him enough for one day. She didn't want to give too much too soon. So she just listened to Alex talk until it was time for her to leave. She was somewhat encouraged by the progress Alex was beginning to make, though. She thought he'd made a huge breakthrough in his ability to really see things from Drew's perspective and start thinking about how to be a friend to Drew instead of how to change his beliefs.

Annie and Sara were able to meet at the regular time on Wednesday night. But they met at a Thai food place and chatted over green curry and Pad Thai noodles. They had a free and easy discussion about how each of their weeks had gone. Annie described the tennis lesson with Oliver and the cookies at the Bixly's.

Then she asked, "So Sara, I've been wondering about something. I have this friendship with Oliver, right? And we've been hanging out since I started working with him. So I feel like it's sort of a mutual relationship–we play tennis, we complain about work, that kind of thing. But then there's the Conrads. I really, really want to be a friend to them. And I've been really trying to help them, you know? But it ends up feeling like the relationship is one-sided. It's always me pursuing them or helping them. And I don't mind that, but it just doesn't feel the same as with Oliver. I'm afraid that they're beginning to feel as if they were a project of mine."

"Ah, you've hit on something that's really important. It's the mutual give and take of relationships that is so beautiful. There may be times when it's appropriate and necessary to pursue someone

294

unconditionally and in the face of rejection or scorn. But ultimately, being able to give and take and learn from one another is a beautiful, beautiful thing. But it is sometimes hard to shift a dynamic that's already been created. If you start out pursuing and loving someone in need, do you think there's a way to change the dynamic?"

Annie scrunched her nose as she thought. "Well, I don't know. Maybe by asking for help yourself?"

"I think that's a great idea, Annie. In fact, I've found that there are many times when being vulnerable about your needs with other people is a really good thing. There was a time with this professor that I worked with, where we'd been sort of friends for a long time. But she had me in this weird category because my life was so 'perfect,' or seemed to be. Life was relatively calm for me. But then, when Barry died, I was able to call and ask her and her boyfriend for help with moving some things around the house. She jumped at the chance to help me, and she began to see me as more of a normal human being." Sara paused and looked out the window.

"You know," Sara continued, "one of my friends described it to me like this. She said, 'Your life is like a car wreck that I can't look away from, Sara. I want to stop paying attention, but it just looks so different than mine. So I walk along, rubber-necking.' I think being vulnerable with my professor friend really helped to make me seem more human and more normal. It moved my life a step closer to human and a step away from car wreck."

"I have a hard time, Annie, allowing other people to do things for me. It's natural for me to want to do things myself–just to see if I can, sometimes–but it's been really important for me to show my vulnerabilities to the people around me."

"Hmm . . . ." Annie said. "So maybe I could ask Josie or Patti for help with something?"

Sara nodded, "Sure, Annie. I mean, you don't have to orchestrate a need or anything. But maybe next time you do need something and you're thinking of calling your family or Alex, you could pop next door instead."

"That makes sense, I guess. I'll try to remember to do that." Annie took a bite of curry and then continued. "I have another question for you. I'm not really sure what to do about Patti. I mean, she's still so quiet. She barely talks about anything. I don't know if she needs to talk or if she needs to forget what happened to her. But I'm worried about her keeping it all bottled up inside. Is there anything I can do?"

"I don't think you can force her to talk. So I'd say just keep being available and showing her that you care. She may open up to you. And she may not. But at least she'll know that you care about her. Recovering from abuse is a long process that usually requires professional counseling."

A Delicate Dance

Alex and Drew worked the same shift on Thursday. After the lunch rush, Alex headed upstairs to the office to catch up on a little paperwork. As he entered the room, he found Drew sitting at his desk. Alex still wasn't sure where things were at, but he strode into the room and said a gregarious hello. Drew just mumbled a hello and didn't even look up from his work.

Alex walked to his desk and started rummaging around his papers. "Hey, Drew, have you seen my inventory sheets? I thought I'd try to get a jump on tomorrow's ordering."

Drew just shrugged and kept working. So Alex kept rummaging around until he found them. He sat down and looked at them for a while until he sighed dramatically and asked, "So, when can you come over tomorrow?"

Drew swung his chair around. "Really, Alex, why do you want me to come? It seems a little ridiculous, doesn't it. What do we even have in common?"

Alex thought back to when they first started working together. "Don't you remember how we convinced Jackson that we were going to do Halloween in May? So we printed up fake fliers and everything, and he came into work dressed as the Grim Reaper? That was fun, right? We can have fun together. I kind of miss having someone here to joke around with."

Drew just looked at him, as if taking his measure, seeing if he was serious. Finally, he shrugged and said, "I can be there around 6:30."

Alex was thrilled. And before he said anything stupid, he went back down to the café.

That night, Alex and Annie had dinner together at Annie's house. Alex was so excited that Drew was coming over. He tried to talk through acceptable dinner topics with Annie.

"So, do you think it's okay to talk about God at all, Annie?"

"I don't know, Alex. I think that you have to be you and be real. And God is a big part of your life. So if things come up where we would normally have a conversation about God, I don't really think that's a bad thing. But I'd steer away from any kind of condemnation. Drew hasn't responded well to that in the past." Indeed, why would he, she wondered.

"Alex, do you even like Drew?"

Alex fidgeted as he thought. "Well, yeah, kinda. I mean, I used to really like him. We used to do practical jokes, of course, but we could also talk about baseball. And he's a huge fan of Comedy Central, just like me, so we were always talking about shows on there."

"So what changed?"

"Oh, Annie. Everything changed when I found out

about his boyfriend. I mean, I just couldn't get over that. I can't really stand the thought of two men together. So it just made it hard. Whenever I'd see him, that's all I could think about. It's mostly all I think about now."

"Here's what I'm wondering, Alex—and don't take this the wrong way—but do you think that your desire to see Drew's life changed has more to do with your feelings about homosexuals than with how it would affect his relationship with God?" Alex immediately started shaking his head, but Annie continued. "I mean, I know that God hates sin, and that it separates people from him, but I don't see you walking around calling out all the gossiping old ladies in our church. Why choose this, Alex? Why is this such a big deal to you?"

Alex was still shaking his head, but words weren't coming out of his mouth.

After a minute of silence, Annie changed the discussion to the menu for the next night, and within 20 minutes, Alex was picking up his things to go.

As he left that night, he couldn't get Annie's question out of his head. But instead of allowing it to penetrate his heart and challenge his assumptions, he met her question with an attitude of defensiveness. When he got home, instead of continuing his search for Jesus's interactions with people, he checked out the verses again on homosexuality. He went to sleep that night satisfied that his was a holy cause. Yes, he wanted to love Drew and get to know him. But ultimately, Alex would not be satisfied unless Drew could walk away from his homosexuality in the name of holiness.

As Annie was winding down for the night, she thought of the Conrads. She needed a pie recipe because she was in charge of dessert for the next night. So she took the opportunity to go next door and ask if they had one. Josie was at a friend's house, so Patti was alone. Annie made her request, and Patti invited her in for tea. After the water was hot, Patti sat down at the pristine table with Annie and pulled out her highly organized recipe box.

"So what kind of pie were you thinking of making? Homemade crust, or no?" Patti asked.

"I don't think I have time for homemade. I have to work a half-shift in the morning. So I'm going to have to throw it in the oven when I get home."

"Ok. What kind of pie do you like?"

"Well, I really like blueberry. I could get some vanilla ice cream on the way to Alex's, and that would be perfect."

Patti said, "Well, I don't have to do anything tomorrow. Why don't you just let me make you a pie?"

"Oh, Patti, I couldn't ask you to do that. I felt bad enough for coming over this late. I wasn't sure if you'd be sleeping."

"No, no, Annie. It's no problem. And you've been doing so much for Josie, and for me, and well, I'd like to do something in return. Please let me." Patti's face looked drawn, but the thought of being able to help Annie had brought a spark of life to her eyes–more than Annie had seen in the last couple of weeks. So she relented. "That would be really, really nice. Thank you."

That settled, they sat with their tea for a while longer. "How do you think Josie is doing, Patti?" Annie asked.

Patti shook her head. "I worry about her. She's had to carry a lot of the load around here. I don't know if she's even really had time to grieve losing her dad."

"Have you heard from him recently?"

Patti's jaw tightened, and her eyes flashed. All she said was "no." Jake was obviously not something Patti wanted to discuss. Annie was tempted to talk to her about Alex and their difficulties. She thought maybe Patti could give her some advice. But would she understand? She didn't even believe in God. Could she understand their differences? But Annie thought back to her conversation with Sara and jumped in.

"So I know it's late, but can I ask you a question?"

"Sure, Annie, go ahead."

"Ok, well, Alex and I are having some problems. Mostly it stems from how we put into action what we believe. I'm having a really hard time because so much of

301

what I hear coming out of his mouth is judgmental. Sometimes it seems that he cares more about the idea of truth than about the people that he's spending time with. I'm not sure what to do. I mean, I'm even thinking that we might have to break up. It just seems like this giant chasm. Even though we say we both believe the same things, we're putting them into practice so differently, you know? And I don't like to see people getting hurt."

Patti quietly sipped her tea, in no hurry to respond. Finally, "Well, Annie, I think you have to make a choice. You know who Alex is. You know what he stands for. You know what his character is. What I can tell you for sure is that things that bother you now will bother you a hundred times more when you're married to someone. Things that you can take a break from now, by going home or having your own space, they don't get better in closer quarters. It's something you have to deal with. So you have to decide whether it's something you want to live with."

"But isn't it possible he can change and grow?"

"Of course it is. It's always possible. But you can't go into it with that expectation. You can hope for change, but you have to be okay with your life and what it would mean if it never does."

Annie pondered this for a moment. "Thanks so much, Patti." She took the last gulp of her tea, and then rose to leave. "I really appreciate the pie, Patti. And thanks for the tea. And for listening to me. I'll let you know what happens." Annie smiled, a little sadly, and made her way home.

The next day, Alex spent the whole afternoon preparing for dinner. He had to clean the whole house, of course. He couldn't remember the last time he or one of his roommates had cleaned the kitchen or the bathrooms. And everyone was always leaving all their stuff all over the living room. By 4 p.m., he had things pretty much spiffed up, so he started in on the meal. He was just going to grill chicken and veggies outside. It was a little bit cold, but he thought he could manage it.

When Annie arrived at 6 p.m., Alex was finished with just about everything. All that was left was to set the table and put the food on the grill. He didn't want to do that too early, though, so they set the table together.

"Are you ready for this, Alex?" Annie asked.

"Of course, Annie. It's no big deal."

Annie just smiled. "Is there anything special that you want me to do or say?"

"Not that I can think of."

They sat for a minute, and then Alex jumped up to put everything on the grill. He ran around like a madman until the doorbell rang at exactly 6:30. Alex vaguely heard it but continued his ministrations at the grill. Five minutes later, he entered the living room.

He was prepared with an enthusiastic welcome, but

303

it died on his lips as he saw Drew. Right beside him stood another guy, who was introduced to Alex as Jonathan. Annie saw the look on Alex's face and said, "Alex, why don't you go finish up in the kitchen. I'll just get the guys some drinks and we can eat when you're ready."

Leaving Annie to do just that, Alex rushed to the kitchen and leaned up against the counter. Never in a million years had he expected Drew to actually bring someone along. Sure, he'd told Drew he could invite his boyfriend, but he didn't actually mean it. And as Alex thought back to the scene at the doorway, he could almost read a challenge in Drew's eyes–"What are you going to do now, buddy?"

And what was he going to do? Alex believed very strongly in hospitality and didn't want to be rude. The thought of having to watch them together at the table, it was almost too much to bear. How was he going to get through this?

He suddenly remembered the chicken, so he rushed outside to check on it. It was just done, so he pulled that and the vegetables off the grill. He returned to the kitchen and pulled some bread he'd been warming out of the oven and started bringing the dinner, piece by piece, to the dining room. He could faintly hear Annie entertaining the guys in the living room, and they sounded like they were having fun. Annie must be telling one of her stories. *Better her than me.*

Finally, Alex popped his head into the living room and called them into dinner. Everyone sat down, and there was an awkward pause while everyone waited. Annie nudged Alex's foot under the table, and he shook himself and said, "Dig in."

Annie kept the conversation going through dinner. She seemed to be trying hard to draw Drew and Jonathan into sharing their stories. She learned that Drew was a drama buff and had played the starring role in several plays in high school. Both Drew and Annie had parts in *Fiddler on the Roof* in high school, so they talked about that for a while. Jonathan just smiled and looked interested in the conversation, while Alex had still not recovered. He ate with just an awkward word here and there.

Finally, it was time for dessert. Annie went in the kitchen to dish out the pie and ice cream, and the guys headed back to the living room, coffee in hand. They all sat, and then there was an awkward silence. For the life of him, Alex could not figure out what to say or what topic might be safe. Jonathan and Drew started to chat among themselves. Finally, Alex asked, "So Jonathan, what kind of work do you do?" *Wow, Alex, that was exciting.*

Jonathan answered, "Well, like I said during dinner, I work at a commercial printer in town. I do design work there." He rolled his eyes at Drew. Alex immediately felt as if they were making fun of him. He bristled, but he tried to salvage the conversation.

"So where did you go to college?"

"Oh, I went to a private Christian college out east. Until I got kicked out, that is. So then I finished up at Virginia State."

"Why were you kicked out?" Alex couldn't resist asking.

"I could no longer live by their lifestyle commitments, so they kicked me to the curb. Good riddance, I'd say."

"So do you consider yourself a Christian?"

"Yeah, I do, not that it's any of your business."

Again, Alex bristled. Rising to the implicit challenge, he asked, "So how do you reconcile your faith with your sexual orientation?"

At just this moment, Annie walked in carrying two plates of pie and ice cream. She was just in time to see the rage building on Drew's face as Alex's question hit the table. Nobody moved for a minute. Annie stayed frozen in the doorway. Alex broke the tension by jumping up to help her and placing pies in front of Jonathan and Drew.

But Drew and Jonathan stood up in perfect unison. Drew said, "Thanks so much for your hospitality, Annie. I think it's time that Jonathan and I head out." Without another word, they collected their jackets from the couch and walked out the door. They didn't even acknowledge Alex.

As they left, Annie turned to Alex and asked, "What

306

did you do?"

"I don't know what happened," Alex said, bewildered. "We were having a good conversation, at least I thought it was, and then all of a sudden, they left. It was weird." He shook his head.

"I cannot believe you said that. I just can't believe it. How could you ask such an inappropriate question?"

He shrugged, "Inappropriate? I don't think it was inappropriate. I was curious."

"For one thing, how do you even know he's gay?"

"What do you mean? Of course he is. He's here with Drew, isn't he?"

"Alex, I don't think that's quite enough proof. I know this is hard for you to imagine, but it is possible for a heterosexual person to be friends with a homosexual one."

Alex said, "Well, why'd he even bring Jonathan, then? I only invited him and his boyfriend, and I didn't even mean to have him come."

"Perhaps he felt he needed reinforcements. Look, Alex. I'm going to go too."

And with that, Annie quickly picked up her things and left too. Alex stood for a moment, wondering what was wrong with Annie and then grabbed some pie and ice cream.

A Map for the Journey

Annie and Alex spoke little in the following days.
What conversation they did have was stilted and
unnatural. Annie was brewing over the conversation they
had with Drew and Jonathan and couldn't figure out how
Alex could so lack sensitivity and care for the people
around him. She kept thinking that he obviously did care,
but his was a care with an agenda. It had never been more
clear to her that he cared about the people around him with
just one purpose–to convert them to his way of thinking.
She desperately wanted to believe that this was out of a
genuine concern for their well-being. But she knew that
Alex, once he got into his head what he believed was right,
would stop at nothing to try to convince those around him
to follow along.

She just kept going back to what Patti had told her.
It gets worse, the closer you get to someone. The things
that bother you now will bother you more in closer
proximity. And she could barely stand the thought of even
talking to Alex right now.

She had half a mind to go to Second Story when she
knew he wouldn't be there to apologize to Drew. But what
could she say, really? I'm sorry my boyfriend's such a
jerk–don't take it out on God?

She sighed. It was Wednesday and time to go to
Sara's. She kind of wanted to skip out, but she couldn't

think of a good excuse. Besides which, she actually really wanted to see Sara and hear what she had to say. These past few months, she'd grown a ton. And Sara was a gem. She was learning so much about following God and sharing his love and light with others. She wasn't ready for that to stop.

So she grabbed her keys and said goodbye to Herman. She prayed for Patti and Josie on the way out of the apartment and spent the ride to Sara's praying that she would have patience with Alex. She didn't know what this discussion was going to look like.

When she arrived, Alex and Sara were calmly talking in the living room. She helped herself to some tea and sat as far away from Alex on the couch as she could. Sara immediately felt the tension between them but didn't say anything.

"Well, you guys, how was your week?" Neither Annie nor Alex jumped to answer, so Sara turned her attention to Alex. "Alex, did you manage to spend some time with the stories of Jesus's interaction with people?" Alex nodded. "So what did you observe?"

"I think it's just like you told me, Sara. Jesus told a lot of stories. In response to questions, mostly Jesus asked questions back or told a parable."

"So what can we learn from that?" Sara asked.

"Well, that stories are powerful," Alex answered, "And it's okay to use them to tell people about truth."

"What about the morals of the stories? Did Jesus ever tell people what those were?"

"What do you mean?" Annie asked.

"Well, did Jesus tell people how they should understand his stories or what they meant?"

Annie answered, "I think he did sometimes. Like I remember the story of the four soils. Jesus definitely told the disciples what that meant."

"Sure he did. But very often he didn't give the meaning at all. He seemed to trust the Holy Spirit, and the people he told the stories to, to discern and apply the truth to their own lives. Why is that important?"

They all thought for a minute. Annie answered, "Well, maybe it shows us that we don't always have to draw all the conclusions for people. Maybe we don't have to tell them all the answers. Maybe it's enough to share part of the journey with them and tell them stories and ask them questions. Maybe we can trust the Spirit too."

Alex became even more tense, if that was possible. He said, "But how do we know that they'll get the stories right? Like the story of Abraham, for example. Is your friend Patti going to be tempted to go out and kill her own daughter to prove that she loves Jesus?"

"Ah, Alex," Sara said, "that's a good point. There's a process to learning discernment and obedience. There's certainly a place for teaching. That's why community is so important. It's much harder to misinterpret what God is

311

saying in our lives when we have a community around us that's helping us discern."

Alex squirmed a little, but held his peace. Sara waited to see if there would be more questions, but as none were forthcoming, she continued.

"I want to talk with you about something I've noticed over the years while I've been working with people. One thing that I've noticed is that there are certain times in a person's life when he seems prone to ask and be open to the spiritual questions in life. I first noticed this when I was in college. Every time one of my friends would get engaged and start planning her wedding, she would begin to think about going to church, getting her life started in a healthy direction. And then again, as my friends transitioned into parenthood, every time someone learned she was pregnant or had a baby, she seemed much more likely to be asking spiritual questions. So I started watching people at other times in life. Similar things happened at funerals, at graduations, at the times when kids move out of the house. Any kind of life change, people seem to pause for a moment and seek the spiritual realm."

Sara paused. Annie noted that Alex barely seemed to be listening. But she was interested. Sara must have noticed the same thing because she asked Annie, "Why do you think this might be important?"

Annie thought about it for a second, "Well, I guess

so I can be prepared. I mean, I think that you're right. Josie's world has been blown apart, and she's totally seeking right now to find answers to her questions in a way that she clearly wasn't before. If I had known that ahead of time, maybe I could have been prepared for it."

Sara nodded. "One thing that I sometimes do is just think about where people are at in life. I try to see where they are and what kind of life events might be coming up for them. That way, I can start to pray about being prepared for the questions and hurts that might surface. It just gives me one more opportunity to be ready to walk alongside people."

Annie's mind immediately turned to Oliver. He'd just had a major breakup with his girlfriend, Heather. She wondered if he was seeking spiritual things. She wondered if she'd missed being a part of his questioning process.

Sara must have been concerned by Alex's silence and obvious lack of participation because she asked, "Alex, is something wrong?"

He shook his head, as if to clear it. "I'm sorry, Sara. I just don't think I can do this anymore. I mean, I really appreciate everything you have done for us, being willing to talk with us and everything, but I just don't think that what you're saying is really biblical. What about the truth? Isn't it my job to make sure that the truth is being told? How can I just let the story sit there, for itself, to be interpreted any old way the listener wants to hear it? That

313

can't be right."

He rose to leave. "I think I'm going to get going, Sara. I really appreciate your time." He leaned over and kissed Annie on the cheek. "Are you coming?" He asked.

"I'll leave in a bit, Alex. You can call later, if you want to." So Alex walked out the door.

Annie and Sara just sat for a minute in silence. Annie gave a great sigh. "Well, I guess that's that, Sara. It sounds like he's done here, and I think he really is. Did he tell you what happened with Drew this week?"

When Sara said no, Annie filled her in. Sara asked, "How are you feeling about all this, Annie?"

"Oh Sara, I don't know!" Annie jumped to her feet and started pacing. "I love Alex, so much. I really do. He's a sweet, special, good-hearted guy. But far from drawing us together, meeting here with you has really illustrated how we're different. I know that Alex loves the people around him, and I spend so much time right now trying to convince myself that he's not hurting them on purpose. I keep telling myself that he is learning and growing still. But he seems so closed off to these ideas." She paced the room some more as Sara's eyes followed her back and forth.

"Sara, you should have seen the look on Drew's face. I mean, he was beyond insulted. And I was mortified. And Alex doesn't even see it. He's so full of his cause, he can't see that he's hurting people. And not just hurting their feelings. He's getting in the way of how they see God. Sara, I don't think I can stand that."

"I mean, I feel like my life has been transformed. I am living with purpose and vision that's bigger than me and my own life, and I want to be with someone who can be a partner with me in that. But all I've seen Alex do in the last months is alienate people–from himself and from God."

She flopped on the couch. "What am I going to do?"

Sara sat for a minute more, "I don't have the answers for you, Annie. But I'd be happy to pray with you."

So they sat and prayed that God would lead both her and Alex. Annie wanted to be hopeful that he could change, but she just wasn't. A few minutes later, she headed for home.

After an hour or two, Alex called her on her cell. After little introduction, he said, "Annie, I'm kind of concerned about you. It's hard to say, but I'm not really sure that you're concerned about the truth. I know that I introduced you to Sara, but I really don't think that we should meet with her anymore. I am just not sure that she's really on track, biblically speaking."

Annie held her tongue and let Alex talk. She didn't want to say anything that she would regret later, but she could barely make it through the call. After just a couple minutes, she begged exhaustion and hung up the phone.

Her spirit was not at rest as she prepared for bed and then attempted sleep. She couldn't get Drew's face out of her mind. And she knew Alex. She knew she couldn't make him see what he wouldn't see. He would see what he would see, and no one could tell him any different.

Annie did her best to avoid Alex on Thursday, but Friday he insisted that they meet for lunch at the old diner. So she showed up around noon and reluctantly joined him at their regular booth. She was feeling too nauseated to eat, so she just ordered a soda.

Alex started talking a mile a minute about an evangelism curriculum he'd found on the web. He had done some research and ordered it, and he was wondering if Annie wanted to go through it with him, now that they were done meeting with Sara.

"Wait a minute, Alex, you cancelled on Sara?"

"Well, yeah. Obviously, we can't go and see her anymore. And I don't think it's really helping us, you know?" He grabbed her hand. "I still want us to grow together. I think it's so important. And I'm so thrilled that you are so passionate about reaching out to the people around you. I couldn't be happier. We just have to learn to do it the right way." He smiled at her.

She asked quietly, "So you're really convinced that

316

Sara is leading us astray?"

"Well yeah, aren't you? I mean the story stuff is fine, but it really has to be tempered by the truth. There are a lot of false religions out there, Annie, and there's a lot of untruth. Someone has to guard the truth of Scripture."

"And what if I don't agree, Alex?"

"Don't agree? How could you not see it, Annie?" Alex seemed perplexed for the first time. "You really don't, do you?"

Annie shook her head. "Actually, Alex, I'm kind of concerned myself. I'm concerned about Drew. Did you see the look on his face as he left your house?"

"Yeah." He frowned. "I really didn't understand why he was so upset."

"Alex, he was really offended. Why did you have to bring up their sexual orientation? And really, why is it any of your business how they act and live?"

"Annie, do you hear yourself? God hates sin. It separates us from him. It has to be confronted."

"By whom? Do you really see that as your main job on earth, to walk around convincing people of what sin lives in their hearts? Isn't that what the Spirit is supposed to do?"

"Well, sure, Annie. The Spirit convicts. But don't we have a responsibility to tell the truth?"

"Maybe. But there's a time and a place for truth-telling. I think there's also a time to love. You have to earn

317

the right to be heard, Alex. You have to have a relationship with someone–a mutual, caring relationship–before you can usually speak to them about such deep things as spirituality. And I don't actually remember any place where Jesus condemned someone who wasn't claiming to follow him."

Annie took a sip of her soda and then said, "Alex, I really think you need to apologize to Drew."

"He's not speaking to me right now, Annie. I doubt it will do any good. Besides, what would I be apologizing for?"

"For offending him. For speaking out of turn. For turning a nice dinner into a confrontation."

"Is that really what you think I did?"

"That's what it felt like when I got back in there. I'm not saying it's all your fault–I don't know because I wasn't there. But seriously, Alex. They were deeply offended. And probably hurt."

"Well, I'll take your word for that, Annie. You're much better at reading people than I am."

Alex chatted on, and Annie sat there sadly. They were at such different places. Alex didn't even see it.

Sharp Turn

The next day, Annie found herself back at Patti's house. Josie was there, but she never really liked to talk when her mom was there. So Annie got settled in with tea and some fresh cookies at the table with Patti. Josie sat just around the corner in the living room, her face just visible beyond the bar. Annie asked how Patti's search for work was going, and Patti didn't sound too hopeful. She had not worked since Josie was born, and she didn't have many skills. She explained she was thinking about going back to school for some kind of medical assistant position.

"Oh," Annie said. "There's an orderly position available on my floor. It's not super exciting, but I could recommend you. The hospital's obviously pretty big, but sometimes it helps to have a recommendation on the inside."

Patti looked at her. "You would do that for me?"

"Of course," Annie said.

"Well, okay. How do I apply?" So Annie filled Patti in on the application process. After a few minutes, Patti asked how they liked the blueberry pie.

"Oh, man. It was one awful night. I told you about how Alex and I are on different pages. Well this was terrible." She told Patti about how Alex had offended the guys and they walked out without eating the pie. "I didn't even get a piece. I was so upset, I left right after the guys."

Josie interjected from the living room, "So what are you going to do, Annie? Are you going to dump that guy? Oliver's available, I think." Annie could just barely see the mischievous grin on her face. Annie couldn't help but laugh. "I don't know, Josie, I don't know. Your mom gave me some pretty good advice though." She winked at Josie.

Patti changed the subject. "Annie, I really do want to thank you for everything you've done for us. Honestly, I don't know how we would have made it through."

Annie was embarrassed. "It was really no problem, Patti. I was happy to help. And Josie has been such a pleasure to have around." Josie was still nearby, pretending to be engrossed in an art book. But with that comment, a warm flush spread up her cheeks.

"I do have a question though. I don't understand why you spent so much time with us. I know you have your family and your boyfriend, whatever your problems. You've invested a ton. Why?"

"I'm not sure that you'll want to hear this Patti, given Jake, but honestly, it's because of how much God cares about me." She paused, to make sure Patti was tracking. Instead of looking hostile, she just looked peaceful, so Annie went on. "I was explaining to Josie just the other day, actually, about how when Alex was in the hospital, I was having a really hard time believing that God was there with me. The only reason I could have faith that he was, and that he cared, was because of how the people

320

of God, the people from my church, mostly, were acting toward me. That's how I felt his presence."

"And honestly, a couple of months ago, God really transformed my life. I suddenly understood that being a Christian isn't about going to church or doing the right thing, but it's about a relationship with God. But it's not a relationship that's centered around me–it's centered around me surrendering to God–living for him and for something bigger than myself. As part of that realization, I started looking around for people around me who needed to know how much God loved them. So I wanted to share that with you. Not necessarily with words, though I'd love to talk about it more. But by my actions toward you. I wanted you to have what I had when Alex was sick."

Annie looked over at Patti and then at Josie. They both looked a little uncomfortable. Yet they seemed curious too. So Annie just said, "Anyway, I hope that you know that God loves you."

Patti started to object "But–" and then stopped. She held her tongue. Annie knew that she must be struggling with how belief in God could lead to such different outcomes–hers and Jake's. So she told a story. "You know, Jesus told this story once. Do you mind if I share it with you?"

Patti and Josie shook their heads. "He was talking about how they would know his followers at the end of time. And he told them that his followers would be known by what they did. Those who clothed him, who fed him, and visited him in prison would be the ones who were his followers. And he explained to them that these people would say, 'but when did we feed you, clothe you, or visit you in prison?' And he said, 'whatever they did to others, they did to him.'"

She paused for a minute and forced herself not to explain the meaning of the story. The women were subdued, but they did seem to be thinking about the story. So Annie quickly finished her tea and then made her excuses and headed home.

As she unlocked her door, Josie burst out of the door behind her. "Annie!" she said.

Annie turned. "Yeah Josie?"

"Are you saying that my dad's not a Christian?"

"I don't think I can answer that, Josie. I can't know what's in his heart. But Jesus pretty clearly said that we would know his followers by how they treat others."

Josie nodded. "Okay. Thanks." And before another second passed, she was back in her own apartment, locking the door.

Friday Alex was back at work, working in the office for most of the day. He was surprised to find Drew not there, as they both worked every Friday. He began to worry after about an hour, and then he got a phone call.

"Hey Alex, it's Drew. I'm not coming in today. I'm

in the hospital." Before Alex could even say anything in response, Drew hung up the phone.

Alex knew that Drew had been getting chemo and radiation treatments pretty regularly. Apparently this one hadn't turned out too well. He'd been thinking about what Annie said about hurting Drew's feelings. That certainly wasn't what he meant to do. He really wasn't sure what made Drew so mad the other day. By bringing up the topic of sexuality, he'd expected they could have a rational discussion about it. He'd been able to talk with Drew about that before. But obviously it hadn't worked out that way. Well, he thought after work he might stop by and try to bring Drew a balloon or a get-well card or something.

A few hours later, he went down to the café for the end of the shift. Omar was working the counter, and the store was dead. Omar and Alex sat at a table drinking coffee and talking.

"So, Alex, I return to my country in only a few months. Have you ever traveled overseas?"

"Not to the Middle East. The only trip I ever took was to Manila, in the Philippines."

"What was that like? I have never traveled there."

"Well, we went to a very poverty-stricken area. There were whole cities that grew right around the city dump. It was so hard to see those kids sitting there, playing there, living in such squalor."

"Why did you go there? Were you there as a

323

tourist?"

Alex noted some skepticism on Omar's face. He answered, "Not really. It was a trip I took with some people from my church. We called it a missions trip. We did some evangelistic meetings and then assisted with health clinics in the poor areas."

"Interesting. I have not taken a trip like that before. Indeed, when I travel I like to see the nicer side of life." Omar smiled. "We ordinarily stay in hotels and enjoy the city life. What was the best part of that trip for you?"

Alex thought for a while. Omar seemed really interested, and perhaps this was an opportunity to share from his heart. "Well, I really enjoyed being able to share about my faith. I believe in Jesus, you know, and I got to talk with people who had never heard his name before. It seemed such a privilege to be able to tell God's story to the people."

Omar nodded. Alex couldn't really read the expression on his face. He seemed open and accepting, but he had no way to know whether what he was talking about was penetrating. Omar continued, "We have had Christian missionaries who have come to my country. It is generally understood that they are trying to tear apart the cultural fabric of our country by asking people to stop being Muslim." Omar shook his head. "I do not think you would be welcome in Qatar to do these things."

Alex felt very out of his element here. His first

instinct was to defend the Christian missionaries. Perhaps this didn't make sense, since he didn't know them. But still. If he didn't defend them, how would Omar know what the intentions of their hearts really were? He didn't give a thought to potential emotional barriers or a story he might tell to answer a question behind a question. So he just tried to explain the reasons. "Christ does demand that people follow him with all their hearts, souls, minds, and strength. So it's true that, where Muslim culture and spirituality conflict with Jesus's commands, then we must submit. So I can see how you would get that impression. But God doesn't wish to have the whole fabric of any community destroyed. Just the parts that are not the best."

Omar nodded as if he understood, but he didn't say anything more. Alex wondered about whether there was something else he could say to keep the conversation going, but then another customer walked in.

After work, Alex stopped by the hospital bearing a get-well balloon. He found Drew's room and stopped in for a moment. Jonathan was standing near the door with his coat in hand, and Alex approached just in time to hear a soft goodbye. When Jonathan spotted him, he looked back at Drew and asked, "Do you want me to stay?" Drew shook his head, "I've got this." So Jonathan left.

"You've got a lot of nerve showing up here Alex. What religious platitude have you come to offer this evening? Something about the supposed love of God? Oh, I know. I'm going to hell because I haven't turned away from my homosexual ways. Why don't you just take yourself and your balloon and go home, Alex. I don't really have the energy to deal with you today." And he turned his head toward the wall and closed his eyes.

Alex stood there in the door for a minute, but couldn't for the life of him figure out what to say. And indeed, what could he say, now? His words and actions up to this time had alienated Drew to the point that nothing could be said to make things right. It would take years to undo the damage he did in his own relationship with Drew. And God only knew the damage that had been done to Drew's relationship with God. But Alex didn't think about any of this. He just shrugged and walked out the door.

Saturday neither Annie nor Alex had to work, so they spent a few hours hiking in the cold. Conversation during the hike was focused around their respective families and stories from work. Nothing was said about evangelism or Sara or any of their friends. Alex felt a little tension though. There were times when he felt that Annie wasn't totally with him. But he made the best of things, telling entertaining stories and goofing off.

Occasionally, his mind flickered to where they were headed. He'd pretty much decided that he was done meeting with Sara. He just couldn't handle how wishy-washy things seemed. It seemed such a far cry from the certainty that he'd grown up with. And it seemed not to be concerned so much with the truth. And how can a person share faith without being concerned with communicating the truth? Alex didn't understand how that was even possible.

He was really glad they'd met with Sara though. Even though he wasn't comfortable with everything they'd discussed, he was thrilled that it had seemed to bring such a change to Annie. She really seemed passionate about reaching other people now. She finally seemed to have the same passion that he had to share the story of God. Now it was just a matter of figuring out how to move forward from here: where to go, what to study, how to keep growing.

After the hike, Annie and Alex stopped for hot cocoa and some lunch. As soon as they sat down, Annie sighed. Alex looked up from his cocoa and asked, "Why the sigh, Annie? What's up?"

"Alex, I've been thinking. I know that you've decided that you are really uncomfortable with the ideas that Sara presented. But I think you should know that they've been really important to my life and my growth. I've learned so much! And I think that what Sara shared is actually helpful. So anyway, I just wanted you to know that."

"That's funny. I was just thinking about that too. I'm so happy that we met with her because it's made a huge difference in your life. I'm excited that you've moved to a place where you can see the mission that we're on. I'm really excited to see what God might be able to do with us together in the future." He smiled a big smile and squeezed Annie's hand.

Annie's squeeze in response was halfhearted. Alex asked, "Is something else wrong?"

"Well, I'm not sure, Alex. I'm having a hard time with things. I'm still thinking about Drew and the look on his face when he left your house the other night. I feel responsible for that."

"I know, Annie. It's really hard. I stopped by the hospital with a balloon yesterday and he was really rude. He asked me to just go and leave. I couldn't even leave the balloon. I guess he's still mad about things. I don't really understand why."

The look on Annie's face was troubled as she asked, "Alex, why did you feel like you needed to ask about Jonathan's sexuality just then? I mean, we were having a really good conversation together. They were feeling pretty warm and open."

"Well, Drew and I had had conversations like that before in the office. So I was just curious about how they worked through those issues, you know? Drew obviously knows what he's doing is wrong. I wondered where

328

Jonathan stood on the issue."

"But Alex, how did that improve your relationship with Drew? How did that open the lines of communication? How did that open anyone's heart toward God?"

"I was just trying to make connections, you know? Open the lines of communication about faith, talk about things that are important. I do enjoy goofing off, as you know, but I was hoping to bring things around to a more serious conversation."

"Do you think it worked?"

Alex frowned, "Well, no, it didn't seem to. I'm not sure where I went wrong." He shook his head.

Annie paused. Her face was sad. Then she blurted out, "Alex, I'm just not sure that we can continue this way. I mean, I don't see how you can sit here and say you don't understand why Drew rushed out of the house or why he wouldn't let you visit him in the hospital. I know that you mean well, I do. But I just can't see how this will work out. What if I bring Josie over sometime for dinner? It seems like you could undo all of my months of relationship-building in just an hour. I don't think I can handle that."

Alex was shocked. Where was this coming from? They were finally on the same page with values and mission. What more could they need?

"Annie, I don't understand. What are you saying? Are you breaking up with me?"

Annie's face looked even more sad. She bent her head to her mug and just nodded. Tears gathered in her eyes. She looked up and looked him in the eyes, "Alex, I can't tell you how much I love you and how much I used to like being around you. I have been so happy to have you in my life and to learn from you. And I can't thank you enough for introducing me to Sara and walking with me through this time. But I don't see how we can go forward from here. You want everything to be black and white and certain. I don't live in that world, Alex, and my friends don't either. I don't even think that it's necessary to see the world that way to follow Jesus." She just sat, looking at him.

Alex was flabbergasted, and then he got mad. His voice was cold as he said, "Well, Annie, if that's what you want, I guess I can't change your mind. I'm happy for your life change; I'm just sorry it doesn't include me." With nothing else to say, and nothing coming from Annie, he got up and left the restaurant, leaving Annie to find another way home. He just couldn't handle being in the same car with her right now.

As Alex traveled home, his mind reeled. As the days passed, Alex alternately grieved his loss and was relieved that things had played out this way, before they were married. In some ways, he could see the wisdom in splitting, as he couldn't imagine having someone as his wife who valued "story" and "relationship" above the truth. He wished it would have turned out differently, and he wondered if Annie would ever change her mind and come back to him, but he wasn't about to seek her out. She'd made the decision, and she could live with it.

He was grateful that no harsh words were said. At least they could part somewhat amicably.

A New Chapter

Annie was heartbroken. When she started out on this journey, she had never imagined that they would end up here. She was less than hopeful at the beginning, thinking that Alex had lost his mind. But as they had worked through ideas and tried to live them out, she had begun to understand where he was coming from. And she was deeply saddened that it was not enough for them. But it wasn't.

To her own surprise, she now valued her relationships with Patti, Josie, and Oliver, among others, so much that it was important to her who she introduced these friends to. And she couldn't picture putting them in the same room with Alex. He meant well, she knew he did, but he had consistently alienated all those around him who didn't consider themselves Christians. As much as she loved him, she couldn't handle that. She actually felt a calling to be one of God's storytellers in her world, and to make that impossible by being with Alex was not something that she could do.

In the back of her mind, she hoped that Alex might be spurred on to ask some questions and reflect on how people were perceiving him and his statements and questions. But she was doubtful. As they'd walked through this process with Sara, she saw him gravitating toward what he felt was secure and comfortable and certain. But that wasn't the world she lived in. Things in her world were not black and white, and relationships with people, even those who don't believe in God, were to be treasured.

Monday after work Annie and Oliver went to play tennis. Over the course of the game, it came out that she and Alex had split up. Oliver was surprised that she was doing so well.

"When Heather and I broke up, I had an awful time—you remember—I could barely go outside in the sunlight unless I had to. You're doing amazing. So what happened? Did Alex cheat on you or something?"

"No, we just weren't on the same page with some things, you know? It wasn't going to work out."

"Wow, Heather called me to swear at me once a day for at least a month."

"Well, I think we both still love each other. I still want to see the best happen for him. I just don't think the best is me."

"I still don't know how you do it. Aren't you hurt or upset or frustrated? Something?"

"I can't say I'm not upset, Oliver. But this is where I feel like the love of God makes such a huge difference in my life. If it was just me, I am sure that there are hurts that I would be holding onto right now and even hateful things I might be tempted to say. But instead, I can view Alex as a brother, as someone who is valued by God and should be valued by me. I can hope that God will do the best for both of us."

Oliver didn't say much in response, but he seemed to be pondering it. Conversation drifted to other things, but Annie was glad she'd been able to share from her heart. She'd been able to share with him about a real difference that God had made–or was making–in her life. So she prayed that that story might be a small seed in Oliver's heart that would grow into questions and eventually even faith.

Tuesday came, and Annie was feeling down in the dumps. Instead of going to her parents' to hang out after work, she thought she might see if Patti or Josie was home. So she went next door and found Patti alone. She invited herself in, and Patti boiled water for tea.

Annie sat at the table and waited for Patti, tapping her finger on the table. She was upset. Patti was attuned enough by now to Annie's normal state of being that she was concerned. She asked, "What's going on Annie? Is anything wrong?"

So Annie described the breakup with Alex. She framed it as a mostly positive thing and struggled to explain the reasons. "I think, Patti, that I just realized that Alex comes across as one of those really judgmental Christians. He can't really see what people's pain in life might lead them to do or so say, and he's not willing to be patient to walk through those questions or issues with people. He expects that people will all believe and do the same things he does, and when they don't, he feels the need to change them. At the end of the day, I don't actually think that's what Jesus asks us to do. And I don't want to put that kind of pressure on the people around me, you know?"

Patti just held her peace. Annie continued, "But it's really, really hard. I really miss him already, and it's only been a day. But I guess I've been missing him for a long time. I've missed who he was before the accident. Do you miss Jake?"

She immediately thought that maybe she shouldn't have gone there. She'd asked without thinking. She had never before been able to get Patti to talk about it. But Patti didn't seem upset. She was just quiet for a while, until Annie thought she wouldn't answer at all. But then she said, "Yeah, I do. We were married for a long time." She didn't elaborate. Annie desperately wanted to talk to her about faith–about whether she had faith, or whether she had walked away from God when Jake walked away from her. But she knew that Patti was still that mousy woman who looked only at her own feet in the hallways. She didn't want to scare her away, and she wasn't sure that now was the right time anyway. Someday, she may have that conversation, but it still felt too soon.

So Annie changed the subject. "Hey–did you get

that application filled out for the hospital?"

"Yes. I actually have an interview next week, and they sounded really positive, actually. Thanks again for giving me such a great reference. I'm actually hopeful that I have a shot."

The ladies finished up their tea and Annie got out of Patti's hair. Later that night, Josie stopped by.

"So, Annie, I heard you and Alex busted up this weekend."

Annie laughed a little. "Yeah, Josie, we did."

"Are you okay? What happened, anyway?"

"Why don't you come in? Soda? Brownie?"

Josie accepted and then made her way to the couch. "Well, what happened? Spill."

Annie was amused. The barriers between Josie and Annie were all but gone, and Josie had just made herself at home. "Well, Josie, we just weren't on the same page anymore. We've been struggling for a while–I told you about his accident right? He was never really the same after that. It gave him kind of a picture of what he wanted his life to be. We've worked really hard to get to the same place, but we're headed in entirely different directions. It's sad, but I think it will be okay."

"So what were you fighting about?"

"I don't know that we were even fighting, really. But we disagree on how to build relationships with people who don't believe the same way we do. Alex thinks it's important to change people's minds about how they believe by confronting those beliefs head on. I don't really think that's an effective way to engage people on the important issues of life. I feel like there are all kinds of opportunities to share my own stories and stories from the Bible with people around me. I guess I think it's okay to let God worry about changing people's hearts. I can't do that no matter what I say. But I'm boring you, aren't I?"

But Josie asked, "What kind of heart change, Annie? What kind of change is supposed to happen in someone's life?"

So Annie told Josie the story of how they started meeting with Sara and the things that God had done in her own heart. She told about God's call to love him with her whole heart, soul, mind, and strength, and the call to be a part of walking with people through life and helping them find healing in their relationships with God and others.

Josie's eyes lit up. "So that's why you have been helping us, right? Because you are trying to walk with us? Because of how God walks with you?"

Annie was surprised that Josie seemed to understand the big picture. But she was glad. "Yep, that's exactly right, Josie. Because God loves you so much, I wanted you to know that you were loved and cared for too."

They continued talking for some time, and when they were done, they prayed that Josie and Annie would both be able to keep learning how to love and walk with God.

Wednesday came, and Annie went to see Sara. They had a comfortable conversation about where to go from there. They decided they would like to keep meeting to talk through the stories of God and to think about how they could be applied and shared in their own lives and the lives of those around them.

Acknowledgments

I never would have gotten here without Cathy, who encouraged and taught me to live these ideas long before I could put words around them. It's as much her book as it is mine.

Thanks to Taryn Myers, Kara DeBruyn, Melinda and Jeremy Bouma, Pam Butler, Sarah Rapa, Travis Hill, Cheryl McKeel, and Sharon Brown for early feedback, publishing information, and help with marketing and branding.

Thanks to Mary Engelsman, who provided the idea for the book; Courtney Waid, who both listened and asked questions; and to Dean and Susie Heino, for opening their home at just the right time; without them this would have been a nonfiction book.

And thanks to my copy editor, Beth Simonton-Kramer, who was detail-oriented so that I didn't have to be.